YOU WILL BE MINE

🦋 🦋 🦋

YOU WILL BE MINE

N.J. ADEL

To girls who think red flags make excellent decorations, who know falling for a masked stalker serial killer is a terrible idea but proceed anyway, who think 'restraining order' is just a love language, who definitely wouldn't survive in real life…

Your therapist is gonna have a field day.

To the masked man in the shadows with a tragic backstory and abs and a big pierced… "nose"—thank you for making bad decisions look so good. Next time, bring chocolate…

CHAPTER 1

Birdie

What if the only way to get your happy ending was to let a killer get away with murder?

Image after image flickers in my head, one lifeless face after another. What would the people behind them think of as they took their last breaths? I imagine I could dig my way through each of their skulls and sift through their thoughts until I find that final one. Would they know why they were going to die? Would they regret what brought them to their demise? What would they pray for, forgiveness or second chances? Would they think they could still be saved?

I hum my imagination to sleep, the cool scent of the ocean a helping hand to sooth me. I head down the stairs toward my home office. My assistant, Gia, waits for me next to my desk, holding a manila folder. A man in a navy blue suit rises from his seat. "Good morning, Mrs. Abel. Tristan Morra."

"His face could have been forged in the wettest of dreams or the worst of nightmares."

Gia clearing her throat alerts me this isn't the best thing to say when I first greet a stranger, let alone the security detail I'm supposed to interview. *Goddamn you, words. You always get me in trouble. If it wasn't for you, I wouldn't need a bodyguard in the first place.*

"I'm sorry. I didn't mean to say that out loud." I lower my eyes from his face. He is at least a foot taller than I am, though, and my gaze hits his broad shoulders and puffed-up chest under the white dress shirt. Are you kidding me? The man is a living, breathing character begging to be written in one of my books. My brain is having a field day with all the lines I can scribble just by looking at him. "Please take a seat, Mr. Morra."

His lips twist into a smirk, accentuating the scar above them rather than softening it. "Are you writing a new book?"

I sit at my desk. "I wish. But under the current circumstances, I…" *Can't trust the consequences of writing another book?* "…prefer to take some time off. Fortunately, my publisher agrees. At least, until they find me proper security to make sure the stalker never enters my house or comes near me again. That's why you're here, Mr. Morra."

He sits across from me. "Your publisher? I was under the impression your husband arranged for this interview with my firm."

"Blake Abel is also my manager. He and the publisher serve the same interest." Protecting the golden goose that makes them rich.

Gia sets the folder aside and gives my shoulder a reassuring touch. "Which is your safety, Birdie."

The safety of my future manuscripts. I plaster a smile. "Of course. What else?"

Morra's eyes, more green than hazel with flicks of gray, harden at me as he gives me a curt nod. "Noted."

Does he understand what I'm saying between the lines or is it a mere acknowledgment of who is hiring him?

"After the incident, Birdie has become extremely paranoid," Gia volunteers, as if she knew how I felt or what kind of thoughts were gnawing at me. "She fired all the house staff. She doesn't trust anyone anymore."

"Can you blame me? A man broke into my house without any sign of forced entry. He was in my bedroom. He watched me sleep and…" My stomach lurches at the thought.

Morra's forehead creases with a scowl. "And

what, Mrs. Abel? Did he touch you?"

There is an edge to his voice I don't know whether to appreciate or be concerned about. "No." Not that I know of.

"Did he come close enough for you to see him, his face, any remarkable features or identifiable tattoos?"

"I didn't even know he was in the room until I woke up and found his note on the bed."

He leans forward. His scowl seems permanent now. "I see. But how do you know he's a man?"

I cock an eyebrow at him, unappreciative of the inquisition. First, I'm supposed to interview him, not the other way around. Second, he's acting like the police that dismissed me once they knew *what the fuss was all about*. Apparently, a crazed fan that sneaks his way into a female author's home to leave her a sick note isn't something important enough or dangerous enough to be worthy of their precious time. I rub my fingers over my mouth, cursing myself for thinking for one moment a man could be genuinely concerned about what happened to me. "Have you signed the NDA form, Mr. Morra?" The last thing I want is some idiot spreading the details of this nightmare for money or for kicks.

"Yes."

"Good. Before I answer any more of your

questions and spill, to a complete stranger, more details about the horrific incident I'd like to keep private, let's hear more about your qualifications and why I should consider you for the job."

"With pleasure," he says, unfazed by my enforcing control over the conversation, and then he babbles the information on his resume, which I already know.

Tristan Morra, twenty-seven, ex-military, honorable discharge after two tours. When his father died, he was the sole caretaker of his sick mother, until she, too, passed away. He used to work for Triad, a major security firm, where he's been the personal bodyguard of several businessmen, celebrities and politicians. Then he left and opened his own firm, Monarca, in Boston last year. Small but efficient. Reasonable prices with the experience and the qualifications needed. Neither overwhelmed by having too many clients nor arrogant. The boss himself is here for the position. In other words, the firm and he, with his physique and record—all his previous clients are safe and sound—are perfect for the job.

If only he wasn't mansplaining me…

The only reason I continue this interview is to see the look on his face when I reject his application at the end. I love it when I put a cocky man, who thinks he knows better than a woman, in his place.

To show him I'm not making arbitrary assumptions, I nod at Gia to show him the evidence. She opens the folder and hands him a clear plastic bag with a yellow piece of paper inside. The stalker's ominous note.

He's professional enough not to take it out of the bag, I'll give him that. It's criminal evidence that should have been tested for prints and DNA had the police believed me. But they ruled the note as nothing but a publicity stunt just like the bruises I've shown them before. *They could be anything, Mrs. Abel, they said. You might have taken a nasty fall. You might have even inflicted them upon yourself to promote your books. Aren't you that author who writes about abused women and the villains that save them? They laughed.*

Figures of authority have always disliked me, starting with my parents. When you're raised by narcissists who falsely believe they're smarter, more confident, more successful than you'll ever be, you turn into their enemy. It doesn't matter if you're their own blood. It doesn't matter if you're an innocent child who wants nothing but their love. They try to destroy your confidence and any positive image you have of yourself. They try to convince you you're nothing without them, and you'll never earn their love because of your many faults. Until you believe them. Until you're broken and desperate. Until you're forever a puppet under their control.

If, for any reason, you try to break out of their cage, you get punished in any way they see fit. And if you have the audacity to object or seek help, guess what? You get the blame. They're your loving parents who have done everything to raise and nurture you despite your shortcomings and lack of potential. *How can you not see that everything they do is for you? Is that how you repay them, you ungrateful brat?*

It wasn't very surprising I received the same response from the police when I tried to complain about my violent husband. After all, they think their ex-cop friend is the kind of husband who supports his wife financially while she writes fictional stories about ungrateful wives who dare complain about domestic violence and emotional abuse. *These stories are all made up. She lied about the bruises, too, just to sell more books. There's no way she's making ten times more than him with that crap she writes. There's no way he abuses and controls her to live off her, right?*

Wrong.

Morra's stare goes over the words that are now engraved in my head; I wrote most of them.

You look so peaceful in your sleep.
You're my obsession, my addiction, my salvation and my destruction as I will be yours. You're the reason

I breathe, the reason I live, the reason I kill. I love you so much that I'll kill everyone who has ever hurt you, anyone who will ever touch you again, darling.

Morra peers at the dried off-white blobs that stain the yellow background. Then he brings the bag to his nose. "Is this—"

"Ejaculation? Yes, it is, and before you ask me how I know for sure, I'll answer you. When the police refused to take the case seriously or even run a few tests, we did. The tests confirm it's semen on the note."

He hands the bag back to Gia. "Can I trouble you for some water?"

Is he nervous? I can't help the smirk that tugs at the corner of my mouth. "Oh, where are my manners? Bring some coffee, too, Gia, please. Perhaps some hot chocolate or even something stronger? Vineyard Haven in March can be cruel."

"Coffee is fine. Thanks," he says.

She tucks the note away in the folder. "Sure. How do you take yours, Mr. Morra?"

"Black, one sugar." He pauses until she leaves the room. "Mrs. Abel, I'm so sorry you had to go through this. I understand how you feel and how grave the situation is."

Does he? Should I give him a medal or something?

"Don't think I didn't pick up on what you were trying to say earlier when your assistant jumped in. I just didn't want to speak in front of her. You have every right not to trust anyone right now."

Interesting.

His gaze pins intensely on mine. "You're my obsession, my addiction, my salvation and my destruction as I will be yours. You're the reason I breathe, the reason I live, the reason I kill."

I freeze for a second, taken aback by the way my skin breaks out in goosebumps as he recites that part of the note. "Excuse me?"

"He quoted from your latest book, *Twisted Obsession*. It's about a stalker obsessed with a woman prostituted by her husband. He kills the husband and kidnaps her for himself."

"Yes… You read my book?"

"Of course."

Blake must have briefed him about the quote. Morra read the book and came prepared. I'll give him that...too.

"Not just because of the case," he adds, as if he can read my mind. "I truly love your writing. It's like you nail every emotion with a sledgehammer. The intensity and authenticity in every story are so relatable you can't help but fall in love with them. My favorite book is *The Nightingale's Whispers*."

I blink, frowning.

"What?"

"You're not exactly my target audience, Mr. Morra."

His smirk makes a reappearance. "Men read, too, and not just the stereotypical genres."

Not the men I know. Blake never reads my books, and he makes a living out of them. Have I been so prejudiced that I judged Morra too quickly?

"Is this the first note he sent you?" he asks.

I look down and shake my head. "Wouldn't call him a stalker if it was. There have been several over the years of my author career."

"Where did you find them?"

"Fan mail mostly. A few at signings. They'd magically appear in the merch boxes or in my books at readings. But one time I found a note slipped under the door of my hotel room while I was on my book tour. When I opened the door, no one was there.

"I told Blake. He checked the hotel security cameras, but they found nothing. We decided to put the whole thing behind us because the notes were merely quotes and words of admiration. Harmless. But now they've escalated to sickening violations, dark obsessions and threats of murder."

"How do you know it's the same fan? Do the notes have the same handwriting? And please don't think my questions earlier or now are skeptical or condescending. I know you must get that a lot, especially from the police. I'm only gathering facts and evidence because if you choose me to be your bodyguard, I won't only protect you. I will catch that bastard for you."

A strange feeling washes over me, one that is as soothing as it is alarming. It's like I can finally let go of the weight I've been carrying for so long. It's a moment of strength when I can stand up to the fears that have held me back for so long. A moment of hope, of believing things can be better. It's also a moment of vulnerability, of opening up to a new world and trusting that it will be kind.

"The other notes were typed, not handwritten. I know it's him, though, because of the butterflies," I answer.

"The butterflies? Like the one drawn at the end of the note you showed me?"

"Unlike other fan mail, his notes are never signed with a name, but he always leaves an illustration of a butterfly. We've been calling him Butterfly Man because of his signature."

"Let's stick with *stalker*. Giving him a name like the press does with serial killers legitimizes him. It's what he's after, creating a rapport with you, his *victim*. Do butterflies mean anything to you? Do they hold any significance in your life or in your books?"

"No. The only thing I can think of is that

my name is Birdie. Butterflies and birds have wings, and both words start with a *B*." I chuckle at how silly I must sound. "I don't think it has anything to do with me. It's obviously significant to him, though."

"Don't worry. We'll get to the bottom of this. I'll do everything I can to keep you safe. No woman should be afraid in her own house because of a man…stalker or otherwise."

I stare at him for a few moments, and he respects the silence. His words sink deep, more than any have in a long time. It's like he understands, like he truly gets it. I haven't cried in years, not in public, but tears jump to my eyes, threatening to spill. I swallow to contain them. Is this real? Can I finally break that thick surface of fear and pain? Can I finally breathe?

Perhaps I've been wrong about Tristan Morra after all. "Thank you. I must say, you and your company are perfect for the position, Mr. Morra."

"It'll be my honor to protect you. You have no idea how thrilled I am to be your security detail."

"Because you're a big fan?"

"Because, for years, I've been waiting for an opportunity to repay you."

"Repay me? For what?"

"You don't remember me, but I can never forget the face of the person that changed my life. I used to be nothing but a scrawny boy whose parents whisked him from Argentina to start a new life in Miami when he was three. They couldn't afford a good school, and I was dyslexic. At nineteen, I was unable to graduate, so I saved some money and enrolled in the adult English classes for students with learning difficulties at your school. I was lucky enough to have you as my teacher. You were amazing. You gave me an opportunity to continue my education. You—"

"You were a student of mine?"

"Yes, Mrs. Abel. Well, your name back then was Ms. Fletcher," he continues. "I had a different name, too. I figured Tristan Morra would be much easier to pronounce than—"

"Shut up." The gentle breeze soothing my soul turns into a cold chill down my spine, shattering every shred of hope and replacing it with dread.

"I'm sorry?"

I hurry to the door and open it with more force than necessary. "Get out."

"I don't understand. Did I say something wrong? I'm just showing my gratitude."

A wave of nausea threatens to knock me out. "Do you have any idea why I quit teaching? Why I moved halfway across the country to a cold isolated island where no one knows who I really am? Why I hide behind that stupid pen name?"

He looks like a deer in the headlights. "I thought you left to start a new family with your husband. To pursue your dream as an author."

A bitter scoff escapes my mouth. "Oh I wish it were that simple and dreamy." But it's dark and painted with blood. In a way, I'm glad he doesn't know the truth, and the secrets that I've paid a heavy price to bury remain safe.

"Then what happened?"

"This interview is over, Mr. Morra. I'm sorry to have wasted your time. Please remember that you signed an NDA, and *everything* we talked about can't be disclosed to anyone at any time."

"Of course. You can trust me. I'd never say or do anything that could cause you any discomfort or harm. Please—"

"To keep it that way, this is the last time we'll ever cross paths. Now, get out of my house and never come back."

CHAPTER 2

Birdie

There's a story in everything. Why, for the past seven years, I've been a brunette instead of a blonde. Why I put on twenty pounds and glasses I don't need. Why my author photo is a logo. Why I don't show my face on social media. Why I refuse to go to signings or readings unless my publisher threatens to terminate my contract, and when I do go, it's never to any event in Florida, and I don't allow pictures.

Why I can't let Tristan Morra be my bodyguard.

There's a story behind all the big fat whys, but like all stories, it has multiple sides, most of them are fictitious. The truth… That's a different story.

"Birdie, you can't kick out every bodyguard

you interview. There's no one else left on the list," Gia says as I watch Morra leave my property on my laptop monitor. Blake has installed a simple security system in the house after the incident. I didn't want him to. If Gia hadn't called him that morning, I wouldn't have told him about the note. I don't want to open any door that allows Blake to snake his way back into my life, not after I've finally found an opportunity to kick him out. I never want him to set foot in my house again.

"Birdie? Are you even listening?"

"Go home, Gia," I sigh, closing the laptop and getting off my desk.

She sets the tray that holds Morra's drinks on the coffee table between the two guest chairs. "And leave you all alone in this house after what happened? No way."

What happened could be a darkly twisted answer to my silent prayers—a chance to escape the bruises and fear, to start anew far from Blake and the shadows of the past. The thought of freedom is intoxicating, even if it comes at a cost as pricey as blood. What if the only way to get my happy ending *is* to let my stalker get away with murder?

I pick a book from my own little piece of heaven—the custom-made bookshelves that entirely cover three walls of my office. "Nothing is going to happen. There's a security alarm on both the front and back doors, and the house is peppered with cameras."

"Courtesy of Blake."

"Go home, Gia," I say in warning this time.

She hovers around as I place the book on the side table next to the velvet, teal sofa bed and remove the decorative cushions so I can sit. The color is in stark contrast to the black and gray minimalist furniture and eggshell walls. While blue and its derivatives aren't my favorite colors, that sofa bed is my favorite part of the room. It used to be my book nook and sometimes workspace. Now, it's my bed, too. I can't bring myself to enter my bedroom after what happened.

The second I sit, she plops down next to me. "Look, I don't know what's going on between the two of you, but whatever it is, it can be fixed. He loves you to death, Birdie. You have no idea how worried he is about you. When you won't return his calls, he calls me, at least three times a day, just to check on you. Didn't he come home rushing after you found the note? Didn't he install the security system himself on the very same day? Didn't he literally beg you to come home just so that he could protect you?"

Oh, Prince Blake Charming. My knight in shining armor. I do a mental eyeroll while I stifle a snort. How can people choose to notice every detail about something when it suits them and become utterly blind when it doesn't?

Blake did rush to the house the second Gia called him that morning, but it wasn't because he loved me to death. It was about control.

It's always been about control.

When he insisted on installing the security system himself, it wasn't for my protection. I bet my own life he has, on his device, the same application he installed on my phone to access the house security cameras. To watch *me*.

When he begged me to come back, it wasn't to protect me. Blake sees the stalker situation as an opportunity to slither his way back into my life. To show me I still need him. To convince me that even after all these years, I'm nothing without his protection.

It must be aching for him to have lost control over his possession. He must be going insane that I finally have the filmed evidence I need to file for divorce, or better yet, to put him in prison. He couldn't say a word when I showed him the video of his downfall. He went on his knees and begged for forgiveness. *"You can have anything you want, baby. Just don't leave me."* He even faked some tears.

There's nothing this excuse of a man can give me but his signature on the divorce papers and the termination contract of his managerial duties of my business.

18

His response when I made myself clear about my demands was no surprise. He yelled, and when it didn't scare me or back me into a corner, he lifted his arm, fist ready to throw a punch. I stood there, waiting for the blow, praying for it to land on my face, while my phone camera was on, to capture that video, too. Only this time, he punched a wall. He wouldn't let me catch *that* piece of evidence. Then he told me he'd leave for a few days to let me think. *"Take all the time you need. Don't rush into any decisions we may both regret. I beg you."*

He wasn't begging. Just like all his pleas over the years, it was a threat laced with emotional blackmail.

Gia drones on about the fine qualities of my husband. Maybe she wishes he was *her* knight in shining armor. With the way she idolizes him, I'd say those two were hitting it behind my back. I know better, though. *Sorry, Gia. The hero you worship, while he'll never admit it in public, doesn't go for confident, full-figured women with work efficient haircuts that make them look like they're in charge like you do.* He goes for women who look like the eight-year-younger version of me. He wouldn't be with me now, after the drastic changes my looks had to undergo, if it wasn't for my money.

"Would you please stop zoning out when I'm talking to you? I—"

"Gia, I'm going to read my book, take a little nap and then go out. Your services aren't needed today. Go enjoy the day off."

"Where are you going?"

"I have an appointment."

She checks her phone erratically. "There's nothing on the calendar."

Because it's something I've scheduled on my own and am not planning on telling anyone about it just yet. "It's the gynecologist, Gia," I lie. "You don't need to keep track of my pelvic exams and pap smears, do you?"

"Sorry. What time is the appointment? I can give you a ride."

"No thanks."

"How are you gonna get there? Your car is old and hasn't run in years. Blake drives you everywhere."

Another form of control. Because he needs to know where I am at all times. He even had a tracker on my phone for fuck's sake. I managed to remove it the night he left. All these years he's posed as the dedicated husband who would take the burden of driving off his beloved wife's shoulder, it's been nothing but a façade. He just won't let me go anywhere by myself. Another power he takes so that I'll always rely on him, even for the simplest life tasks, while he monitors every move I make.

I glare at her. "Then, with your permission,

I'll Uber, unless Blake has given you a direct order not to leave my side and report to him every fucking move I make!"

"Of course not. What are you…" She rises to her feet. "Birdie, I know you're under a lot of pressure, but your paranoia is getting out of hand, so is your lack of self-preservation. In case you haven't noticed, there's a deranged, murderous man who is dangerously obsessed with you, stalking you, and you choose to throw out every potential bodyguard we can hire and ride with strangers to God knows where."

"The gynecologist's, Gia. I'm going to the gynecologist's. Don't forget when you tell him."

She throws her hands in the air, shaking her head, as if she's given up on reasoning with me, and stomps her way to the door. Before she leaves, she turns and says, "Butterfly Man's actions are driving you to push away the only people who care about you. He wants you isolated, Birdie, and you're letting him win. Don't turn into your worst enemy."

CHAPTER 3

Butterfly Man

No one can escape their past. But I do when I read her words.

They're a lifeline, a thread that connects me to a different reality where I can leave behind the shadows that haunt me. In her stories, I forget the memories that torment, the regrets that consume, the sins that stain. My pain, guilt and shame no longer exist. The faces of those I've lost, and of those I've destroyed, blur in the pages until they disappear.

Until there's no one there but you and I, darling.

Lost in her lines, I become someone else. Someone who deserves her attention, her trust, her love. The only one who can make her happy, who can save her, who earns the right to be with her.

She doesn't see me, but I see her. In those universes she crafts for the two of us to secretly meet away from the cruel world that's keeping us apart, and through the words she nonchalantly writes on her social media accounts and speaks in interviews and podcasts, I've learned everything about my little bird. Not the outside shell she allows fans to dissect, not the lies she makes them believe, but the real her.

Birdie Abel, although she made it official, isn't her real name. She tells everyone her favorite color is blue, but, even though it matches her eyes, she never ever wears it. Her glasses either—when she thinks no one is looking. She sings about how much she loves her housewife mother and accountant father, how supportive they are, but they're never in the picture. They don't have names known to the public. No one can tell for sure if they're alive or dead—or made up.

But I do.

I've dug deep underneath that surface to learn about the things she doesn't let anyone else see. The secrets. The lies. The desires. The darkness. They don't scare me. They entice me. I've devoured them all to the point of obsession until I worshiped her through them. They're not easy to decipher, but for me, they're loud and clear. The hidden messages between her lines, they speak to me, calling out to me, because she, too, escapes her past when she writes those words.

"I see you, my little bird. I see you in every way possible." I caress the image of her face on the live feed streaming from the hidden cameras I planted around her house when I stole that moment in time to be so close to her beauty, to hear her peaceful breaths, to inhale her addictive scent, to finally confess at her altar my feelings and my sins, while I whispered a prayer of love.

Will her security guard—if she ever chooses one—find my little windows of heaven? It can be a problem, but in a way, I hope he will. It'll prove he's competent enough to protect her, not that she needs anyone but me to protect her. Her husband didn't bother checking the house for bugs before he installed that flimsy security system I could hack easily. If I'd known, I wouldn't have wasted the precious minutes I had in her house hiding my expensive high-tech cameras. I'd have spent every second with her.

What did she see in a guy like Blake Abel to choose to share a lifetime with? "Big mistake." I nod at her. "I know. It's okay. It doesn't matter. Soon enough, he'll be out of our way. Don't worry, darling. No one can come between us. No one can take you away from me."

She's ready to get lost in a book. *What are*

we reading today, darling? In the brief time I was in her office, I took pictures of the stacks on her bookshelves. Then I ordered all the books I didn't already have. Now, we have matching TBR lists. We can have our first reading date today.

I zoom in on the footage to see what book she's reading. *Forced* by Katie Saldana. "In a mood for some cookie cutter, flat, dark smut written by a white trash wanna-be who won't dream of becoming half the storyteller you are? Hmmm…"

The tiny wheels of the work chair I sit on glide toward my little home library, and by little, I mean floor to ceiling bookshelves that cover all four walls of the loft I've recently rented in Vineyard Haven. "Well, it's our first reading date. I'll let you call that shot." I fetch the book and roll back to the monitors, to her gorgeous face that haunts my waking hours before my dreams. "Who am I kidding? I'll let you call all the shots." I smile, but she doesn't. Does she not believe me? After all these years, she still doesn't know how much I love her. "Of course I will. I'll do anything for you, darling. You're my queen."

She opens the book in the middle. "Oh, already started it without me? Let's see what page you're at."

Her eyes, bare, bluer than the clearest of

skies, move with the lines, as she lies back on the sofabed. For a moment, I forget to look for the page number and trace the shape of her body instead. Long neck. Elegant and inviting. I can bury my head there for days to taste the delicacy of her skin and breathe the smell of her hair. I close my eyes, conjuring her sweet scent, and my breath shudders. *If that's what you'll do to her neck, what will you do to her pussy?*

Snapping my eyes open, I silence that voice. I don't like that voice. *But you like her. And her pussy. You want to fuck that pussy so hard and hear her say your—*

I flip through the pages fast and find the right one. Then I read out loud to distract myself. "*She is my life, my soul, my reason for being. She is the only one who can save me from my past. She is the only one who can make me whole. She is the only one who can make me happy. She is mine, and I am hers.*" My eyes squint at the paragraph as I reread it. "Wait a minute. This sounds so…familiar."

I roll across the loft to the side where my bed is and grab a foxed paperback copy of *Until I'm Yours* from the stack on the nightstand—where I keep my favorite rereads of Birdie's masterpieces. The sticky tabs tell me exactly where to look. Yellow for the hidden messages she knows only I can find. Red for explosive steam. Blue for inspirational quotes. Purple for power statements. Magenta for the absolute best I can't get enough of.

The magentas in this mastery of storytelling are abundant, but I know exactly where to look. Page eighty-three. My stare lands on the marked paragraph automatically. "Aha! *She is my light, my breath, my reason for being. The only one who can rescue me from my past. The only one who can make me whole, who can make me fly. She is mine, and I am hers.*"

Birdie slams the book shut and bolts upright. "That bitch."

"Right?" I look from the book to her and back to the book. "She stole your work…and turned it into some tacky, boring lines in cheesy book porn without a hint of a plot."

She rubs her fingers over her mouth, a gesture I've learned she makes when she's angry… or horny. For the latter, it comes with a gentle flutter of her eyelashes that floors me. Then she uses her phone to take a photo of the plagiarized page, finds her own book and takes another photo of the original she wrote. She hits send and makes a call. Who is she calling? Her assistant? Her editor?

Lucky for me, she puts the call on speaker. "Hey, Birdie." I know that woman's voice. It belongs to Martha Goldman. Birdie's agent.

Birdie leaves the sofa bed, clenching her jaw. "Did you see the screenshots I've just sent you?"

"I…have. Yes."

"I'm sure if I read through her book I'll find more. This is not the first time, Martha. I ignored it before like you asked me to, convincing myself it's just a coincidence, imitation is the best flattery and all that bullshit, but this is plain patchwriting. She practically used a cheap thesaurus to replace a few words, *my* words, and used them in her pathetic excuse of a book. Why does she keep targeting my works?"

"You know why. You're at the top. Your books have been high on the charts for months. Everybody wants to be you. All you need to do is relax and enjoy it. Then write the next bestseller. Worrying about a minnow that rephrases a paragraph of yours here and there won't get you anywhere. It'll only give you hemorrhoids." Martha laughs.

"I can't just stand by while she steals my stories right under my nose and makes a fortune out of them."

"First, she isn't stealing your stories. Those come with signature plot twists that are hard to replicate. Saldana will be too stupid to just copy them, and she knows it. What she does is borrow heavily from your finely crafted words, butcher them, and then try to make them fit in her weak prose."

Good point.

"Which is the definition of mosaic plagiarism, and it is selling her books like hot cakes."

Also a good point.

"She is not a threat to you, Birdie."

"I don't care. She stole from me. She won't stop unless someone makes her stop."

Yes, darling. I hear you.

"I understand your frustration. What do you want to do?"

"I want to sue her."

"Sue her? Birdie, do you have any idea how long copyright infringement lawsuits take or how much money they cost or the statistics of winning them? Unless she published something that's word for word or plot point for plot point, the chances to win are slim to none."

"We can't just do nothing. At least, tell the publisher to issue a cease and desist. It's my right!"

"It is. But have you thought about how much attention you'll be drawing to her books if we do, attention that will be taken away from yours? Because she has a good reach on social, and she'll use it to twist things around. You know the drill. She'll hold a cat and blubber ugly on camera while she begs for forgiveness and blames the whole fiasco on depression medications. She'll do it over and over until she turns your own readers against you, making you the villain."

"The villain? For claiming back what's mine? This is ridiculous."

"I totally agree, but it's the culture we live in, my friend. *The world, as my villains, is morally gray…*"

"*And so are the rules of vice and virtue. Neither can claim supreme authority,*" I say with Martha. One of my absolute favorite quotes by Birdie.

"…your words, not mine." Martha chuckles as if anything about this situation can be humorous.

Birdie wipes a full hand over her mouth. "You're my agent. You must figure something out."

"There are only two options, Birdie. We take the legal route or the public route. One is a waste of resources if we don't have more than a few rewritten, too generic paragraphs, and the other… Well, let's face it, you can't win unless you're willing to put your face on a camera all over social in a vicious war that can last a while, which is something you don't do, and she does...pretty well."

"Well, there must be something else that can be done."

There is, darling. There surely is.

"I'll tell you what," Martha says after a long pause, "I'll set up a meeting with Blake and see what we can come up with."

Birdie's eyes widen with rage. "Get him out

of this."

"He's your manager, Birdie. It's what he's here for. Unless something has changed?"

Birdie swears under her breath. "You know what. Forget it." She hangs up and tosses the phone on her desk.

I touch her hair, imagining how it feels draped over me while I have my arms wrapped around her. "Oh, please, darling, don't get upset. Leave it to me. I'll take care of it. She's not worthy of your time or anger. Let me take care of my little bird. It's what *I* am here for."

She lets out a heaving breath, and then she looks up at one of Blake's cameras. Her eyes narrow for a moment before she opens her laptop and presses a few buttons. She waves in the direction of the camera and gazes at the screen. Then, when she doesn't see herself on the monitor, she takes *Until I'm Yours* and lies on the sofa bed.

"Did you just turn off the office security cameras? Why?"

When she resumes reading page eight-three and her slender fingers slide down her pants, I have my answer. From line twenty on page eighty-three to the end of page eighty-nine is one of the most epic spicy scenes she's ever written, and she's touching herself to it.

And I can see her touching herself to it.

My breath snags in my chest. I swallow, hot

blood pumping through me. Call me crazy but having sex with a woman is great, watching her work on herself to word porn is... "Fuck."

Pinching my upper lip, I listen to her laboring breaths that quickly turn into moans, and I imagine how loud she can be when she orgasms. Then she does that thing when she rubs her lips and flutters shut her eyes.

"Oh God." I can't stop my hands from unbuckling my belt and freeing my now painful erection. *Yes, she turned off the cameras so her husband wouldn't see. She's putting on that show only for you. You might as well enjoy it. Don't let it go to waste.*

Her back arches, and her breasts thrust up. My tongue darts out and licks my lips instead of her pebbling nipples, but in my head, I'm feasting on her plump flesh and filling my hand with it while my cock is giving her pleasure and inducing those delicious moans.

When her mouth forms a silent O, and then she breaks into a crescendo of successive gasps and curses, I allow myself the release, too. I know I'll be allowing myself more releases today and the days to come watching this footage over and over and over until I learn every sound, every move, every contour of that face she makes when she climaxes.

"Thank you, my love. You don't know how long I've been waiting for this."

I'm about to clean myself when she grabs

Saldana's book and opens it. She takes the fingers that have been inside herself and smears the page. It isn't hard to guess which paragraph she's just stained.

"Oh. My. God. Wow," I laugh as she uses her laptop to write something. Her printer whistles, and a paper comes out of it. She takes it and pastes it on the front page of the book. I adjust the camera range to see what's written. *Congratulations.* Then her index finger dips back in her pussy, and it traces her initials on the paper, as if signing her name with her cream. She puts the book in a yellow envelope, seals it and writes an address on it.

I look it up. Yes, it's Katie Saldana's address. "Holy fuck. This is gold. I love your mind, little bird." I think about doing the same with my cum, painting her most beautiful quotes with it and mailing it to her. Not as a statement or a threat, but as proof of how much power she has over me.

She turns the cameras back on, shoves the envelope in her purse and leaves the office.

"I thought we were taking a nap first before you left for the *gynecologist's.*" I chuckle because I know she was lying to Gia. "Where are you flying so fast, little bird?"

CHAPTER 4
Birdie

I text Gia the Uber car and driver's information and description. I'm still livid that Blake could be using her to keep tabs on me—how pushy she's become to know where I'm going and to drive me there herself arouses a lot of suspicion in me—but unlike what she's said, my self-preservation skills are intact. If the driver turns out to be Butterfly Man…I mean, the stalker, and I end up being taken, Gia and Blake will know where to look. I doubt he's a fifty-year old male who hangs cute pictures of who seem to be his grandchildren on the dashboard of his car, though.

GPS announces I've arrived at my destination as a white. A Victorian house restored into a café attached to a mini bookstore appears on the right, Sweet Home written on its book-shaped sign. It's my favorite hangout where I can get a nice lunch or a cup of coffee, surrounded by people who appreciate books as much as I do. Today, I'm not here to dine or read. Still, it's the perfect place to be without raising any suspicion from Blake, if he's following me.

As I get out of my ride, I scan the area for Blake's face or his car and find neither. The street is quiet. There are barely any cars passing by. A few people are walking on the sidewalk or entering the deli at the corner. After seven years of living in a universe where he controls every aspect, every move, I can't shake the feeling that he does follow me, always watching, even when there is no evidence that supports my claim.

The constant sensation of someone observing me accompanies me inside the café like a disease with no cure. When I sit, and the waitress immediately brings my usual coffee, I regard, behind the sunglasses I never take off outside, the faces scattered around the tables. What if it's not Blake who's watching me? What if it's the stalker that's triggering my gaze detection?

It should have been my first thought, but

when I think of the stalker, I treat him like one of the villains in my stories. Attracted to the dark, lurking in the shadows, stalks his prey at night. He won't be following me in the middle of the day to a neighborhood where there are no crowds to blend in. And, as in my books, he ends up being the one who saves the girl. Never the hero, it's always the villain that gets the girl.

Except Butterfly Man—sorry, but my writer mind needs a name for him—isn't a character I've created from a fantasy or an unspoken need. He's real. A man, psychotic enough to vow murder. That kind of villain doesn't save the girl, even when he thinks he does; he kills her in the end.

The door opens with a jingle as a tall, black woman in a green suit enters the café. A blue coat dangles over her arm and cascades down to the briefcase in her hand. I watch through the line of steam as her heels echo toward me, and my heart bangs with every step. She is making a turn to her table of choice when she casts a look at me over her shoulder. I busy myself with my phone, the shake in my fingers giving me away.

"Excuse me? Aren't you Birdie Abel? The author?"

I slightly lift my head toward the voice. It's coming from the same woman. She's standing closer to my table now, smiling in anticipation. I nod, worst case scenarios blistering my brain.

She's sent by Blake or Butterfly Man to watch me.

She's sent to give me another note from Butterfly Man.

She's sleeping with Blake and has come to play games with me.

He's sent her to intimidate or threaten me. She's—

"Oh my goodness. I'm a huge fan. If you're not too busy," she opens her briefcase and gets out a copy of *You're Not Alone, Darling* and a pen, "would you mind signing this for me?"

I close my eyes for a second and take a deep breath. I don't know why I'm letting my nerves get the best of me, but I am, and for all the wrong reasons. Perhaps I am too paranoid for my own good like Gia says.

You have every right not to trust anyone right now.

Morra's words flash in my head as I take the book and pen from the woman. "What's your name?"

She slips in the chair next to mine. "Adriana."

It's normal for fans to ask for my signature, especially here, but to take a seat without an invitation is rather strange. The waitress glances at me, a question on her face. Should she intervene?

"It's okay," I mouth at the waitress as I open the book cover, and she walks away.

"I'm sorry," Adriana says quietly. "Did I ruin it? It's my first time having to meet a client this way."

"Not at all. You did great." I sign the book. "I'm the one who should apologize for dragging you from Boston to make you meet me like this. I just… If Blake finds out I've been going to a law firm, it won't end well. With this little charade, if he comes to snoop around here later, they'll tell him you're just a fan."

"I understand." Pity crosses her face. As a divorce attorney, specializing in domestic abuse cases, Adriana Lockwood must have seen many women like me. She knows what people like Blake are capable of.

After a thorough search for divorce attorneys, her firm came highly recommended. I orchestrated an *accidental* meet at the coffee place across the firm building where I pretended to ask her about their best coffee I could order, and then explained the situation and how much I needed her help. She was more than understanding and accepted me as a client. Her ways of keeping our arrangement as confidential and discreet as possible assured me she has the right expertise to help me. She's the one who created an unmonitored email for our correspondence and provided me with a burner phone to contact her.

We never meet at her office. We never meet. Period. Even when she sent me the burner, I had to claim it from a post office in Edgartown, prepared to lie to Blake if he asked. *It's a card from a fan. She wrote down the wrong P.O. box. When they saw my name, though, they knew where to call. I'm so glad they did. I hate it when they return fan mail. I don't want my readers to think I don't receive their kind gifts or that I don't appreciate them.* Adriana did send a fake card with the burner, in case he needed proof.

"Eventually, we had to meet in person to get your signature on the papers. They're inside the book," she says.

The divorce papers. I sign them, too, and slip my burner phone among them as I return the book to her.

"Can I see the video you said you had? You said you wouldn't send it over the internet, which I think is smart. Once something is out there, it never goes away."

"Excuse my trust my issues. I've been going through something that has been driving me insane. I literally considered walking out of here when I saw you come in. I'm too scared. I even had crazy thoughts that you might be working with Blake—"

"Hey, let me stop you right here. All of what you're feeling is comprehensible. Your husband has been manipulating you for years. Emotional and psychological abuse often accompany domestic violence. They are equally painful and destructive." She gives me a kind smile. "Rest assured I'm on your side, Birdie. You know you can trust me. I can't be working with your husband. You can have me disbarred if I were. Our firm is the best in the county, and we have a reputation to keep. You wouldn't be working with us otherwise."

"I know. I'm sorry. The video is on the burner. It's inside the book."

She pretends to be looking at my dedication while she plays the video I had of Blake. The one I used to finally kick him out of my house. A grin stretches her lips. "We got him, Birdie."

"You think?"

"I don't think. I know. I thought you got him screwing someone else on camera, but this…I salute you."

I don't feel as confident as she seems to be. "Will he go to prison?"

She plays the video again and zooms in on Blake's face while he draws his gun at the drug dealer from whom he's buying his psychedelic amphetamines. After Blake's therapist cut him off last year because she suspected he was abusing the drug, he's been getting his supply illegally. I don't know why he was threatening the dealer with the gun, and I don't care.

Blake always has a gun on him. With his anger issues—among several others—it was only a matter of time before he used it. I was lucky enough to be there when it happened to get him on the video that would buy me my freedom. "Possession of a controlled substance while armed is a felony."

Fear spreads under my skin. "I…I don't want him to go to prison. He… He will retaliate."

"Don't worry. Domestic abuse is difficult to use as grounds for divorce if there's no physical evidence, but with this," she chuckles, "we won't even have to go to court. Blake will happily sign the divorce papers and waiver any claim of any marital rights he might still have after the prenup to avoid jail time."

"I don't know. What if that felony isn't threatening enough to bargain with? What if he thinks he won't be charged?"

"Because he's above the law?"

"Because he's an ex-cop." I curse the day I thought I should marry one. Protect and serve my ass. "You know how it is. The police are his friends. What if he pulls a favor, asks them to tamper with evidence, bury it, so he can walk away? Like he did when I reached out to them all black and blue?"

"They can't. Not this time." She looks me in the eye, smiling with certainty. "Birdie, we won.”

I want to believe her. I want to believe her so badly. Is this real? Are we really going to win? Can I finally be free of that monster? “What about terminating his contract as my manager?”

“Corporate law isn’t my specialty, but according to the contract you showed me, termination must be in writing with a minimum notice period of thirty days. All you need to do is send him a termination letter, wait for thirty days, and the contract will be terminated.”

“I’ve already done that, but what if he goes behind my back and does something unexpected or I find myself in an Elvis and the Colonel situation? I don’t want him to take another dime of my money.”

“Like I said, I’m not a corporate attorney, but I can refer you to someone trustworthy. Meanwhile, it’s best if you email the termination letter to the entities he mostly deals with, like your agent and publisher.”

My personal phone rings. The caller’s number I don’t recognize.

“I’ll let you take that call.” Adriana leaves her seat. “See you soon.”

“Thank you, Adriana.” I answer the call as she puts the book with the burner in her briefcase. “Hello?”

“Mrs. Abel?”

"Yes."

"This is Detective Jacob Torrance, Oak Bluffs police department."

"Detective?" I squint at Adriana, and she halts in place.

"I'd like to have a word with you, ma'am. It's important. I stopped by your house, but it seems no one is there. Can you drop by the station? Or if you're somewhere close, we can meet and save you the trip."

I gulp. This must be Blake's doing. He wants to know where I am, what I'm up to, if he hasn't already figured it out. He's sending a friend of his to find me.

To scare me into silence.

Putting the call on hold, cold sweat trickling down the back of my neck, I stare at Adriana. "He knows. Blake knows, and now he'll make me pay."

CHAPTER 5

Birdie

My hands tremble as I collect my things. All I can think of is the pain that awaits me, and if I'm going to make it through the night without Blake's rage marking me. I've hoped to hide my plans, at least, until I'm sure he doesn't have any other choice but to let me go without consequences. But he found out. He always does.

"Where are you going?" Adriana asks as I try to leave the table.

"I don't know." Over the course of the eight years I've spent with Blake, I've come to know there's nowhere to run from him. He'll always find me. He's worse than a stalker. I should have hired Morra. I need a bodyguard to protect me from my husband more than I'll ever need one to protect me from anything else. "I can't do this anymore. You don't know Blake like I do. You have no idea what he's capable of."

"Birdie, you don't know what that detective wants from you. Let's hear him first before you make any decisions."

"Blake sent him, Adriana."

"You don't know that. Listen, I have an idea. Tell the detective to come down here now. I'll be sitting there," she points at the table behind me, "and I'll film the whole thing. If he is really sent to intimidate or coerce you in any way, we'll have proof. It'll strengthen our case immensely."

I shake my head. "It'll only make things worse." All I can do is try to calm Blake down, lie to him and do whatever I can to mitigate his anger.

"I know you're scared, but you don't have to be. This is going to play in our favor, Birdie. If we get that new video, we can easily get a restraining order. You will be safe. He can't hurt you anymore."

Fear a vice around my heart, I choke on a tearless sob. Adriana doesn't understand how unpredictable and dangerous Blake can be when provoked. A restraining order would only enrage him further.

She puts a hand on my shoulder. "I know what you're thinking. A piece of paper won't stop him. It'll only make him more determined to retaliate. Maybe you're right, but if we have tangible proof of his coercion tactics along with the other video that incriminates him in a serious felony, he will have no choice but to comply with your demands."

I stare at my phone, and she says, "You're stronger than you think, Birdie. We can do this. That's why you hired me. We're going to outsmart Blake for once. He will never come near you again."

"If he already knows, it's too late to back down anyway," I mutter, logic and maybe despair rising above the dread.

"Exactly. Finish that call. I'm right here with you."

I retrieve Detective Torrance's call. "Are you still there?"

"Yes," he says.

"I'm at a café nearby called Sweet Home."

"I know the place. I can be there in fifteen."

My chest flutters with anxiety, but I ignore it. I repeat Adriana's words in my mind. *We're going to outsmart Blake for once.* No more cowering in fear. "I'll be waiting."

CHAPTER 6

Butterfly Man

I didn't follow her. I'm not a stalker.

All I did was check the location Birdie put in the Uber app, and it happened to be the café across the street. There's nothing wrong with having a cup of coffee while reading my favorite book at the place right around the corner from my loft.

We are bound to meet. It's not intentional. It's destiny. She just doesn't know it yet.

My heart skitters when she climbs out of the car in the same outfit she's just masturbated in. If I concentrate hard enough when she comes in, will I be able to catch the scent of her wet pussy? I curl my lip under my teeth, imagining her taste.

She's anxious, looking for something…or someone. *I'm right here, darling, and I'm harmless.*

You should never feel anxious around me.

When she enters, her gaze is still wandering restlessly behind her shades. It falls on the large Ficus Ruby that obscures my table for a split-second, but she doesn't see me. She gives me her back and sits, bestowing me with the gorgeous outline of her ass. I'm dying to know if she's going to make the same orgasmic sounds I've heard today when it's my face instead of that chair.

"God, you're gorgeous. Have I ever told you that you look even more marvelous with dark hair? Don't get me wrong. I loved your blonde waves, but this…is *you*. And I love *you*."

I smile as she glances at me over her shoulder and says it back. Then she's on my lap, her ass bouncing on my thighs while her hair is brushing my shoulder, and her mouth is wide open with her screams of pleasure.

"Is there anything else I can get you?"

My eyes snap open. I sit upright and make sure my cap and the hood on top of it are in place. "No thanks," I tell the waitress without looking at her, pushing my sunglasses up my nose and covering my crotch with my book.

A woman approaches Birdie's table. Her clothes are expensive. Tasteful jewelry. No wedding band. The briefcase in her hand gives a clue about her job. An ambitious African American woman who has a job that pays for nice expensive things. Corporate? Banker? Lawyer?

She's giving Birdie a book to sign. A fan? I haven't seen her around here before. A woman as busy as she seems won't have the time to read recreationally. But if she does, she won't randomly and accidentally walk into the same café the author of the one fiction book she has in her briefcase has just entered.

Who are you and what are you doing with my Birdie? I strain to overhear their conversation, but I'm too far away to catch anything. I fish my phone out of my pocket and resort to my best friend: technology.

A reverse image search tells me who she is. Adriana Lockwood, senior partner at Abbot and Lockwood. Ms. Lockwood is a family law attorney specializing in divorce.

"What are you doing, little bird?" Is she divorcing Blake? It'll only make him angrier, nastier to her. This isn't the way to resolve things with him. "I have a plan, darling. I will fix everything for you. All you have to do is wait and watch it all go away."

But she doesn't know that. The promise I left her isn't clear enough. She doesn't trust me yet. I have to show her that she can believe and rely on me. I must send her another message, louder and much sooner than I've planned.

She gets a call that riles her up. My protective instincts flare. *Who is that dick? Just tell me and they won't get to live another day.* I hate to see her like that, scared and insecure. The urge to intervene is strong, but I force myself to remain still. For her sake, for our sake, I can't expose myself just yet.

Ms. Lockwood talks to her, and it seems to ease my little bird's anxiety. They go back to their tables. A few minutes later, a man in a suit enters the café and approaches Birdie's table. A cop. I don't need a search engine to tell me. I know a cop when I see one.

I don't like this. I don't like this at all.

I slide lower in my seat and feel the cold metal of the gun in the inside pocket of my hoodie. I always have a gun on me. You never know when you need one. It's best to be prepared.

Birdie is tense, on edge. My fists clench. If that man dares threaten my Birdie, I will not hesitate to act. She's mine. I protect her at any cost.

Eyes pinned on the target, I do what I do best. Watch. Observe. Wait for the right moment to strike.

CHAPTER 7

Birdie

Adriana gives me an assertive smile and takes her place, phone ready in her hand. I sit back and hum—a technique I've learned to stimulate the vagus nerve—feigning a calm I don't feel. Thirteen minutes later, the café doors chime with the arrival of a man in a gray suit. He has dark hair and is built like a football player. No, a freaking wrestler. It must be Detective Torrance. Blake chose the biggest man in the precinct to scare me, and it's working.

I steal a glance at Adriana, and she gives me a subtle nod as she positions the phone in my direction. Torrance's strides approach, long and firm. His face is unreadable.

"Mrs. Abel?" he asks as if he doesn't already know.

My hands wrap around my coffee to conceal the tremors in them. "Yes."

"Detective Torrance." He flashes his badge at me and takes a seat. "Thank you for meeting me."

"Like I have a choice."

He stares at me for a moment, his eyes the color of steel. "I'm sorry if I gave you that impression over the phone. I'm only—"

"Let's cut to the chase. I know why you're here and who sent you."

"Sent me?"

"Please, Detective. I know you're friends with my husband."

He gives me another long stare, as if he's studying me, weighing my words. Then he leans forward. "No, ma'am. I'm not. I'm here to talk to you about the report you filed."

Losing my patience, I rub my mouth. Fine. I'll bite. "Which report? The domestic disturbance or my stalker's promise of multiple murders in my name?"

"Domestic disturbance?" He muses for a second. "I'm very sorry, Mrs. Abel. I wasn't aware you filed one. I was recently transferred to Oak Bluffs."

I squint at him. "So you really don't know

my husband?"

"All I know is that Blake Abel is an ex-cop, which drew my attention to your case, the stalker case."

"Why?"

"Because no one followed up on it. There was no investigation whatsoever. Usually, cases that involve a cop's family member are prioritized."

"Well, your colleagues dismissed both my *claims* as publicity stunts, but I think we all know they did it as a favor to my husband."

"And when I called, you must have thought I was coming on his behalf, to do him another favor."

"Can you blame me?"

Pity jumps to his expression, maybe a dash of anger, too. "Again, I'm very sorry, ma'am. When I called, I wanted to help. I'd like to follow up on the stalker incident."

I glance at Adriana, and she gives me an encouraging smile. Detective Torrance seems to be the only one at the police department that isn't influenced by Blake. He could be of real help with the stalker. Maybe even with my husband.

You never learn from your mistakes. You're gonna trust another cop? Are you insane? How do you know he's telling the truth? How do you know this isn't just another game to get you to trust him? To open up and tell him about your plans with Adriana only so he would report back to Blake?

"You mentioned there was a note. I want to run forensics on it so—"

"Detective Torrance, I appreciate what you're trying to do here, but I'm taking the whole thing to a private sector."

He leans back, pursing his lips. "You don't trust me."

Trust is a word long erased from my repertoire. "Even if you mean well, and you really want to help, they won't let you. I don't want to waste your time or mine."

His chest puffs up with a long inhale. He reaches inside the pocket of his jacket, which allows me a better view of the definition of his bulging muscles underneath his shirt. My mind races with all the lines Jacob Torrance's physique could write for a character of mine, just like it did with Tristan Morra. Except this time, I'm able to swallow the verbal vomit early on.

"Here's my card," he says as he gives it to me. I lift my eyes to his, and a hint of a smile crosses his lips. *Did he notice I was staring?* "Give me a call if you change your mind…or if you need anything." He stands to leave. "We're not all the same, Mrs. Abel. I hope you know that."

I read his card as he steps away. "Detective…"

He turns, his eyes hopeful when they meet

mine.

"Grab a book of mine from the mini bookstore and let me sign it for you. Don't worry. I'll pay for it myself."

Confusion shadows his face for a moment or two, but then he does as I say. When he leans over to give me the book, he whispers, "What is this about?"

"I believe Blake is watching me. When he asks you what you were doing with his wife, tell him yours is a fan. You wanted to surprise her. What makes a better gift than a signed book from her favorite author."

Disappointment erases his confusion. "You're quick with making up stories, Mrs. Abel."

"It's my job."

"But I don't need a story. I'm not scared of your husband."

"That makes one of us, Detective." I open the book. "What's your wife's name?"

"Sign it to Nancy, please. While I'm buying your book, I had to call to make sure she really is a fan. It turns out she is."

He bought the book when I said I would. A show of dominance. I personalize the signature with one of my quotes. My readers love it when I do. "A man who doesn't know what kind of smut his wife reads is a miserable man, Detective Torrance." I hand him the book.

"You should read it. You might learn a thing or two."

A chuckle rips out of his throat. "I'm not married, Mrs. Abel. Never have been. Nancy is my little sister."

Heat bursts in my cheeks. What's wrong with me today? The urge to get back at any man who tries to show me he has the upper hand has put me in an awkward position twice in one day. "Oh...I... How old is she?"

"Twenty-one."

At least, she's not a minor whose dirty little secret I revealed to her older brother. I clear my throat. "And you?"

"Forty-two."

The answer hangs between us for a while. I'm sure he can read the question in my gaze. Why a man like him, good-looking, with a decent job and an excellent physique, a man who has reached the emotional maturity that allows him to settle down and start a family, has never been married. He chooses not to answer it, though. "Don't read too much into it. There's no story there."

"Everything is a story, Detective."

Another chuckle. "I just never happened to meet the one."

I don't know why he needed to tell me that. "Well, there's nothing wrong with waiting." I collect my belongings. It's getting dark, and I should go home before dark. "I got married in my twenties. Suffice to say, it wasn't the best decision I've made."

He sighs and waves the book at me. "Thanks for this. If you're heading out, I can give you a ride."

You should know better, Detective. "I'll walk. I could use some fresh air. And, Detective, I'd appreciate it if you could keep both complaints I've filed confidential. I don't want the press creating a scandal."

"Of course. You don't have to worry about my tipping the press. I'll be busy reading your book. I might learn a thing or two."

Something in the way he says it puts me on edge. Is this merely a throwback or something else more sinister?

He winks. He fucking winks at me. What the hell?

Karma punishes his arrogance instantly. He pumps into a man in a hoodie on the way out so hard he almost trips over his feet. Almost. Shame.

Torrance apologizes awkwardly to the man and leaves. I stop by Adraian's table. "Sorry about dragging you into this. False alarm."

"No problem. But…what's the deal with that stalker? Why didn't you tell me?"

"Not here, Adriana. We'll talk later. You have a ferry to catch, and I have to go home, but if it's not too much trouble, could you send this package with your outgoing mail at the firm?" I hand her my gift to Katie Saldana. "Gia mailed my signed book orders but forgot this one on my desk. I hate it when I disappoint a fan, and you'll save me the trip to the post office."

CHAPTER 8
Birdie

The sky is dimming black, and the crisp air stings my cheeks. My footsteps echo on the sidewalk beneath the soft glow of the streetlights. I'm practically alone on a dark, quiet street, probably for the first time since I moved here, but I'm not afraid. Walking by myself gives me a sense of freedom I've long forgotten. I hold on to it like a lifeline. How long will it last, if at all? I dare dream. A happy ending of a story yet to be written, where I control the narrative. A book to call mine.

I check the security app on my phone. The feed from the rooms remains as I left it. The security alarm is beeping green. No one has broken into my house or left more promises of mayhem. I'm both free and safe for tonight.

A faint scuff on the sidewalk asks if I've spoken too soon. Is that a footstep behind me or a trick of the wind? I glance over my shoulder, but the street is empty.

Nonetheless, that elusive freedom slips away. The sick feeling that I'm being watched creeps up my spine. My pace quickens. Just my imagination. The wind is innocent; it's my mind that's guilty. I try to reason with myself that it's all in my head. When you live in the dark long enough, the light becomes the monster you fear.

But then I hear it again. A crunch, somewhere in the pitch-black alley. Not a rat. Not a cat. A footstep.

My body tenses, ears straining over the sound of my racing breaths. Another step. The foot hits the ground firmly now. Deliberate.

I get my phone and a can of pepper spray out of my purse, but I don't dare turn around or wait for the footsteps to reveal their owner. My body breaks into a desperate run. The decision to walk home turns into regret. I should have gotten a ride. I should have gotten a gun and carried it with me everywhere like Blake does.

Blake. My first thought is to call him despite everything. My heart hammers as the footsteps behind me advance, louder, closer, steady in their pursuit. They tap out a terrifying beat, like the pulse of fear thrumming through me.

I run as fast as my legs allow me. My lungs burn. The cold air does not help. Outrunning whoever is following me doesn't seem like a viable option now. If I fall, I'm as good as dead.

Who is this? Why are they following me? It can't be Blake. I know the sound of his footfalls like the back of my hand. He won't be sending someone to follow me in the dark like a creep either. What if it is some random creep, though?

What if it isn't random? What if it *is* Butterfly Man?

My feet freeze at the thought, and so do the footsteps behind. I can't hear anything but the echoing of my heart. *Think, Birdie. Every crime has a motive. Every goal needs an obstacle. Be the obstacle not the victim.*

I clutch the pepper spray can with one hand, the other ready to tap Blake's number. Slowly, I turn and aim the can at the shadows. I can't see who is there because bright headlights down the street flash in my face. The roar of a motorcycle engine shatters the night. In a split-second, the bike screeches to a halt at my side, and a leather-clad rider hops off. He rips off his helmet, revealing his face.

CHAPTER 9

Birdie

"Mrs. Abel, are you okay?" Tristan Morra asks.

Eyes wide, I stare at him in his biker clothes, unable to comprehend what's happening. Then my head whips between him and the pepper spray I'm aiming at…nothing.

His gaze follows the same path. "Mrs. Abel?"

"Someone is following me," I say.

His posture changes, fully alert, and his stare darts around. "Did you see where they went?"

I just shake my head.

"The sound of my bike must have scared them off. They wouldn't have gone far, though." He pulls a gun out of the back of his pants and steps in the direction where I was pointing the can. "Wait here. Get that mace ready. If you see anything, call 911."

"Wait. Do you have another gun?"

"Do you know how to use it?"

"Yes."

He opens his jacket and hands me a Glock. I shove the pepper spray can in my pocket and hold the gun, and then he starts down the street.

The last few minutes play in my head on repeat. Someone was there. I heard the footsteps. I ran. They followed. When I stopped, they did, too. I aimed the pepper spray at them, but…they weren't there. No one was there.

No one but Tristan Morra.

"I didn't find anything, Mrs. Abel," Morra says, and I flinch. He approaches, a creature cut from the canvas of the night. A dark angel or a devil in disguise? My grip squeezes the gun.

He puts his weapon back in his pants. "Sorry, I didn't mean to startle you."

I swallow. "I didn't see anything on the other side of the street either."

"Are you okay?" He comes closer. "You look so shaken."

I take a step back. "What were you doing here?"

His brows hook, but then realization hits his face. He points behind me. "My hotel. It's three blocks away." He reaches inside his pocket, and I take another step back. "Here's the keycard. It has their number. You can call to verify."

I stare at the keycard, Madisson Inn logo printed on it—a hotel I *know* is three blocks away because I stayed there a couple of times—and curse myself under my breath. "I'm making a fool of myself again. You must think I'm crazy."

"Men have called me mad; but the question is not yet settled, whether madness is or is not the loftiest intelligence—whether much that is glorious—whether all that is profound—does not spring from disease of thought—from moods of mind exalted at the expense of the general intellect."

"Quoting Poe on this dreadful night? A simple no would suffice next time."

"Next time? Well, here's another quote from another writer, whom I think is one of the most talented, brilliant artists of our gener-ation, and not crazy at all. *This is the last time we'll ever cross paths, Mr. Morra. Now, get out of my house and never come back.*"

I bite my lip on an apology I can't seem to verbalize. "And yet here we are."

"Almost like destiny. Do you believe in des-tiny, Mrs. Abel?"

"Destiny can be rewritten." I hand him his Glock. "Thank you for trying to save me tonight. It looks like it was all in my head. I troubled you for no reason."

"But there is also always some reason in madness."

Nietzsche. "You read a lot, Mr. Morra."

"Thanks to you…and audiobooks. They're a dyslexic man's best friend." He smiles. I can't ignore how charming he is. Be it in a suit in the middle of the day or a biker attire in the embrace of the night, Tristan Morra is a dangerously attractive man.

He gives me a spare helmet from his bike. "Let's get you home, Mrs. Abel."

I scowl at it. "I…I don't think that's—"

"There's no way in hell I'll let you walk by yourself when you thought someone was following you. I *will* be your ride home."

"That's not up to you to decide."

He pushes the helmet over my head and buckles it, his scent, leather, musk and a hint of spicy cologne penetrating my nostrils, shifting the ominous energy that has been coursing my body into something more…dreaded. An uninvited delight is as frightening as fear itself. "I'm not taking no for an answer."

"You can't force me to ride with you."

There's a glow in his eyes as he holds my gaze and cocks a brow at me. "Hop on, Mrs. Abel."

"Is that an order, sir?" I mock with a salute.

"No, ma'am. It's a request."

"Can you, at least, say please?"

His lips twist with a smirk. Suddenly, his hands are on my waist lifting me and placing me on his bike. "Please."

A gasp escapes me, the only form of protest I manage to push out before he straddles the bike and revs the engine.

CHAPTER 10

Tristan

The second I pull over at her house, she jumps off the bike, unbuckles the helmet and shoves it in my face. "Thank you for the ride."

With a chuckle, I roll my eyes toward the little camera nestled at the top corner of the front gate. "My pleasure. If you have an app for that security camera feed, show it to me… please."

She fumbles with her phone and lets me check the footage. The house seems empty, and the alarm is intact. "Happy? Now, off you go."

"I'm not leaving until you're safe inside."

"You're not my bodyguard, Mr. Morra."

Whose fault is that, Mrs. Abel? I'm tempted to say it, but I don't. "*And yet here we are. I save* you from a potential stalker, give you a ride home and make sure you're safe for the rest of the night. *Almost like destiny."*

She shakes her head with a scoff when she realizes I'm not going anywhere until she enters her house. As she lets herself in and climbs the stairs to the front door, I regret that this is probably the last time we'll cross paths. Repaying her for how much she helped me wasn't just something I said. I meant it. It bothers me that this wonderful woman has been going through all that pain, and there's nothing I can do to help. Well, there's plenty, but she won't let me.

Keys in hand, she stares vacantly at the door. Her steps falter back as she throws me a hesitant look. She's scared to walk into her own house.

I kill the engine and hop off my bike. "On second thought," I walk through the gate and climb toward her, removing my helmet, "I will check the house and secure the parameter myself before you go in." It is what she wants me to do, but she's too proud to show me her fear, too stubborn to ask me for help.

Her face, as pale as the moonlight, softens for a fleeting moment. Then she squares her shoulders and sticks her chin up. "Knock yourself out. It's not like I can do anything to stop you."

Good girl. I use her keys to unlock the front door and step inside. The house is quiet except for the soft ticks of the heating system. When I turn on the lights, everything looks exactly like in the feed. "You can disarm the alarm and wait in the foyer as I check the rooms."

I do a quick sweep of the first floor. Living room, kitchen and dining room are one large space with no doors. There's a guest bathroom, a small bedroom, and the study where she interviewed me this morning. All clear.

Upstairs, I check each room of the three besides the master suite. Then I nudge open the door to Mrs. Abel's bedroom and tread slowly. The lights reveal a world of her own, glimpses of her tastes and habits, that engulfs and swallows me whole the second I dare cross the threshold.

Her essence, not only the faint floral fragrance that lingers in the air, but the hints of the complex soul she is, is imprinted everywhere. The black furniture dressed in elegant gold flicks. Books and trinkets arranged the way they are on the nightstand and dresser. The wisps of dark hair on her pillow. The lavender sheets rumpled from her slumber…where she's been violated.

Anger and protectiveness take over me. She shouldn't have to feel unsafe here. Why can't she just let me protect her? Mrs. Abel has so many fine qualities I've always admired. Stubbornness isn't one of them.

I check the bathroom and the terrace thoroughly. When I'm satisfied, I return downstairs. She's waiting in the foyer, clutching her purse, eyes darting around nervously. "All good. No one is here." I assure her.

She shuts the door and sighs in relief, but then she crumbles down on the couch and bursts into tears.

"Hey." I hurry to her side and crouch down in front of her. "It's okay. You're safe. *You're safe*, Mrs. Abel."

She covers her face with her hands, crying harder. Then, as if that isn't enough to hide her tears from me, she buries her face in my shoulder, her sobs sifting through me.

I don't talk or ask her to stop crying. Part of it is out of respect, the other part is that physical touch I don't initiate triggers me. She doesn't know that, though, and right now, she needs me, so I push past my own conflicts and dare wrap my arms around her. A proud woman like Birdie Abel won't be crying her heart out in front of someone like me unless she's truly in pain and needs a shoulder to cry on. If that's the only thing she'll let me be, I'm here for it. I wouldn't be where I am today if it weren't for her. I owe her that much.

However, it hurts to see her suffering to the point of breaking. It hurts to go back to a place where all I can do is watch helplessly. It's the worst feeling ever, and I've promised myself never to be in that place again.

"Mrs. Abel, I—"

"I'm sorry, Mr. Morra." She yanks herself away from me and wipes her face.

"For what?"

"This. I should have had more control over my emotions. I'm very sorry."

"You're apologizing for crying?"

She takes a moment before she says, "I guess I am. Crying in front of someone else isn't something…I allow myself to do."

That pause is holding more than just air. I can feel it. This isn't a statement of pride. There's something heavy behind it she won't reveal in words. I sit in the armchair across from her. "There's nothing wrong with showing emotion. If it's any consolation, this isn't the first time I've seen you cry, so let it all out."

Her face, her whole body goes rigid. She looks at me like I stabbed her. I was only trying to make her feel less vulnerable. Now, I've made things worse. "I'm sorry. I shouldn't have said that."

"But you did. When did you see me cry before?"

"It's nothing really. I'm sorry to have brought that up."

"*When*, Mr. Morra?"

Fuck. Here goes nothing. "Eight years ago,

at school, you were talking to another teacher at the pantry. The door was open, I was passing by and overheard parts of your conversation. You were crying, the name Blake came up," I swallow, "and you had sunglasses on…barely hiding the bruise under them."

She jumps to her feet and turns, raising a hand at me to stop talking. Her steps drift away, but her chin and fingers visibly shake as she places the back of her hand under her nose. She's crying again, and I hate myself for it.

I leave my seat and approach her carefully. "Mrs. Abel, please, I—"

"This morning when you said no woman should be afraid in her own house because of a man, stalker or otherwise, you knew, didn't you?"

That Blake Abel, her fiancé eight years ago and now her husband, has been abusing her? Yes, I knew. "I'm so sorry for what you had to go through. I didn't know how long it's been going on until I met you again. All this time, in my heart, I was hoping it was just that one time. I guess I was being naive because it's never just that one time."

"Never meet your heroes, Mr. Morra. They can turn out to be utterly pathetic."

"You're *not* pathetic. You're an amazing person."

She spins, her eyes and cheeks wet and

struck by red. "You know what was the first thing I did today when I left the house? I texted Gia the driver's info because I thought she'd report back to Blake, and he'd know what to do if anything happened to me. And when I thought I was being followed, who was the first person I got my phone out to call for help? It's not 911, not the one cop that's actually on my side, it's fucking Blake. My idea of protection is replacing one monster with another. What does that make me if not a pathetic imposter?"

"It's not your fault. You can't blame yourself. You've been conditioned to think he's the only one who can protect you." I hold her arms gently. "It doesn't have to be that way anymore. I know you don't want me as your security, but I can give you reliable referrals that you can hire. I can arrange for meetings first thing in the morning. The cycle can be broken."

She sniffles, a broken smile on her lips. "You know a lot about abuse, Mr. Morra. I wish you hadn't. Who was the victim? You? Someone you loved?"

A lump clogs my throat. "I'm going to check the backyard and the surrounding areas of the house."

"Did you save them, Mr. Morra?" she asks as I walk to the door, the question a dagger in my back.

I stop for a second, memories attacking me. I shake them off and continue. "I won't be

CHAPTER 11

Birdie

long."

"There's nothing outside, but your security system is basic and can be easily hacked. The security firms I recommend will replace it with a more advanced system." Morra puts a few business cards on the kitchen counter. "Who is staying with you tonight?"

No one. "I'll call Gia."

He nods and looks at the phone in my hand.

I squint at him. Is he waiting for me to make that call? "Thank you so much for everything, Mr. Morra. I've troubled you enough for one day. You're most likely going back to Boston in the morning. I'm sure you need to rest."

He takes a seat on my couch and makes

himself comfortable. "New York."

"Excuse me?"

"I've been planning on opening a new branch there, but I postponed it to come here. When I didn't get the job, I decided to go straight to New York and get on with it."

"I'm truly sorry you didn't get the job, and I wish you all the best with your future endeavors." I don't sit so that he can take a hint.

He flashes a smile at me. "I'm not leaving until your assistant arrives, Mrs. Abel. If you want me out of your hair, now would be a good time to call her."

He's on to me. I fold my arms across my chest, too exhausted to argue. "And if I don't?"

He stretches his arms and then slaps his thighs as he leaves the couch. "Then we're going to need a lot of coffee."

As he helps himself to my kitchen, I realize what he means. "No. No, that's not happening."

"Well, you have three options." He's already pouring himself a cup of coffee. "First, you call your assistant, and the second she's here, I'll bid you both farewell and be on my way. Second, you take my room at the hotel, and I'll stand guard outside the door all night. Third, I do it here, in the comfort of your own house." His strides close the gap between us. His gaze, a mix of concern, intensity, determination and desperation, holds mine. "There's no way in hell I'll let you stay here all alone unprotected, so which is it gonna be?"

I throw my hands in the air in exasperation. "I know you think differently, but eight years ago I was nothing but a woman doing her job and getting paid for it. You don't owe me any-thing, Mr. Morra."

"Yes, I do. Why do you have to be so stub-born all the time? It's just one night. Why can't you just let me help you?"

I wish I could explain, but I can't. Being associated with him in any capacity, long term or one night can open a can of worms I can't contain. It's a risk I'm not willing to take be-cause if it goes south, I'll lose everything I've worked hard for in life.

"I'll call Gia." Begging her to come over af-ter what I said to her this morning will hurt my pride, but I'll take that pain over the alternative.

A long sigh seeps from his chest as I walk toward my office. I feel terrible. Tristan Mor-ra is a good man. He doesn't deserve the way I treat him. Under his dominant bravado, he must be questioning himself and his abilities. He must be wondering why a woman who's supposed to be one of the most supportive and encouraging people in his life would make him feel inadequate and unworthy. I wish there was a way to make him believe none of this is personal or intentional. I'm only doing what I have to do to survive.

I toss my purse on the desk as I scroll through my phone to dial Gia's number. Before I tap the green icon, my fingers tremble, and the phone slips from my hand. A gasp chokes in my throat. I grab on the desk so I won't faint. "Mr. Morra." I try to shout but my voice is trapped. Summoning all the power I have, I yell over the panic attack about to hit me, "Tristan!"

"Mrs. Abel!" His footsteps scurry toward the room, my heartbeat louder. He bursts in, guns out. His stare darts around, unable to locate the threat. "What is it? Are you okay?"

My legs can't carry me any longer; I crumble on the chair. His eyes zero in on me and then on the desk. Then he freezes when his stare, too, falls on the yellow note with the butterfly signature.

CHAPTER 12

Birdie

My breath snags inside my chest. "He was here. He was inside my house again."

"I've just finished reviewing the feed between the time you left and the time you returned. There's nothing on the cameras. The alarm is intact. There's no breach detected," Morra says.

"How? He's not a ghost."

"This security system is basic and can be tampered with. He must have hacked it. It's the only explanation."

I pace my office like a trapped animal looking for a way out, my fingers rubbing frantically over my mouth.

"Mrs. Abel, please calm down. We'll figure

this out. Do you want me to call the police?"

"No!"

The severity of my reaction strikes his face with confusion for a second before he nods. "Okay. I understand."

Does he? He must think it's because of my history with them. He'd have been right with previous incidents. This time, though, I'm not worried about their dismissal. It's quite the opposite. I don't want them to believe me and investigate, not with what's written in that note.

He holds it with a tissue and reads. "*She is my life, my soul, my reason for being. She is the only one who can save me from my past. She is the only one who can make me whole. She is the only one who can make me happy. She is mine, and I am hers.* Is that a quote from one of your books?"

I shake my head. "It's by someone else. Katie Saldana." The quote that bitch patch wrote in her book. The same one I marked with my arousal and sent over to her.

"Do you know that author?"

Author? She's a cheap hack. "She has a big following on social media. Don't *you* know her?"

"No, ma'am, but *you* do, and not because of social media."

I throw a glance at him over my shoulder. "You should have joined the police force, not the military. You'd make a good detective."

"What kind of beef do you have with her? How did she hurt you?"

"What makes you think that worm can hurt me?"

"In the note you showed me earlier, he said he'd kill everyone who hurt you." He brings the note he's holding to my face. "Look, under the quote there's another line. *She is MINE, and I am YOURS*. What do you think that means?"

"Why don't you tell me?"

"She did something to hurt you, and he's about to prove to you he'll keep his promise. This note is a clue…for an upcoming murder."

It's one thing to think of the possibility of evil, it's another to hear it said out loud. Putting it out there for the universe makes it real. It carries a weight, and it smacks me like a wrecking ball. "No."

"You don't want to believe that there's someone out there, a fan of yours, who is capable of taking a life because of you. I get it, and I hope to God those vows of murder are empty threats, but what if they're not? What if Katie Saldana is going to be his first victim?"

His first murder in my name. One in which I could end up a suspect if the police traced back the book I mailed her. What if Butterfly Man doesn't only know about the feud between me and that bitch? What if he knows about the book, too, and he is counting on my silence?

That son of a bitch. How did he find out about either? I was all alone this morning. Could he have hacked my phone, too, like the security system? "Do you know of a way that can detect if my phone has been hacked?"

"Yes." He stretches his hand at me. "Give it to me. I have the necessary tech to check on my phone. If you'll let me use your computer, I can do it right now."

I hand him my phone and watch him work, my heart racing. If it's the phone that's bugged, Butterfly Man must have seen my messages to Martha or heard our phone call. He wouldn't know about the book in the mail, though. I prefer this scenario to the alternative. "Please tell me it's the phone."

He removed both of our devices from my computer. "It's clean."

My heart dips. If Butterfly Man hasn't hacked my phone, there's only one more explanation left. He hasn't hacked into my cameras just to leave his note without getting caught. He did it to watch me, and not only tonight; he's been watching me in my own home for God knows how long.

"Goddammit!" My eyes dart around from one corner to another as I remember I turned off the office camera after I ended the call with Martha. If he's been watching me through it, he'd only know about the plagiarism. Unless…

All the blood rushes away from my body. "Oh my God. What if there are other cameras in the house?"

"What?"

I stare at the bookshelf opposite the sofa bed, my chest heaving, before I lunge at it and rummage through the books. They drop painfully on my feet, Morra's perplexed inquiries in the background, until the bookshelf is clear.

That's when I stop. That's when I see it staring back at me, turning all doubts into certainty. "There are hidden cameras in this room, ones that Blake didn't place."

Morra steps forward and examines the little spy hidden at the back of my shelf. I falter back and drop on the sofa bed. Butterfly Man did watch me while I was touching myself. He has a recording of me fucking myself before I stained Saldana's book with my cum and put it in a package ready to be mailed.

A whirlwind of disgust, apprehension and anger spirals inside me. I grab the side table and smash it on the floor. "Where else are you hiding them, you piece of shit?!"

"Hey." Morra rushes to my side and holds my arms. I yank them out of his grip and dash toward the other bookshelves.

"Hey!" His embrace envelopes me and swirls me to face him. "Look at me. No need to destroy your furniture. I have the right equipment that can find them for you. It's in my hotel. Let me bring it, and we'll find them all."

"I can't live in this fear anymore."

"You won't. I'll take care of this tonight. Then all you have to do is hire one of the firms I recommended. They'll make sure he never sets foot in your house or plants any bugs in it ever again, but you have to promise me you'll act fast. This can't wait."

"No."

"No? Mrs. Abel, you're not dealing with an overly enthusiastic harmless fan. This man is a criminal and a psychotic creep. You are in danger. You *need* professional protection asap."

"That's why I'm saying no. No more waiting. I must act fast like you said…and hire you."

"Me?"

Yes, hiring a former student of mine is a risk that could cost me a lot, but it doesn't compare to the risk of being at the mercy of a deranged potential murderer's whims. I hope my beseeching gaze will let Morra forgive my rudeness to him today and accept my offer. "Please don't go to New York and be my bodyguard, Mr. Morra."

CHAPTER 13

Tristan

"We removed them all…and the tracker we found in your vehicle. He must have planted them the first time he was in your house," I tell Mrs. Abel.

Her lashes cast a shadow over the dark circles hollowing under her eyes. She hasn't slept a wink. The rays of daylight streaming from the windows on her face can't conceal how drained she is.

"Thank you, Mr. Morra. I don't know what I'd have done without you." She gets off her chair and brings a folder from her desk. "Will you walk with me, please?"

I follow her to the backyard, past the team I've sent for this morning that's now swarming the house, securing all entrances and installing an adequate security system.

She regards the shrubberies and the garden seats. "Are there any cameras here?"

"Only at the doors. Nothing on this very spot."

Her gaze still wanders restlessly, covering every corner, even the sky above.

"We're alone, Mrs. Abel. Whatever you want to say, it's safe with me."

"You always seem to understand me without words." A nervous smile twitches on her lips as she opens the folder. "I can't thank you enough for accepting the job after how I've been treating you. These are the contracts, already signed by me, ready for you to countersign."

"You? Not the publisher?"

"No. *I* am hiring you. You answer only to me." She stares at me, waiting for confirmation.

"I understand, and I couldn't agree more."

She hands me the folder. "I added another document for you to sign, though. Please read it carefully."

"Let me guess. Another NDA?"

"I'm sorry. It's not that I question your integrity. I just…" She trails off when I sign the document. "You haven't read it."

"I am your bodyguard, Mrs. Abel. I'll do anything to make sure you're safe and secure.

Do you think a man who is prepared to take a bullet for you will hesitate to sign a piece of paper that will make you feel protected?"

She laughs under her breath.

"Something funny?"

"Blake said something similar when I asked him to sign the prenup."

My jaw clenches. I can never win with her, can I? "I'm sorry that all the men you know are deceitful, abusive pieces of shit who want to use you, but I'm not one of them. I'm here to protect you, bound by my word and my code, not by pieces of paper and paychecks. If that's not enough for you to trust me, consider our agreement void, ma'am." I jab the folder in the space between us. "No need to compensate me for my time. You can keep the gear, too, as a gift from Monarca."

I turn to leave, but she jumps in my way. "No, please. I'm sorry."

The desperation in her voice doesn't soothe my anger. "Me too."

"Please." She grabs my wrist as I step away. The way her fingers tremble around my hand lights a fuse inside me, my protective instincts on haywire.

"I don't like to be touched, Mrs. Abel. In my line of work, even the kindest touch could pose a threat."

Her hand drops. "I'm very sorry. I didn't

mean to make you uncomfortable."

Uncomfortable? Unlike everyone else, it's not discomfort she makes me feel. It stunned me the first time she cried on my shoulder, but I managed to ignore it. Now, she does it again, and it drags me to an uncharted territory I don't know how to navigate.

"Please, don't go. Tristan, I need you."

Despite how her touch makes me feel, the way she calls me by my first name and her voice when she says she needs me compel me to stay. "Without trust, I can never protect you. Can you trust me with your life or not?"

"Yes. I can. I do."

I sigh and nod at the folder. "Give me that back."

A swift smile appears on her face as she does. "I feel like I need to explain the document you blindly signed. Primarily, it prohibits you and your team from disclosing any past, present and future business or personal information about me, my family and my works. It strictly and precisely states that you can't disclose to anyone our former teacher-student relationship or reveal my real name."

"I don't need an NDA to know that. You almost didn't hire me because of our former relationship." I finish signing the contracts. "Now that I've proven you can trust me, can you tell me why?"

The softness she's allowed me to witness vanishes. She gives me a look I recognize from her teaching days; the look that says I crossed a line, and there will be consequences. "How did you get that scar on your face?"

My eyes twitch for a second as the memory carves my skin fresh. "That's… I don't see how my past injuries can be relevant to my question."

"Not all of us can wear our scars on our faces. We may trust others with our lives but not with the secrets behind the deepest cuts that can't heal without leaving their marks. When you trust me enough to tell me how you got yours, I'll tell you about mine."

CHAPTER 14

Birdie

"This is my house! You can't stop me from coming in! Birdie!"

My body jolts at Blake's voice. Angry footsteps stomp down the hall, a prelude to a hurricane.

Morra's forehead creases. "You don't have to see him. Let me deal with it."

I shake my head. "If he feels he has no access to me, he'll flip. Blake is unpredictable when it comes to losing power. I have to talk to him."

He nods reluctantly as he walks ahead of me. I rush forward to cut him off. "Uh…perhaps alone?"

He stares at me as if I'm out of my mind. "I'm your bodyguard. That man is a threat. You're not going anywhere near him without protection. Please follow me, Mrs. Abel."

Blake storms into the house, barely contained by Morra's team. "What the hell is this?!" he bellows when he sees my face.

"Blake, please," I begin, barely meeting his gaze, my voice trembling despite my efforts to appear composed, "I hired one of the security firms you vetted." I gesture at the four men in suits surrounding Blake, "That's the team responsible for the house security," and then at Morra, "and this is Tristan Morra, my bodyguard. I believe you've already spoken."

"You hired a damn bodyguard without consulting me?!" Blake's voice booms through the house. "I'm your husband and manager. *I* make these decisions."

I swallow, my throat too dry. "Not anymore."

"Oh yeah?" Blake scoffs bitterly and glares at Morra. "Well, you're fired. Get the fuck out."

Morra doesn't flinch. "I don't work for you. Mrs. Abel hired me herself, as an individual, which means neither you nor any other party you represent has any authority here. She's the only one I answer to."

Blake switches his glare toward me, and I notice how red and glazed his eyes are. He's on something. "Still scheming behind my back, aren't you? You think this glorified babysitter can protect you?"

My heart pounds. Blake's temper is unmanageable when he's wasted. "Blake, please. Why don't you leave now? We can talk later."

"There's no later. I'm heading upstairs to take a shower. Escort your guests out before I come back down and throw them out myself." Blake moves toward the stairs, but the men block his way. He pushes the two in front of him. "You can't stop me from going to my room. This is my house!"

"No, it's not," I say to end this conflict before it escalates more violently, drawing strength from Morra's presence amidst this chaos. "This is my house, and you don't live here anymore. We have an agreement."

"What fucking agreement? To stab me in the back and kick me out of my own house? What did you do, Birdie? What the fuck did you do?"

"Blake, please don't make a scene."

"That's all you care about. Your image, always protecting your dirty secrets, always pretending to be the fucking victim. Who has been protecting those secrets for you all these years? Who has been running to your rescue all this time like a damn dog? I ran down here the second I…"

"The second you what? The second you lost the live feed from the security system you installed? The one you used as an excuse to watch my every move?"

He stumbles on his words, proving my suspicions true. "Everything I do is to protect you."

"No. If that's true, you would have been here last night when I was terrified out of my skin because that psycho broke into my house again. You'd have been by my side instead of spending the night with God knows whom, getting wasted in a shithole. But no, you only rush down here when you lose control over your possession. That's what you do, Blake."

"What about you? What did you do, Birdie?"

"What are you talking about?"

"After your call with Martha, what did you do?"

The patches of my courage rip. Is he referring to what I did to Saldana's book or what I've planned with Adriana?

"Why wouldn't you let your agent call your manager to resolve the problem with Saldana?" Blake insists. "Why would you turn off the cameras in your office before you leave without telling anyone where you're going? What did you do, Birdie?"

He knows. Blake knows everything. "You're wasted. Please leave."

"I know you better than anyone, sweetheart. Why did you turn off the cameras, Birdie?

What did you not want me to see? Will you tell your new savior? Do you think he's gonna stay and protect you after he finds out what a monstrous little bitch like you is capable of?"

Morra steps in between us. "That's enough! She asked you to leave, Mr. Abel. If you don't remove yourself, we'll have to remove you by force."

Blake shoves Morra but barely moves him an inch. "Don't tell me what to do in my own goddam house! I'm not leaving!" Blake's expression darkens, his gaze boring into mine with an intensity that sends a shiver down my spine. "I can't live without you, Birdie. I did everything for you. You can't leave me. You're mine."

"Please, go, Blake. I'm begging you," I plead, my voice thick with choking tears.

His face twists in fury as he pushes past everyone and lunges at me. I scream, my steps faltering back, but Morra uses his body as a shield between me and Blake. He grabs Blake's arms, incapacitating my husband in swift moves.

"Get your hands off me!" Blake barks, struggling against Morra's iron grip. "This is my wife! I do whatever I want to her whenever I want. If I wanna fuck her in front of all of you right now, you can't stop me."

My skin crawls at the obscenities streaming

from his mouth. How did we get here? How could I've been so blind all these years to what my husband is capable of? How did I end up dragged to this level of disrespect and malice?

Morra's hand balls into a fist and punches Blake in the face. "This is not a way to talk in front of a lady. Apologize."

"Apologize?" Blake laughs hysterically. "To the *lady?* You don't know what you've gotten yourself into, boy. You're nothing but a fucking pawn in that bitch's game."

Morra growls, his fist ready for the second punch, but I yell, "No, Mr. Morra, please just let him go."

He glances at me over his shoulder for a second before he nods at his team. "The next time I hear you disrespect a woman, I'll punch you silent."

Two of the men take Blake by the arms and drag him toward the door. He kicks and flails, and then his wild eyes meet mine again. "This isn't over, Birdie. I'm not letting you go. You're mine, you hear me? Mine!"

CHAPTER 15

Tristan

Mrs. Abel excuses herself without a word. I follow her up the stairs, but she says, "You don't need to follow me around inside the house."

She needs some time alone after all that's been happening, but I have to do my job. "To ensure your safety, I must be always aware of your location and make sure said location is secure. It's in the job description. Literally."

Anticipating her proud sass to pop, I brace for whatever comment she's going to dish out to dismiss me, but she walks to her room without so much of a glare. "I'm just going to take a bath," she mutters as she opens the door, hiding her face from me. "Maybe it'll help me sleep a little."

To help her sleep or free her tears without being seen? I can hear them in her voice. "Mrs. Abel—"

"Please, from now on, call me Birdie."

"I… That's gonna be very difficult for me to do, considering, you know, that thing that shall not be named." She was my teacher. I've never called her by her first name before.

"You'd better get used to it because I don't want to hear his name ever again, not if I can help it."

"I understand. Are you okay?"

She steps inside her bedroom. "I'll be fine, Mr. Morra."

"C'mon now, for this to work, you gotta call me by my first name, too."

She nods solemnly. "I'm sorry you had to see that, Tristan."

A surge of anger jolts through me. First, she apologizes for crying, and now she apologizes for that piece of shit abusive husband of hers, who should be locked up for what he's done to her. How badly has he messed with her head? Is it only him? Are there others before him that started the cycle? "Mrs. A—Birdie, I know you're a woman that values her pride, but you should know that what he did is in no way a reflection of who you are. You can't apologize for what he's done. He's responsible for the damage he's caused. None of it is your fault."

She finally lifts her eyes to mine. "Thank you…for not judging me. Your parents would have been so proud of you, of the man you've become. You're very mature for your age."

"I'm no longer nineteen. I'm a twenty-seven-year-old man. I should be that mature." I don't know why I had to say that. I should take her words as a compliment, but I end up in defensive mode, offended even.

She regards me for a while before her expression hardens. "I can see you are a man, but are you a violent man, Tristan?"

"Excuse me?"

"That anger I detect in your tone, does it come out solely every time my husband is in the conversation, or is it always there?"

My whole life has been a front row seat to the horrid games people play to dominate those they think are inferior. The threat, the potential of violence, I see it in everything, everywhere. "I'm a soldier, a guard, violence is part of my job, but it's not who I am. I'm a *protective* man, Birdie. That's why I don't tolerate people like Blake Abel."

"Is that why you punched him when you had him completely incapacitated? I don't think *that* is in the job description."

There it is, the sassy snark biting me back in the ass. In a way, I'm glad she's no longer so distraught that she wants to hide in her room and wallow. That man doesn't deserve her tears.

"Mature people know when to apologize, Tristan."

"I agree, but I'm not sorry I punched your husband." I cock a brow. "Are you?"

Her brief silence and the shadow of the smile on her lips satisfy me. "I was worried he'd hurt you and the team. He's always armed. I'm surprised he didn't draw his gun at you."

I can't help smirking as I reach into the back of my pants and bring out Abel's gun. "The team and I can handle ourselves."

Her eyes widen. "You took it from him?"

"The second he tried to lunge at you he became a violent threat that needed to be neutralized. I felt the gun he was hiding under his clothes when I grabbed him. Once he was secure in my grip, I disarmed him."

"You're so fast. All I saw was your immobilizing Blake and then punching him."

"Fast is in the job description."

She laughs under her breath. "Thank you for everything you've done."

"It's nothing." Nothing compared to finally hearing her laugh after the daunting events that have been happening to her. That is my greatest accomplishment today.

"I'm getting a divorce, you know?" she whispers. "He'll never grant me one on his own, so I've been consulting with a divorce attorney in secret. Yesterday when you found me, I'd just finished a meeting with her. No one knows about this yet, but it won't be long before she sends him the papers."

I'm elated she entrusts me with this information and relieved she's leaving that monster, but underneath her words there's something else. There are fear and shame, and a reason for sharing them other than confiding in me. "That's wonderful news."

"I know you don't judge me, but it's important for me that you know the woman you respect isn't such a weak doormat that lets a man like Blake walk all over her without doing anything about it…or, at least, trying."

"You're afraid of what he can do to stop you, but I'd like to see him try. You will get that divorce, Birdie. You have my word."

"You don't know him. He's capable of so much evil. You heard the things he said, how he tries to turn you against me. He always does that to anyone on my side he can't control."

"There's nothing he can say or do that's going to change how much I respect you or how much I want to be here to protect you." I level my gaze with hers. "There's nothing *you* can say or do that's going to change that either."

She folds her arms over her chest. "What's that supposed to mean?"

"What happened after your call with your agent?"

Her lashes flutter, and then her jaw clenches. "See? Blake is already getting into your head."

"No, Birdie, but something happened yesterday. It can't be a coincidence the stalker sends you a note threatening to kill that writer the very same day you're talking to your agent about her."

"I'm tired, Tristan. We'll talk later."

She tries to shut the door, but I hold it and step inside. "As much as I'd love to leave you to get your much needed rest, this can't wait." I close the door, not leaving until I get answers. "There's a woman's life on the line here. What did she do to you that the stalker is set to kill her for you? What are you hiding from me?"

Her fingers rub over her mouth as she sits on her bed, and then she crosses her legs and looks me straight in the eye. "When you found the hidden cameras, you told me the stalker planted them the first time he was in my house and not yesterday when he left the second note. How did you know that?"

CHAPTER 16

Birdie

My question is merely a deflection so I won't have to answer his. I expect him to give me one of his clever explanations or lash out about not trusting him, but this, the silence, rigid and intense, sends me spiraling.

His unfazed gaze knocks the air out of my lungs. Am I looking at the monster that has been terrorizing me all this time? In this game of cat and mouse, have I ended up the prey?

My heart echoes over the silence. This can't be my plot twist. I'll be damned if it is, if Tristan Morra turns out to have anything to do with Butterfly Man, if I haven't seen it coming before I let him in my house, before I made him my protector, before I sit in my bedroom in front him, isolated and unarmed, while he holds a gun in his hand.

Staring at Blake's weapon in Tristan's hand, I reprimand myself for not thinking this through. I should have chosen a better timing for blowing the cover of the man posing as my bodyguard.

Tristan drops his stare to the gun for a heartbeat before he returns to regard me. My fingers twist the sheets, looking for something, anything I can use as a weapon. "You should give me Blake's gun. It's evidence that can help with the divorce."

"*Bueno. Si es necesario que cada uno de nosotros dé un paso atrás para que podamos avanzar juntos, hagámoslo así.*"

"What? I'm sorry I don't speak Spanish."

He strides toward me, and I jump. Stumbling on my feet backwards, I hit a wall. In a flash, he's in front of me, his palms caging me in. He doesn't lay a hand on me, but I feel invisible chains holding me immobile, defenseless while he's in utter control. If he wants to do anything to me, I won't be able to stop him. My eyes dart sideways at his palm on the wall, at the gun that is now an inch away from my face. "Tristan, what are you doing?"

His gaze travels down my body and then back up my face. He halts at my trembling lips and inclines his head. My chest heaves with fear and…twisted desire. It's my brain turning danger into something enticing to make it more tolerable. That and the fact that Tristan Morra's lips blur the lines of logic and sanity.

His breath fans my skin, the scent intoxicating. "Do you like to be afraid, Birdie?"

"No," I whisper.

"I don't like to see you afraid either."

"Then why are you scaring me?"

He smirks. "I'm not trying to scare you. I'm only giving you a taste of your own medicine."

"What are you talking about? Why don't you just put the gun down and answer the question?"

"Which one? How did I know when the cameras were planted?" His smirk stretches into a full grin, a predator about to lock his jaws around his catch. "Or am I your Butterfly Man?"

A harsh tremor vibrates through my body. "Are you?"

"What if I am? You shouldn't be scared of me. I won't kill or hurt you. I'm obsessed with you. I'm doing all this to have you, aren't I?"

A chaotic storm of emotions engulfs me. My thoughts, a tangled mess, contradict each other. My heart catches between the hammering beats of betrayal and the flutters of relief, terrified yet inexplicably drawn to the man who embodies both danger and safety. If Tristan is Butterfly Man, he is a twisted answer to my prayers. A dark angel sent to take away the pain caused by those who really hurt me. I shouldn't be afraid of him. I'll be safe in his arms.

For now.

"God, you really think I'm your stalker." He chuckles, shaking his head, as he takes the magazine out of the gun. "From the second I set foot in your house, I've done nothing but show you how much you can trust me, how far I'm willing to go to protect you, but you…"

He takes a couple of steps backward, his invisible grip on me lifting, releasing me out of a cage that looks like I've sketched for myself. "You want to know how I figured out when he installed the cameras? I knew that from you."

"I only deduced there were hidden cameras. I never assumed the timing of their installation."

"It was only when you saw the note about Saldana that you realized there were hidden cameras. That means whatever she did to provoke that reaction from the stalker happened before he broke in last night, and you knew the only way he could have known about it was either by hacking into your phone or watching it happen in your office through those cameras. Your phone is clean, which means it's the latter."

Shame constricts my throat as I revise last

night's events and realize he's right. His mimicry of Butterfly Man, though brief, has shaken me to the core. Blinded by doubt, I've assumed the worst of the man I should trust the most.

"Add this to what your husband said, and your reaction when I asked you yesterday if you want me to call the police, do you know what else I can tell for sure?"

"I said no police because they always dismiss me," I lie.

"Don't insult my intelligence as you continually do with my loyalty. I know fear when I see it, Birdie. You were afraid of calling them, of what they may find if they investigate. This whole charade you've just put together, doubting me, pretending you're terrified I might be your stalker, is nothing but a way to distract me, to evade telling me what you're really hiding."

"I wasn't pretending. You were very convincing." I collect myself and move off the wall, away from the scrutiny of his gaze.

"Sorry. If it is necessary for each of us to take a step back so that we can move forward, so be it."

I take a deep breath, letting that sink in for a minute. "That's what you said in Spanish earlier, isn't it?"

"Like I said, I was only giving you a taste of your own medicine. I'm tired of the way you keep distrusting me.”

My eyes travel back to his sheepishly. “I’m sorry, too, Tristan. I keep offending you. How can I make it up to you?”

“Your trust is all I need. No more secrets. I signed your contracts blindly. I’ve just told you there’s nothing you can say or do that’s going to change how much I respect you. You can’t hide things from me no matter how dark they are. I can’t protect you if I don’t know what I’m protecting you from.”

“You’re so convinced I did something questionable to Saldana. What if I told you I committed a crime? Our conversations aren’t privileged. You’re obligated to report me. How can you protect me then?”

He closes the distance between us, his face no longer angry. “I’m gonna say it again and again, until you believe it, do you think a man who is prepared to take a bullet for you will hesitate to lie to keep you safe?”

The sincerity in his words penetrates the darkness betrayal has long wrapped around my ability to trust. I want to believe him so badly. Can I truly trust Tristan Morra? He knows I’ve done something wrong, but he chooses to stay, protecting me with no questions asked. Everything about him invites me to drop my guard and lay myself bare, promising, no matter what, I’ll be safe. There’s nothing that should stop me from trusting him.

Yet here I am, trembling at the threshold, unable to cross once and for all. There's something about Tristan, a darkness of his own, that stands between me and that leap. I hear it in his voice, in his promises. I see it in his eyes. It marks him whole. Or is it all in my head? Am I becoming my worst enemy like Gia warned?

"You would do that for me?" I search his eyes for a definitive answer to put me out of misery.

"In a heartbeat." He puts the gun and the magazine in my hands. "Now, please tell me, if Saldana winds up dead, will there be anything the police can find that ties you to her murder?"

Yes, but should I tell you about it?

Something flickers in his gaze, and it clicks. All the conversations we've had, everything he's done for me, the lines he's willing to cross. Suddenly, all the pieces fall in place. That darkness isn't malicious. It's a vulnerability.

A yearning for a second chance to save whom he once couldn't.

Who is it? A friend? A lover? A family member? I've asked him before, but he evaded my question like I'm evading his. One day, he'll tell me about her and his scar, when I show him I'm worthy of his trust. Is he worthy of mine?

My doubts teeter at the edge, and I make my choice.

CHAPTER 17

Tristan

irdie lets the water run in the bathtub and rests on the porcelain edge. "There are no cameras here, I presume."

"Of course not." I lean against the doorframe and fold my arms over my chest. "I'm listening."

She tells me, eyes barely looking my way, cheeks turning pink, about her beef with Saldana, and what she's done with the book she asked her lawyer to send in the mail.

Birdie, Birdie, Birdie.

She chances a glance at me and swallows. "Say something…please."

I can't because I'm busy stuffing my hands in my pockets to hide the sudden erection I'm having.

"I get it. You don't see me the same way anymore," she mutters.

She's right. A minute ago, she was my former teacher I was indebted to and my client to protect. Now, she's a morally gray woman sitting on the edge of her bathtub, telling me about the time she touched herself and used her cum to stain her rival's book in vengeance, and it gives me a hardon.

My lips press together, stifling a laugh. Is that all she's been terrified to tell me? Is that what makes her so ashamed? Yes, it's wrong and vindictive, but what the other woman did is a crime. Saldana had it coming. *She* should be ashamed, as should I for not being able to stop myself from picturing Birdie's fingers between her legs.

I clear my throat. "I have to go."

Blood drains from her face. "See? That's exactly why I didn't want to tell you."

"Birdie—"

"No, you promised." She jumps to her feet. "You kept pushing me to tell you, and then what? You're leaving."

"Birdie, I have to go get that book before the lawyer mails it." *And to cool down.*

She halts in place and then rubs a thumb over her eyebrow, color flooding her cheeks. "Oh."

Her blushing doesn't help with the cooling

down part. I avert my gaze. "Listen, when I'm gone, Marcus is in charge. If you need anything, talk to him."

She stares at me in confusion, and I realize I haven't introduced the team properly to her yet. "He's the one with the mustache."

"Okay. Thanks…again…for not judging me."

I can never judge her; I'm not a sinless man; Will she do the same for me when she realizes her sins weigh nothing against mine? "There are no saints here, Birdie."

The air hangs heavy between us as we listen to our breaths loud over the streaming water. "Have some rest because, when I return, we're setting a meeting with Saldana."

"What? No!"

"We have to warn her."

"I'm not talking to that thief. What if she doesn't believe me? What if she uses the situation, twisting it around to gain more fans and turn people against me?"

"You really think she'll care about any of that when she knows her life is in danger? There's a deranged man out there who is set to kill her because she crossed you."

"You don't know that for sure."

"Yes, I do. You do, too. So, unless you want blood on your hands, you'd better suck that ego up and listen to what I'm saying."

"And if I say no?"

"Then I'll call the police myself."

"What? Tristan, you gave me your word."

"Which I intend to keep as long as I'm breathing. That's why I'm doing this. I'll protect you no matter what, even if it means saving you from yourself."

I tell her to call her lawyer to get the book ready when I come to collect it and stride out of her room before she gets a chance to argue. Then I brief Marcus on my way out of the house.

The trip to Boston takes a little over two hours between my bike and the ferry. I dust the sand off my boots and gear as I arrive at Abbot and Lockwood's; the roads from the island aren't motorcycle friendly, neither is the ferry ride.

When I reach Birdie's lawyer's office, her paralegal takes my business card and says Ms. Lockwood is very busy, but she can squeeze me in right away. I don't know if it's my mention of Birdie's name that scores me the privilege of meeting busy Ms. Lockwood immediately or it's because the petite blonde is looking at me like I'm a god. Either way, I thank her with a smile that will mean a lot more to her than it'll ever do to me.

My looks—I've learned later rather than sooner—open a lot of closed doors. I've never been a man who relies on charm to get what he wants; I didn't grow up to think I was easy on the eye. For so many years, I was led to believe I was hideous. It's funny how things change when the serpents that hiss poison in your head die. Senses heal and open to a different world, where each imperfection, each scar, becomes a badge, a mark of beauty and strength. It also helps to add fifty pounds of muscle and get a two-hundred-dollar haircut.

Lockwood welcomes me inside her office apprehensively. "Is Birdie all right?"

"Yes. She had an encounter with her husband this morning, but my team and I contained it. She's under my protection now. He won't come near her again."

She regards me longer than normal and then twirls my card between her fingers. "Tristan Morra, head of Monarca security firm himself acting as her bodyguard. Impressive."

I don't like her tone or the way she looks at me. "Birdie sent me to retrieve the book she asked you to mail yesterday. It turned out her assistant left it out of the mailed orders on purpose because the book was faulty. Something about sprayed edges…I don't know."

"And she sends her bodyguard for it?"

She suspects something. I hate lawyers. They're worse than the police. "Yes, ma'am. Birdie needs the package pronto. I'm the one with the motorcycle who can come here the fastest. Hopefully, you haven't mailed it out yet?"

"I haven't," she mumbles.

"Thank God." Now I can get it back and keep Birdie safe. The police won't find anything that ties Birdie to whatever her stalker intends to do to Saldana. "Can I please have it back?"

"As I explained to Birdie on the phone, I'm no longer in possession of the package. She didn't tell you?"

"What do you mean you don't have it? You've just said you didn't mail it out."

She sighs. "Unfortunately, it was lost."

"You lost it? How?"

Embarrassment darkens her face. "Yesterday, when I was walking to my car after I left the café, I bumped into a guy on the street. It was dark, and my briefcase fell open. The man apologized and helped me put everything back, or so I thought. When I checked this morning, the envelope wasn't there. I tore the place down looking for it, but it was gone. I'm so sorry."

A chill runs down my spine as the implications sink in. If this guy is Birdie's stalker... "Can you describe the man?"

"It was dark, and he was wearing all black. A hoodie and a cap. I couldn't see his face because he had a face mask on, one of those that has a custom print on it. Honestly, I thought it was creepy as hell."

"Why? What print did he have on the mask?" I ask even though I know the answer before she says it.

"A butterfly. A big butterfly where his mouth is supposed to be."

CHAPTER 18

Butterfly Man

irdie loves motorcycles. She puts them in all her books, an accessory that adorns her protagonists. Is that what draws her to him, the man with the motorcycle that now calls himself her protector?

What are the odds of his showing up on that street, at that precise moment to scoop her away and play savior? Maybe, it was a mistake not going straight to my place after I snatched the book from her lawyer's bag. Seeing Birdie in the flesh at the café should have been enough. I shouldn't have followed her on her way home. Greed has its way of clouding judgment, but how could I resist walking down the street with her, as if it were our first date and I was walking her home, making sure she arrived safely?

I stole a glance or two at her profile under the moonlight—the curve of her cheek, the way her lips moved when she smiled. She was beautiful in a way that made my chest ache. Did she feel the same electric tension as our footsteps echoed together? Did her pulse quicken as she realized I was there looking after her? Did she sense the unspoken question hanging between us?

"Thank you for tonight," I'd say as we stood at the threshold of her door. "I had a great time."

"Me too." She'd smile, nervous, not knowing I was trembling on the inside.

The moment would stretch as I saw the war in her eyes, the desire to lean in and the fear of where it'd lead. I'd swallow and lick my lips. Then, hopeful, I'd take the first step and lean closer, my breath mingling with hers, my heart a frantic melody, wild yet desperate for permission.

I'd caress her soft skin and kiss her forehead, safe and respectful, but I'd want more. Much more.

Her gaze would flicker to my mouth, and her chest would heave. And then, as if surrendering to fate, she'd tilt her head, closing the gap.

Our lips would meet—a collision of

warmth and need and madness, the first notes of a love song. Time would cease to exist; there would only be this kiss. *There would only be us. But you prefer him—the man desperate to be your hero.*

He, you let into your house. You grant him the pleasure of your company day and night. He gets to earn your trust. He gets to see the look in your eyes when you let him save you.

He enters the law firm building, confident he'll save the day. I smirk at the disappointment in his voice when he realizes he won't. Taking the book from the lawyer isn't the only task I've accomplished when I accidentally knocked her briefcase open on the ground. I put a bug in it, too, and now I can hear every conversation she has.

Birdie thinks I can no longer see her after she's made the man with the motorcycle take away my little windows of heaven. She's wrong. Yes, I can't watch her the same way I used to, but there are so many other ways to watch my little bird. Like placing bugs on people she has contact with. Like watching him.

Through him, I see you, darling. I see you, my little bird.

The book that has started this twisted game presses against my chest underneath my hoodie like a dirty secret as his bike gives a primal roar. I want to follow him. I want to end him and take his place. I'm so jealous. She makes me so jealous I want to kill him. I want him dead. He shouldn't be here. He's not the one who's supposed to be there for her. I am. He has to die. I have to kill him.

My nostrils flare with a deep breath. Birdie's naughty scent lingers from the pages and soothes my compulsions, just enough to clear the haze and bring me back to rationality. I can't kill him now. She trusts him, not me. I have to show her I'm much worthier of her trust than he'll ever be. Then I'll kill him. He'll be out of the way, and I'll be the man she needs. The man she deserves.

I ignore the impatient urges and decide not to get sidetracked anymore. I'm out here on a time-sensitive mission.

Katie Saldana's house isn't far. She moved to Boston less than a year ago after her second book series—a poor rip-off of Bridie's books—took off. It's funny that she's chosen to live in the same state as Birdie. Heck, even the house looks similar to Birdie's, only bigger, much bigger, and tackier. It's like a competition Saldana must win, fueled by envy and spite. Birdie moves to a two-story house on a small island in Massachusetts, Saldana moves to the biggest city in the same state and gets herself a three-story house. It doesn't matter that it lacks taste. It matters that it's more expensive. A show of who has more money, thus more success.

People who measure success solely with money are petty. After taking a good look at Saldana as she's huddled behind her desk, blowing out a breath, frustrated at her own lack of creativity, I get it, though. She doesn't have anything else.

Her creativity is less than mediocre. She isn't much to look at. Her teeth are big—the only thing that's big in her. They're crooked and ugly. When she smiles, she looks like a donkey. Her hair is dull brown, and her skin needs years of facials and expensive fillers. Her husband is grabbing the maid's ass in the kitchen while Saldana tries to patch Birdie's work into hers to make more money that will let him stay with her anyway and tell her that her donkey teeth are the most beautiful thing he's ever seen.

I lower myself behind the wheel of my car when her husband opens the front door. He's wearing blue running shorts and a gray sweatshirt. Is he going out for a run?

He leaves the house and starts jogging down the street, but just as he rounds the corner, he stops. He glances right and left and then at his watch. A few minutes later, the maid leaves the house in her rundown car and picks him up on the corner. Then, as soon as he's settled in her car, his tongue is down her throat.

Yup, they're about to workout, together, in a sleazy hotel room or in the backseat of the rundown car. And my job has become a lot easier. I don't have to worry about luring the thief out without her family noticing or getting rid of them if I have to.

She's all alone, waiting for me.

CHAPTER 19
Butterfly Man

Saldana's head whips backwards, her consciousness kicking back in. A strange noise comes out of her nose as she blinks herself awake. Her body jerks, threatening to knock down the chair I've tied her to. "Where am I?" Her gaze darts around the upper floor of my loft, and when it hits my face, she flinches with a gasp. "Who are you? What do you want from me?"

I clasp my hands behind my head and lean back in my seat. "Your husband is cheating on you with the maid, so you decided to have an affair, too, with me."

It takes her a while to respond. "W-w-hat?"

"That's what the neighbors would say to the police and the press. You were having an affair. I made sure they saw we were intimate when we left your house, and in your car that you let me drive while your lips were pressed to my neck."

"What the hell are you talking about? My husband isn't cheating on me. I don't know you. I didn't let you drive my car, and I didn't... You..." Flashes of memory seem to be coming back to her. "You kidnapped me! Help! HELP!"

"God, you even sound like a donkey. Don't bother yelling. This place is soundproof. No one can hear you. Anyway, I deleted all your security system footage of my drugging you and taking you, your phone and your laptop from your house, so no one is gonna believe your story. The affair scenario, on the other hand, is tight. And your husband is definitely cheating on you, Katie."

Anger colors her pale skin before she blubbers ugly. Then, suddenly, she stops, and her eyes widen. "Why…why would the neighbors talk to the police or the press?"

Realization hasn't fully dawned on her yet. I smile.

"No, no, please. Why?" she sobs. "I don't know you. I haven't done anything to you. Why would you want to kill me? Please, don't. Please."

"You don't know me, but I do, Katie.

You're a thief, a hoax, a filthy imposter that doesn't deserve the air she breathes. While you haven't hurt me directly, you've hurt my little bird, and that is unforgivable."

"A thief? Little bird? What the fuck are you talking about?"

I jump to my feet and jab the air between us with my index finger. "You know exactly what I'm talking about!" I pull the book Birdie was going to send her from under my hoodie, open the marked page and read the stolen words. Then I recite the original from Birdie's book. "Is that enough to refresh your memory or do you want more? There's plenty where that came from."

Sniffling, she shakes her head. "I…I don't—"

"Don't bother lying to me. I know you've been stealing Bridie's words for years."

"No…you got it all wrong. She's…she's the one stealing from me."

My head falls back as I laugh wholeheartedly. "Like that's even possible." Then I draw out my gun.

"All right! I'm sorry! Yes…I've been…borrowing from her books. There, I said it. But… but that's between me and her. Why are you…" She starts crying again. "Who are you and why do you care?"

"Why do I care? Why do I care if a parasite

like you hurts my little bird?" My footsteps echo harshly against the hardwood floor. I bend over and cup her chin to hold her face steady. I look her in the eye as she shudders. "Oh, my dear, you don't understand. Birdie isn't just the love of my life. She's the center of my universe. Without her, I'm nothing. I've woven myself into the fabric of her existence. I've spent my years studying the curve of her spine, the rhythm of her breath, the secrets hidden behind her eyes. She's mine, and I'll protect her fiercely."

"Are…you…her husband?"

"Her husband?" The word tastes so delicious, so fulfilling yet not enough. It's a warm blanket of reassurance, but Birdie sets my soul ablaze with a need to be so much more than just a figure of stability and commitment. She deserves a love that defies confinement—one as wildly boundless as her spirit. A vast, perpetually evolving frontier awaiting exploration without boundaries or limits.

I want to be her safety and her adventure. I want to be not just her partner—a word too frail to carry the immensity of what she means to me—but her inspiration.

I want to be her pain, her darkest of sufferings that I crave with a hunger that defies reason. I want to make her bleed and yet be the fragile beating of her heart that keeps her alive.

For Birdie, I want to be everything. A husband is just a starting point. From there, I'll spend my life aiming to be her muse, the force that stokes her inner fires and emboldens her to burn at maximum brilliance.

My fingers leave red marks on Katie's face as I take my hand off her chin. "It doesn't matter who I am. What matters is that Birdie's pain, no matter how big or small, resonates through my veins, echoing in the dark corners of my mind. Every bruise, every tear, every gasp—it's etched into my soul. When she bleeds, I taste the metallic tang on my tongue. When she trembles, it quakes my being. Do you know what that means?"

"You're a psycho," she whispers.

I wave my gun at her. "I don't like that word, Katie. It brings back bad memories."

"I'm sorry! Please, please don't kill me." Despair drops from her voice. "There must be something I can do. I'll apologize to Birdie. I'll rewrite the books. I don't deserve to die for this."

"Oh, you deserve to die. Anybody who touches her, anybody who ever hurts her, will die. Isn't that your favorite trope that you put in the books you steal from her? Touch her and die, hurt her and die, it's my favorite trope, too."

Her sobs become whimpers. "Please, I'll do

anything. HELP! HEEEELP!"

I roll my eyes. "I said no one can hear you, you dumb bitch, well, except me, and I don't wanna hear that noise ever again, so, here's the deal. In order to spare my ears the ugliness of your voice, I'm willing to make you an offer."

"Really? What offer?"

"If you do the right thing by Birdie and confess right now on social media that you stole her work, I'll let you go home to your cheating husband."

"What? But—"

"Didn't you just say you'd do anything or was it another lie?"

"This will destroy me forever."

"I'm giving you a chance to do the right thing here to save your own life, but you don't want to. Katie, Katie, Katie, what the fuck? Just so you know, I've been recording our conversation from the start, which means I already have your confession. I'm in possession of your phone, laptop and all of your social media accounts and passwords. I can simply hit post on your behalf, and then…"

"No! Please, I…" Her head lowers in defeat. "Okay. I'll do it."

"I knew you'd come around." I get her phone out of my pocket and let her face unlock it. "Once we have a sincere confession and apology, I'll let you do the honors of posting it on all of your accounts." I set a small table in front of her, plug in a light ring and put the phone on it, ready for recording. "Trust me, you'll feel so good afterwards. Guilt gives you wrinkles, you know that? You don't need any more of those."

Her forehead, the corners of her eyes and the skin around her lips crease, proving my point. "You're a monster."

"That attitude isn't gonna help, Katie. There's only one monster here, and it's you. Be a good girl and take accountability for your actions." I look at her face through the screen. "Now, we need to work on your face. This needs to be genuine, coming from your heart. If you look coerced or forced, no one is gonna believe it, and you want them to believe you, right?"

More whimpering. No answer.

I glare at her. "Right?!"

Her eyes squeeze, and her body shakes with tears. "Y-y-es."

I grab a tissue box from my desk and put it in her lap, and then I clean her face. "I'd untie you, but I don't trust you, Katie. I'll just have to do everything myself."

"People will see my arms tied back in the video. They'll know."

"That's why we're only getting a headshot, and don't worry about the backdrop. My library doesn't look like yours, and people might notice, so I'll replace it with the background from your older videos. I have the right app for it."

"You thought about everything."

"I like to be thorough, especially when it comes to my queen. You don't know how much she means to me."

Something flicks in her eyes other than fear and despair. It's jealousy. It's not enough that she envies Birdie's success so much that she copies Birdie's life. Katie is jealous that Birdie has someone like me in her life. A man who would love her to the point of obsession instead of a cheating bastard, a man who would look after her in every way possible, who would literally kill for her just to see her safe and happy.

If I were written in a book, I'd be a red flag. A character readers would say they'd swoon over in fiction but disdain in real life. But the truth is, secretly, I am their darkest desire they wish to come true, and if I were their reality, they'd all turn color blind.

"Speak directly to the camera," I instruct as I adjust the phone camera to capture only her head and shoulders. "Don't let your gaze wander around or look at me, understood?"

She gives a terse nod.

I record her confession. She's blubbering and sniffling, blaming the whole fiasco on imaginary drugs she's been using, and then she apologizes and promises to go to rehab.

"There, I did what you wanted. Now, untie me and let me go," she says.

"You deviated a little from the script, but I'll allow it. Actually, the drug abuse part helps a lot."

"Helps with what?"

I smirk at her and proceed with editing the video and posting it on her accounts. Then I switched off her phone.

"Helps with what?!" she repeats angrily.

"The next step of your redemption, Katie."

"What next step? You said if I did the video, you'd let me go home."

"True. I am sending you home, where thieves like you belong."

She blanches. "What?"

"Hell, Katie. You're going to hell."

CHAPTER 20

Birdie

A knock on the door snaps me out of my nap. "Mrs. Abel, are you awake?"

I shuffle out of bed and open the door. It's the man with the moustache, Marcus. "I am now."

"Sorry to wake you, but there's a woman at the door for you, Gia Conelly. She claims to be your assistant."

"Claims to be my assistant? She *is* my assistant. Let her in, please."

"You must verify her identity once before she's on the system." He shows me his tablet, which has an HD image of Gia on the screen. "Can you verify it's her?"

"Yes, Marcus."

"Thanks. Please tab the authorize button, and she'll be granted access every time she's here once she passes the security check. No need to interrupt you for permission anymore."

I do as he asks, annoyed I haven't gotten as much sleep as I hoped I'd get before the dreaded meeting Tristan is forcing me to have with Saldana, yet glad Marcus is taking his job seriously. Tristan has left me in good hands. His team, so far, is competent, and I should feel safe with them even when he isn't here. "Is Tristan back yet?" I ask, nonetheless.

"No, ma'am. Should I tell Ms. Conelly to come up or should she wait for you downstairs?"

"Send her up, please." I call Tristan when Marcus leaves. Voicemail answers me. I've texted him that Adriana lost my package. He shouldn't have gone all the way to Boston. I'm grateful for the unnecessary trip, though; I don't have to deal with Saldana until he returns.

I splash some water on my face to lift off the fog of sleep, but Gia's voice calling my name all the way up does the job the better. Her eyes are the size of dinner plates as she bursts in my room. "Have you seen Katie Saldana's post on social?!"

My heart thrashes. Any news about that woman after yesterday's note can't be good. "No. What did that worm do now?"

"Oh my God, Birdie. Have you been living under a rock?" She shoves her phone in my face. "You have to see this. It's viral on every platform."

When Saldana's face pops on the screen, I sigh in relief. At least, she's still alive. The video plays, and I can't believe what I'm hearing.

"I can't live with this guilt anymore. I've done something terrible, and all I can do is take accountability for my actions and confess. There's a fellow author whose works, under the influence of substance, I've been borrowing heavily from. It's wrong, and I deeply apologize for my actions." Saldana's voice is broken as her tear-smudged face fills the frame.

"Birdie Abel, please accept my apology. I'll take all necessary actions to rectify this legally and morally. For my readers who have trusted me, I know I broke your trust, but I hope that you'll forgive me. I promise I will go to rehab to deal with my substance abuse so that I'd never do something like this ever again. I'm counting on your support to give me the strength to do so. Without you, I know I'll fail. Acknowledging my mistakes along with confessing and apologizing are the beginning of a long road to redemption. I will make amends to you and to Birdie, my friend and my mentor, whose trust I've abused. I won't stop until I earn your trust and love back. I'm so sorry." She blubbers and whimpers as the video ends.

What are the odds she posts such a video, today of all days, all out of the good intentions of her heart? There's no way she exposes herself like that voluntarily. She must have been forced to do it, and I know exactly by whom.

"This is epic!" Gia squeals. "Your sales have gone up by twenty-five percent since the post went live, and she lost over ten thousand followers and counting."

I stare at her, speechless.

"Hey, why aren't you happy? This is karma at its finest."

"I need to call Martha." My phone vibrates in my hand with my agent's name on the screen, as if she heard me. I answer quickly. "Martha, did you or the publisher talk to Saldana?" *Please, tell me it's you who instigated this.*

"No, hun, we haven't. It looks like you're on good terms with the universe. You put it out there, and karma took care of the rest." Martha laughs.

Karma has a new name. It's Butterfly Man. He promised to get back at everyone who hurt me. His game has started. His first promise fulfilled.

Or is it?

If Tristan's doubts are correct, Saldana's confession is just the beginning, one part of the revenge, and Butterfly Man won't just stop there.

"Martha, I need you to call Saldana now."

"Sure. I'll talk to your publisher and gather the legal team to—"

"Call Saldana now! Her life is…" *In danger.*

The words choke in my throat as my mind wrestles with exposing the truth. If I have to explain to my agent why my rival with whom I have a personal vendetta may be killed in my name, she'll call the police. With the cum-stained book unretrieved, everything I've worked hard for will be in danger, too. I have to decide how much I'm willing to risk playing Butterfly Man's game.

So far, only Tristan knows about the note Butterfly Man sent about Saldana. I intend to keep it this way, at least, until he returns. He will protect *me*. Martha, Gia and my publisher will only protect themselves.

Part of me recoils at the idea of anyone being intentionally harmed, even someone like Saldana. But a deeper part, darker than I'd like to admit, dances with satisfaction at the thought of my rival facing consequences for once. Karma is finally evening the scales. Saying nothing doesn't make me culpable of any harm that comes to her. Saldana reaps what she sows, doesn't she?

"Birdie? Are you still there? What's going on?" Martha asks.

A sick, twisted game we all are sucked in is what's going on, where the lines between justice and vengeance blur, where there's no room for guilt, and self-preservation is the key to winning. "Nothing. Call the publisher and do your thing."

CHAPTER 21

Birdie

"Gia, can you please get me my laptop? I'm going to work until Tristan returns. Please order some food for the team. They haven't had anything but coffee since they arrived," I said. "Get something for Tristan, too."

She cocks a brow at me. *"Tristan?"*

You call him by his first name? is the real question she wants to ask. "Yes, Tristan, my bodyguard. I've just filled you in, Gia. Focus."

"What really happened last night, Birdie?"

I thought I was being followed by my stalker. Tristan saved me and took me home. We found out the stalker had cameras in the house, and he'd left another note implying he'd murder Saldana after he watched me masturbate and stain her book with my cum. Oh, and I intended to send that book to Saldana, but the package was lost, and we have no idea who has it now. But I decided not to share any of this information to save my ass.

"My laptop, please, Gia. I'm finally inspired. I don't want the ideas to flee away."

"You changed your mind and hired Monarca. You're sleeping in your room again. Katie Saldana publicly apologizes to you. And you're ready to write another book. Something major happened last night. What is it?"

"Nothing. I thought about what you said and understood you were right. Thanks to you, I finally have a bodyguard, which means I'm cleared to write again." I approach her, plastering the most genuine smile I can muster. "I don't say it as often as I should, but I appreciate you, Gia. I appreciate that you're still here, by my side, after the way I spoke to you yesterday. I'm sorry. I was out of line."

"The unapologetic apologizes? It must be a heavy secret you're trying to keep from me."

"What are you talking about?"

"I've been your assistant for five years, Birdie. I know all your deflection tactics. Something happened yesterday, and you don't want to tell me about it." Her gaze narrows at a point behind me. "Is that Blake's gun on your dresser?"

I rush and put the gun and the magazine in

the drawer. I was too tired to put them away before I took my nap. "I need to get dressed. Go do the things I asked, please."

"Did you let Blake come home? If you did, why isn't he here and why did he leave his gun with you?"

I stomp my way to the dressing room. "For God's sake, Gia. I don't need this headache right now."

"Birdie, I'm your friend before I'm your assistant. Why aren't you talking to me?"

My steps halt in place, and I spin to face her. "Friend?" I can't help scoffing.

"Of course."

I can't believe the audacity of this woman. She's been discrediting every word I've been saying about Blake, taking his side on every possible occasion, and she may be his spy. How can she call herself my friend? "Cases that involve a cop's family member are often prioritized. When I, an ex-cop's wife, talked to the police about the stalker, they said it was nothing but a publicity stunt. Blake could have talked to them, pulled some strings to make them investigate. Have you ever asked yourself why he didn't?"

She purses her lips. "He must have an explanation. Blake cares about you and your safety more than anything else."

"He cares about my safety as long as he's

the one protecting me. He didn't ask the police for help, heck I bet he asked him not to help on purpose, because he sees Butterfly Man as an opportunity to control me again. He wants me to think I can't be safe without him, and I still need him in my life. Even the police can't help me without his permission. Can't you see? It's his way to have his power back over me."

"Birdie, you're exaggerating."

"Exaggerating?" My voice quivers, the memories flooding back, unwanted and sharp. "Gia, do you remember the time when I was all black and blue last year?"

"Yes, when you fell down the stairs."

I fold my arms across my chest and let out a bitter chuckle. "Well, I didn't *fall down the stairs.*" The lie tastes like acid on my tongue, even now.

"What do you mean? When Blake called that day, he said you fell the night before and he rushed you into a hospital."

I dig my fingers into my arms to steady the trembling. "He was covering his tracks, Gia. He beat the crap out of me that night, and then he left. He didn't even bother to put me in a hospital."

Her eyes widen. "What? Blake?"

The pains of that night shatter through my bones all over again, and I wrap my arms tighter around myself, as if I could hold the pieces together. "*I* dragged myself to the hospital.

They called the police to take my statement, but guess what? The police called Blake, and, instead of saving me, they helped him cover it up."

She shakes her head in disbelief. "That's impossible. Blake would never lay a hand on you. When I came to see you at the hospital, you said you fell. Why didn't you tell the truth?"

Anger and resentment twist my chest. Hot tears prick at the corners of my eyes, but I refuse to let them fall. Can she be that oblivious? "Because he threatened me, Gia. He said if I ever told anyone he hit me, it wouldn't be a hospital he'd put me in, it would be my grave."

"I…I can't… Blake…"

"If you don't believe me, go ask the security team about what happened this morning when he came. Everything is on camera. You can watch when he lunged at me and four men had to hold him back and disarm him so he wouldn't hurt me."

She plops down on my bed, her face pale. "I can't believe this. I don't know what to say. I'm so sorry. Why didn't you tell me? I could have helped. I could have been there for you."

A cold emptiness settles in my chest as I look at her, seeing for the first time how alone I've truly been. "Because you're not my friend, Gia." My voice is barely above a whisper, heavy with pain and betrayal. "A *friend* wouldn't believe me when I said I fell down the stairs."

She lifts tear-filled eyes to me, her lips parting to speak, but I gesture that I don't want to hear it, and then I march to the dressing room.

The bedroom door shuts with a faint click, and a shuddering sigh escapes my chest. I was harsh on Gia, but I just can't take it anymore. How has this become my life? Parents who never loved me. A husband who treats me as his property to use and abuse however he wants. A friend who has turned a blind eye to his monstrosities because she secretly desires him. Why are the ones I love the most the reason I'm suffering? Why am I never worthy of their love? Why is the only kind of affection I'm getting is a twisted sickness from a psycho stalker with murderous tendencies?

I blow out a heated breath and wipe my face to stop the tears before they spill. Now isn't the time for self-pity. To get rid of Blake and Butterfly Man, the monsters that have turned my life upside down, I must be strong—stronger than ever.

The fight won't be easy, but I find solace in the fact that I'm no longer fighting alone. I have Tristan in my corner. With his help, Blake can't scare me into staying with him, and Butterfly Man won't come near me again.

But first things first, I have to deal with Katie Saldana.

I don a long-sleeved, black evening dress with a gold floral pattern embroidered on the fabric—powerful colors with elegant designs and maintain a feminine touch. Perfect for the meeting and whatever statement my publisher will demand I make even though they know I don't do social media. I get my sunglasses ready.

As I look in the dresser mirror, I decide to let my hair down and accessorize with gold earrings, bracelet and lioness-shaped ring. Some concealer, blush and a touch of lipstick won't hurt, either.

There's a knock on the door as I head back to the dressing room to put on my heels. It must be Gia with my laptop. "Come in!"

Footsteps echo against mine. "Just put it on the bed, and once you make sure everybody has eaten, you can—" My words are cut off when my gaze collides with Tristan's face. "Sorry, I thought you were Gia. What took you so long? I was worried."

"My bike broke down. I had to take the bus to the ferry terminal on the way back. Long queues." He stands there, holding my laptop, his stare wide and intense and sparkling. Then his lips part, and his chest heaves before he scowls and swears in Spanish. I may not speak the language, but as a former teacher to upper teens and college age students in Miami, I had to learn all the swear words.

I glance down at my outfit. "Is something wrong?"

"Why are you dressed like this?"

"Like what?"

"Like you're on a mission to make my job so much harder."

I squint at him in confusion, and then I chuckle. "What do you mean?"

He drags his gaze away from me and puts my laptop on the bed. "*Eres increíblemente hermosa. Quiero desgarrarle la garganta a cualquier hombre que te mire.*"

"Tristan, I don't speak Spanish. Out of respect, please—"

"It's my way of saying you look breathtakingly gorgeous." He shoves his hands in his pockets, and his stare returns to pin me in place.

Oh. Heat touches my cheeks. My pulse accelerates at his compliment. The way he looks at me ignites a spark inside me I haven't felt in years—the thrill of being desired by a man—Tristan may be my bodyguard, former student and a few years my junior, but he's still a man—other than Blake. A man whose compliments and admiring looks aren't tinged with suspicion. Too many times, Blake's sweet nothings have turned into cruel words and possessive behavior. And worse…

"I'm sorry if I'm making you uncom-fortable. As your bodyguard, I understand I might have crossed certain lines. Won't happen again."

"It's just a compliment, Tristan," I murmur, tucking a stray strand of hair behind my ear. "There's nothing wrong with that. Thank you for saying I'm gorgeous. I haven't heard that in a while."

Anger flashes across his face for a moment before it softens again. "Then, with your per-mission, it'd be my honor to tell you you're gorgeous every day."

I laugh under my breath, unable to deny how much I'd love for that to happen despite how inappropriate it might be. "Have you heard about Saldana?"

"It's all over the internet, and your assistant filled me in the minute she saw me. That's why I brought your laptop myself so we could talk without her listening."

"My agent called. She and the publisher are going to take legal action. They'll be arranging for a meeting, and they'll ask me to make a statement."

"I get it." His eyes rove over my dress. "It's why you're dressed to slay."

"Is it too much? Should I change?"

"No." His refusal is firm, almost a growl. "Don't you dare. Let your fans before your enemies see how powerful, elegant and gorgeous you are. Let them worship you. Let them fear you."

A shiver runs through me at the undercurrent in his words. They're so empowering yet so…dark. "But you said it was making your job harder."

"Let me worry about that. You wear what you want. It's my job to protect you under any circumstances. It's a good thing I know how to fight."

His confidence and protectiveness wrap around me like a fuzzy blanket. I can't help the joy I'm feeling despite the situation with Saldana and Butterfly Man, despite the looming danger and the secrets we're trying to hide. My eyes wander toward the door to make sure no one is out there, and I lower my voice. "The stalker must be the one who forced Saldana to confess. Do you think *that* is all he meant in the note?"

"I guess…I hope so. We still have to find a way to warn her."

I figured he'd say that. "Even when we haven't retrieved the book?"

He sighs, and I know he'll change his mind. Tristan is smart. He understands the stakes of not having that book back, and he promised me my safety comes first. "How do you know I didn't get it back?"

"Adriana told me she lost it. You were gone before I could tell you, but I left you a message. You didn't get it? Is that why you still went all the way to Boston?" My heart races in anticipation. "Did you get the book?"

"I didn't get the message in time, and I didn't get the book, but it was a good thing that I met your lawyer because she told me who took it."

Cold sweat trickles down the back of my neck. "Hold on a sec, someone took it?"

He nods and tells me what happened with Adriana. "It's him. The stalker has the book."

"Oh God. That means…"

"You were right about last night. He was following you."

My heart dips. I've convinced myself it was only my imagination, but it was true. I can't believe he's come this close to me again. "He watched me in my own home. He knew exactly where I was going. He broke into my house and then followed me around all day." Panic spreads under my skin. "If you hadn't shown up, he could have taken me yesterday. He could have done anything to me, Tristan."

"Hey, look at me. He will never come near you again, not as long as I'm here. I won't allow it."

Tristan is firm and reassuring, but I can't shake the bitterness of violation or the fear of what is going to happen next. "I can't talk to Saldana about him, not when he has the book. It's leverage. We don't know what he's planning to do with it."

"But there's a big chance he'd kill—"

"You asked me to tell her she was in danger. Whatever the stalker did to her to make her go public with her confession means she already knows. There's no need for me to implicate myself any further in this mess."

He is about to argue again as the doorbell rings. "It must be the food delivery," I say as I march out of the room. "Let's eat, Tristan."

When I reach the bottom of the stairs, Gia, as pale as a ghost, looks between me and her phone. My chest tightens. I can't take any more bad news today. "What now?"

"You have to see this," she whispers, giving me her phone with shaking fingers.

CHAPTER 22

Tristan

Birdie takes Gia's phone, and we both watch. On the small screen is a breaking news alert— "Bestselling Author Katie Saldana Dies in Car Accident."

Blood drains from Birdie's face as she scans the brief details. Katie is found dead in her crashed car after texting what seems to be a suicide note to her husband. There's a photo of him crying and a screenshot of the text. *I can't live with myself anymore. I'm sorry.*

"This doesn't make any sense," Gia says. "Why make that video if she was gonna kill herself? Katie wasn't a saint. She was a greedy, fierce competitor that would stop at nothing to be famous and rich. She wouldn't just confess to stealing Birdie's work just to clear her conscience. She made that video with all that bullshit about drug abuse and going to rehab to gain readers' sympathy. She was trying to stay in the industry. She wasn't going to bow out, let alone end her life."

Birdie exchanges a glance with me, a reminder to keep the secret she doesn't want to share with her assistant.

"Cancel culture is brutal, Ms. Conelly. Saldana was hoping to gain sympathy but look at all the negative comments she received. They're literally telling her to end her life." I bring my phone and look up *Forced* by Katie Saldana. I click the book retailer link and check the latest reviews she got. Then I show Gia and Birdie the webpage. "Look, they brought her book rating down to one star. She must have known she wasn't going to survive this blow."

Birdie exchanges another subtle glance with me, a thank you this time. I swear there has been, for the briefest of moments, a smirk on her lips, too.

Gia's phone chimes in Birdie's hand. "It's Martha," Birdie gives Gia her phone back, "she must have tried my phone after the news, but I left it upstairs. Tell her to come over. We can't figure this out over the phone. Katie's suicide changes everything." She walks toward the backyard.

"Where are you going?" Gia asks as she

places the phone on her ear.

Birdie rushes away without looking back. "I need some air."

I follow her to the blind spot in her garden, where I know she'll stop. When she spins to look at me, I try to read her face, what's hidden behind the opaque mask. Is there horror after she's found out her stalker is capable of murder? Is there any guilt in there, because, despite everything, Katie's death is a tragedy Birdie is the reason behind? Or is all what's lying underneath is vindictive relief?

"What are you thinking, Birdie?"

"Saldana didn't kill herself. The car crash has the stalker's fingerprints all over it. You were right. The sick bastard murdered her."

That's not what I want to know. I've asked the wrong question. *What's inside your mind, and how does the murder make you feel, if it makes you feel anything at all?* I should have said, but I don't because a woman like Birdie Abel, one that hides her emotions too well, won't let me find out. "We don't know that for sure. She could have buckled under pressure. You saw the comments and reviews."

"That's something you tell Gia to make her stop asking questions, to protect me like you always do, but you don't believe that."

"You're right, I don't. A woman like her wouldn't crash her car to kill herself. She'd have used drugs or slit her wrists as a cry for help, a last attempt to gain sympathy. He killed her and made it look like suicide."

She studies my expression. "You're mad at me, aren't you? You think if I'd called her earlier, she'd have still been alive."

"There's nothing you could have done to stop him."

"That wasn't your opinion this morning."

"Warning Saldana today like I asked you was only an attempt to do the right thing. It wouldn't have changed anything."

"But if we'd called the cops and warned her yesterday, she might have been alive. Is that what you're saying? You're blaming me for her death?"

Like I, she's asking the wrong questions. "You chose to protect yourself, Birdie, and if you'd told me about the book yesterday," I look her in the eye without a blink, "I wouldn't have called the police or asked you to warn her until I'd gotten the book back for you. I'd have chosen to protect *you*."

"You will protect me at all costs, even if that cost is your moral compass?"

"*I'll sever any ties, discard any shred of my humanity without hesitation. For you, no line is too far, no act too cruel,*" I quote from my favorite book, the best she's written, *The Nightingale's Whispers*.

"That quote…" There's a spark in her gaze

as she holds mine. "Why, Tristan? Gratitude? Honor? Those don't make you remove your soul for anyone. Why would you do that for me?"

Why do you think? I take a step closer, as if closing the distance between us could let me into her psyche and allow me to decipher what's buried behind her eyes. "Are you relieved Katie is dead?"

Her face remains an impenetrable mask. "What kind of question is that?"

The right one.

"Her death goes beyond anything she brought on herself," she says when she realizes I'm not backing down. "The thought of deriving any pleasure from a person's death, no matter how deserved is…"

"Is what, Birdie?"

"Sickening. It's sickening, Tristan."

"What about the thought of him, of someone being able to get that close, to love you beyond obsession, to take a life just to send you a message?"

She cocks a brow at me. "What about it?"

I take another step closer, leaning in until our faces are inches apart. "Does it sicken you, too? A man taken to a murderous extreme to prove his devotion. To show you he'd go to any lengths, cross any line, to rid you of anyone who's caused you pain."

Her breath hitches, but she doesn't retreat from my advance. "You're treading a fine line, Tristan."

"Am I? Or am I simply vocalizing what you've been afraid to admit to yourself?" My voice lowers to a rumble. "Part of you wants this, wants someone so unshakably obsessed with you they'd burn the world down if that's what it took not only to keep you safe, but to make the people who hurt you pay for what they've done to you…"

Her lips part, but no words come out. Pupils dilated, her eyes flash with anger, intrigue and a dark desire even a woman like her can't hide.

"…just like in your books."

A muscle in her jaw twitches. For a moment, I think she'll slap me. But then she moves even closer, so close I can feel her breaths mingling with mine. "I think I'm mature enough to know the difference between fiction and reality. Are you?"

My heartbeat rumbles at her closeness, at her smoldering gaze, at her intoxicating scent. I swallow to fight back the rising tide of feral instincts, the urge to forget our roles and only remember she's a woman and I'm a man. She's testing me, and I can't fail.

Slowly, I draw back until our lips no longer dangerously close, holding on to her gaze as a shield. "He killed for you, Birdie. He kept his promise. Now, he expects you to keep yours."

"I've never promised that lunatic anything."

"Yes, you did. You had a chance to warn Katie last night, but you didn't. You accepted his rules, and he did everything you asked him to. But he understands you might not keep your end. That's why he took the book, to use it if he must, to claim his prize."

Her bravado shatters with fear. "You think he'll set me up? Frame me for her murder?"

"We can't rule anything out. Your *Butterfly Man* has raised the stakes in his twisted game. Katie's death is only the beginning, proof of just how far he's willing to go to get what he wants. A man who is willing to take a life to make you his won't be above blackmailing you or framing you for murder if you don't comply."

She gulps. "What are we going to do?"

Marcus's voice blares through my earpiece. "Tristan, we have a situation. Your presence is required in the control room."

I fight back a grimace, turning on my microphone. "Copy."

"What's wrong?" she asks.

I nod for her to follow me inside. Electric tension crackles between us as she falls into step behind me. Marcus finds me in the hall-way. "It's the food delivery guy. We have him in the control room, ready for questioning."

"What? Why? What did he do?" Birdie asks.

"Upon inspecting the food, we found a foreign box he attempted to sneak in the delivery," Marcus answers.

I reach the guestroom across from Birdie's office that we've turned into the control room. "Have you opened the box?"

"Negative. We checked if it was clean before we moved it inside. It is safe to open, but we thought we should wait for you to open it yourself."

I nod. "Birdie, please wait with your assistant while I deal with the situation. Marcus, stay with them at all times."

"Copy."

"No," Birdie protests. "I must see what's in that box myself."

"We don't know who that delivery man is or what he wants from you."

"You can't possibly think he's the stalker. He can't be that stupid to show up here, pretending to be the delivery man."

"Nonetheless, once I'm positive whoever that man is poses no threat to you, and that box has nothing inside that can harm you, I'll let you in." I gesture for Marcus to take her away, and I enter the room.

Brandon Gatsby, the youngest on the team yet the fiercest in the whole firm, is inside with the delivery…boy.

"Andrew Callahan. Sixteen. We contacted the restaurant and confirmed he worked there." Brandon gives me the boy's driver's license and tilts his head toward the monitors where a box with the restaurant logo is nestled on the desktop. "Upon conducting the preliminary security check, we discovered the contents of that box weren't food. Following protocol—"

"Thanks, Brandon. Marcus filled me in," I interrupt, staring at the boy. I can't waste any time.

Andrew wriggles in his chair where his hands have been zip tied behind his back. "Please, sir, I didn't do anything. It's that man…he gave me five-hundred bucks and told me to deliver that package with the food. He told me to hide it in a restaurant box so it'd be a surprise. I never opened it like he told me."

I hold up a hand to stop Andrew's rambling explanation. "Slow down. Who gave you the package? Describe him."

"I don't know his name. I couldn't see his face either." Andrew's gaze roams between Brandon and me. "He is about your height and build. He was wearing a hoodie, a cap, shades and…he had a face mask on."

My blood runs cold. "Did the mask have any significant print on it?"

The boy gulps nervously. "Yes. A big creepy

butterfly where his mouth is supposed to be."

I exchange an alarmed glance with Brandon, who has clearly made the same terrible connection. Of course, the stalker is the one to deliver this *surprise* under the guise of an innocent transaction.

"Where did the exchange take place?" Brandon asks Andrew.

"The restaurant parking lot. I was just getting into my car with the orders. He walked my way, all nonchalant, handed me the package and the cash and said to deliver it to the writer's house with the food."

He walked. No vehicle to track.

"Which you really shouldn't have done," Brandon scolds. "This was an extremely reckless and dangerous situation you put yourself in."

The boy's eyes widen with a mix of fear and contrition. "I'm so sorry, I didn't think—"

"No, you didn't," I cut him off sharply. "Did the man say anything else? Anything that could hint at what's in the box or who he was?"

"He…he said he was a big fan of the writer who lived here, and it was…a big day for her today, but it wouldn't be complete without this package. He said it was…the second part of his gift."

My gut twists as I look over at the unassuming package. Whatever is in that box has something to do with Saldana's death. What fresh hell could be waiting for us inside it?

I bring out my pocket knife and stand in front of the box.

"Can I go now? Please, man, I'm sorry. I won't do it again. I promise," the boy pleads.

"Quiet," I order and cut the box open with the knife. Squaring my shoulders, I look inside.

At first check, it seems like a box inside a box. I cut open the smaller package, too, and carefully peer at the contents. "What the hell?"

Brandon stares inside the box with me. "What is this? It's just a book."

Forced by Katie Saldana. I stretch my hand at him. "Gloves."

He fishes a pair of latex gloves from his pocket and puts it in my hand. I put the gloves on and examine the book. Inside, there's the note Birdie printed and pasted on the title page and the smudges in the shape of her initials. When I flip the pages, I find the infamous paragraph that she has stained with her cum. This isn't just a book. This is *the* book Birdie was sending Saldana before the stalker stole it.

I feel a bulge in the book's exterior. Examining it further, I find the flaps of the dust jacket neatly folded into a hidden compartment.

"Is this normal in fancy ass books?" Brandon chuckles. "I'm a paperback guy."

"No, they're not, and you're not a reader in

the first place."

He snorts. "Yeah, who am I kidding? Is there something in there?"

I slide my fingers inside the book covert pocket and hit a folded piece of paper. My hand halts, and I speak into my mic. "Get Mrs. Abel in here."

"What…what are you gonna do to me? Please let me go," Andrew sobs.

I roll my eyes at Brandon. "Let him leave."

Brandon sets the boy free and escorts him out. When Marcus brings Birdie here, I order him to give us the room. Then I tell Birdie everything.

She stares at the book. "He must be hiding another note inside. Let's read it."

I take out the piece of paper and unfold it. The note is in the same handwriting as the other two I've seen, and a butterfly is sketched at the end as the signature.

"I'd spill rivers of blood," I begin, "burn this entire world to the ground if that was what it took to let you see me. I'd become a greater monster than any you've faced just to safeguard your radiant light from being extinguished. You're my sole tether to whatever fleeting sanity remains. My obsession. My weakness. My everything. And I will protect you no matter the depravities I'd unleash upon anyone who tried to harm you." My jaw clenches as I glance at Birdie. "It's another quote."

Her face reddens. "From *The Nightingale's Whispers*, your favorite book, the one you've just quoted from. Coincidence?"

"I cleaned the house myself, Birdie, and where we talked in the garden is a blind spot. The stalker couldn't have heard us. It's impossible."

"That's not what I meant. He might not be watching us inside the house anymore, but he is watching from afar. He knows I hired you."

"His cameras were still in your office when you interviewed me. I mentioned how much I loved *The Nightingale's Whispers*."

"The book is a gift like he said. He never intended to frame me. He is protecting me by sending the book back. But the note…that's not for me. This time, it's for you, Tristan." She swallows. "And it's not a gift…it's a warning."

My eyes tighten at the words scribbled in all caps after the quote.

NEVER THE HERO, IT'S ALWAYS THE VILLAIN THAT SAVES THE GIRL.

NEVER THE HERO, IT'S ALWAYS THE VILLAIN THAT GETS THE GIRL.

<h1 style="text-align:center">CHAPTER 23</h1>

<h1 style="text-align:center">Birdie</h1>

Watching the dreary sea from my garden, I pour the last of the chardonnay bottle down my throat. Tristan is standing somewhere behind me, doing his job. I sit upright on the sofa and glance over my shoulder to confirm—yes, he's still there, unfazed by Butterfly Man's warning.

"Are you okay, Birdie? You keep looking my way every five seconds but say nothing," he says.

"Just checking I didn't conjure you from my imagination. I can't hear you breathe. You're a freaking ninja," I slur.

The green in his eyes glints under the moonlight as they bore into me, reading the hidden fears behind my words. "I'm not going anywhere."

"I wouldn't blame you if you ran for the hills after that note."

"I said I'm not going anywhere."

"Well," I dangle my bare feet and let them touch the grass, "I am."

He rushes to my side as I struggle to stand. "Do you need help going to your room?"

"Who said I was going to sleep?" I grab the empty bottle and shake it, stumbling on my feet. "I'm getting another one."

The disapproval in his frown follows me to the kitchen, but his arms stretch toward me every time I stagger, ready to catch me if I fall.

"Let me help." Gia joins us when I slam the liquor cabinets open and shut more times than necessary to find the wine.

"I don't need your help." I wave an arm at her. "Move out of the way."

She glances between me and Tristan and bows her head with a sigh. They both give me space, but then he whispers to her, "Does she always drink like that?"

I roll my eyes. Does he think I can't hear him? Because I do. Or does he want me to hear it?

"No. She barely touches alcohol," Gia answers before a snide comment slips out of my mouth. "Her mother was a bad drunk."

"Was?" Tristan asks as I busy myself finding a new bottle, pretending I'm not listening.

"She died years ago."

"And her father?"

"He's still in Florida, but…they don't keep in touch."

"Do you know why?"

"Birdie doesn't talk much about her parents. It's a sensitive topic." Gia pauses, but I can feel her gaze on me. "You should cut her some slack about the drinking. It's been a rough day with Saldana and Blake. Actually, it's been a rough year. I mean, who would have thought Blake… That woman…suffered a lot. I should have been there for her, but I failed to see the signs. He tricked us all. It's a good thing that you're here, though. I can't imagine how she must have felt, to be trapped in that same kind of marriage all over again."

"Again?"

My eyes snap at them, but they aren't looking at me. Tristan's scowl deepens as he waits for an answer. Gia purses her lips, pity etched all over her face. "Blake isn't Birdie's first husband. Before him, she was married to some asshole who hurt her really bad. That's how she met Blake. He was the officer responding to her domestic disturbance call. Ironic, isn't it?"

My hand squeezes the wine glass until it smashes. "Shit."

"Birdie!" Tristan runs to me, Gia in tow,

and holds my hand. Then he drags me to the sink and runs some water over the gushing blood. "God, there are some nasty cuts in here. Ms. Conelly, do you have a first-aid kit in the house?"

"Yes, it's—"

"This is my house," I interrupt her with a glare. "If you want to know something, you ask *me*."

Gia swallows, her cheeks red with embarrassment. How could she share my secrets without permission? How could she talk about my past to someone she only met today? Even if he's my bodyguard and I trust him, she has no right to lay me bare in front of him without my consent.

"It's been a long day, Gia. You should go home and rest. Good night." Not giving her a chance to respond, I switch my glare toward Tristan, who is prying the glass shards out of my bleeding palm.

Her heels echo out of the kitchen, and I cock a brow at Tristan. "You got nothing to say?"

He drops another piece of broken glass in the sink. "It didn't seem you were talking to me."

"I was. I don't appreciate your fishing for information."

"I only asked for a first-aid kit to help you."

"You know that's not what I'm talking about. You think I couldn't hear your little whispers?"

"Eavesdropping is a very bad habit."

"Tristan!"

Finally, he lifts his gaze to mine. Then his lips curve into his cocky smirk. "Noted. Now, can you please tell me where the first-aid kit is? I need to stop your bleeding."

I yank my hand out of his. "Just find a rag and wrap it around my hand. I'll patch myself up."

"There are tiny shards inside your flesh still. I need tweezers to get them out, and then I'll have to stitch the deep cuts that won't stop bleeding before *I* patch *you* up."

I put some paper towels on the wounds. "*I* will go finish this bottle *now*."

"Are you kidding me?"

"Nope." I grab the wine and sway out of the kitchen.

"Birdie, you're in no condition to…"

My foot slips, and I teeter out of balance. The bottle flies before it's smashed into pieces on the floor. My eyes squeeze shut as I brace for the fall, anticipating the coming pain.

"…drink anymore tonight."

Tristan's voice rings in my ear, and heat engulfs me as I hit something firm. I open my eyes to find myself cradled in his arms, and my head is on his chest.

The heat is coming from his body. The firm surface is his rock-hard muscles. My hero catches me before I fall.

"I got you." He carries me and moves to the stairs.

I gauge his expression, his stance. For a man who doesn't like touching other people, do I make him uncomfortable, having to carry me after I've royally embarrassed myself for no reason other than pride? Apparently, not. He's focused and confident with his step, a man who's simply doing his job. Do *I* feel uncomfortable?

Self-conscious with a shattered pride, yes. But not awkward or uncomfortable. My body eases against his, and if I let myself close my eyes, I'll drift with peaceful dreams. There's something about him when we're this close, about the way his heart beats in my ear, how protectively tight his grip is around me, how his warmth radiates through me, that makes me feel safe in a way I've never known. As if nothing in this world can ever hurt me if I'm nestled in these arms, a shield that won't allow anything through, not even my own demons, not even my own shame.

"Tristan," I breathe, my voice barely above a whisper.

"Yes, Birdie?"

"I don't want you to die."

Charged tension sparks between us as his intense gaze locks with mine at the top of the stairs. Something flickers in his expression—concern, but also something deeper, something that makes my breath catch in my throat.

"Let's get you taken care of," he murmurs, his voice low and strained. He shifts his gaze away as he continues down the hallway towards my bedroom.

Inside, he enters the bathroom and puts me in a chair in front of the vanity. Then he opens the left drawer. "Bingo. The secret first-aid kit has been here all along."

"You have room for humor when there's a murderer out there who wants to kill you?"

He points at the sink. "Put some water on the paper towels before you get them off. They're sticking to the blood. It'll hurt if you remove them dry. Paper towels, what were you thinking?"

"I'm serious, Tristan. Are you not even a lit-tle bit afraid?"

He goes through the kit and sets what he needs aside. "No."

"How? Why?"

He slams the box shut, and his head whips toward me. "Because I'm not the hero in this story, Birdie, even if that's how you want to write me." He leans in, his gaze piercing through me. "Don't think for one second I'm the kind of man that will sit back and play by the rules when there's a madman out there hunting you. I'll hunt the predator who dared make you his prize before he takes another step closer to you. I'll make sure he never hurts you, no matter what lines need to be crossed."

Transfixed by the fervor in his eyes, the unwavering resolve radiating from every inch of his being, I stare back at him. "What does that mean?"

"You know exactly what it means." He starts tending to my cuts. "And don't pretend this isn't what you want. I saw that look in your eyes when you found out he killed for you." The tone of his voice burns harder than my hand. "You never wanted a hero to protect you. Heroes die to save the world, but villains burn the world down to save the girl. That's why you chose me to be your bodyguard. You knew. You can see it in me, in the scar on my face. You hear it in my words, in my promises. You knew I'd be whatever you need me to be to get this done."

From the moment I saw Tristan at the interview, there has been this pull, this undeniable connection building between us. A bond of sorts that doesn't come from compassion or empathy but from the darkest corners of our souls. He's right. I can see it, the darkness we try to bury before it wraps its flames around us, and the pain that ignites it. In those rare instances when the careful mask slips, and I catch a glimpse of the man behind the bodyguard, it calls out to me.

It terrifies me how much I find myself yearning for those instances because I know where it can lead and the complications it can cause. I know I shouldn't want it. I can't indulge it. But God help me, I do. How far will I let it pull me in? How long can I resist before it consumes me whole?

"You know damn well when the time comes, I won't hesitate to become a bigger villain than the one I'm sworn to stop, if that's what it takes to keep you safe."

The weight of his declaration settles over me, a stark reminder that the man standing before me is no knight in shining armor. He is a warrior, a dark guardian willing to do whatever it takes to protect me. And maybe, just maybe, this is exactly what I need.

"Shane," I say, scoring Tristan's undivided attention, "the prettiest boy in school. Notorious. Leather jackets, tattoos and motorcycles. A bad boy through and through but, oh god, so sexy. Senior year, he's flunking English and History, so he asks me, the nerdy girl who is the top of her class, for help and says he'll pay well. I agree to tutor him for the money. That's what I did, tutoring to save enough to leave my parents' house as soon as I can. And, for the time I spend with the hottest boy in school I won't ever get otherwise.

"One day, he's at my place. I'm helping him study for a test and…my mother," I rub my fingers over my mouth, "she bursts into my room, reeking of alcohol, and starts yelling at me, calling me names. She grabs me by the hair, yanking me out of my seat and dragging me across the room… It's not the first time she hits me. It's not the first time she paints my body black and blue. I've been her punching bag since I was four. But it's the first time she does it in front of a witness.

"In that moment, in that look I see in Shane's eyes, I find peace in the misery that has been my life. Finally, I'm not alone. Finally, someone believes me. Even if he doesn't lift a finger and just stands there watching like my father always does, someone finally sees the truth.

"But Shane lifts more than a finger. He stops her before she drags me down the stairs and scoops me in his arms out of the house. He puts me on his bike, rides to his place and says I can stay as long as I need. And I do, I stay, I fall in love. How can I not? He saved the cat, didn't he? A classic bad boy good girl tale where the villain is a redeemable antihero, where he saves and gets the girl.

"A year later, we're married. We move to Miami. I go to college, but he decides to start his own business to provide for our little family. An auto repair shop that barely pays the bills, but it's something. I'm not complaining, I'm happy, but, suddenly, he's not. He drinks the little money we make, screws any skank that spreads her legs for him and tells me I ruined his life. Four months later, he gives me a black eye."

"Birdie—"

"I should have left then. God, I know I should have. I've seen all the red flags at my parents' house. I've lived them until they've become the air I breathed, but I don't leave. I stay and live in denial, believing all the apologies and the promises of a second chance. At least, he says he's sorry. My mother never did. At least, he saved me once. My father never did.

"Then, one day, he brings a *friend* home with him, and Shane tells me to…" I swallow the wave of nausea and close my eyes for a second to stop my stomach from lurching, "he tells me to give his friend *good company* while he runs an errand." A bitter laugh snorts its way out of me. "*That's* when I decide to leave. That's when he smashes my bones. That's when I call the police and meet Blake. Then it's all over again, but this time, it's not with a villain, it's with a hero."

"Birdie, listen to—"

"The point is, Tristan, heroes and villains are the same. Whether they die or burn the world down, it's never for the girl. She's just another thing up for grabs. Once they own it, they use it as a property however they want. The girl is just a means to an end, a tool, a weapon, a treasure, a bargaining chip, a punching bag, a pussy, anything to fulfill the real quest. They don't care if they destroy her in the process, if they leave her in pieces with nothing but shame."

"No!" His roar forces me to look back at him. "I won't let you feel this way. You. Have. Nothing. To. Be. Ashamed. Of."

My breath snags in my chest. "But I do."

"No. A million times no. Say it with me. You have nothing to be ashamed of."

"I have nothing to be ashamed of."

"Everything they've done, it's on them."

"Everything they've done…it's on them," I say as if in a trance.

He keeps saying it and I repeat like a mantra, until I believe it.

"Good girl. You're the strongest soul I've ever seen. Hold your chin high and wear your scars with pride."

The way his eyes meet mine… It's like he can see right through to the vulnerable parts of me that I keep so carefully guarded from everyone else. I feel seen, understood in a way that no one else has ever managed. Unconsciously, my gaze lands on the scar above his lips. "Like you do?"

"Yes, like I do. Our lives are a lot similar than you think, Birdie. You and I are no heroes or villains. We are survivors."

I steal a glance up, and I can swear, for the briefest moment, he's gazing at my lips, too. "I've been trying to tamp down those feelings, those selfish desires, before they burn us both. But then you'll say something like this, and it's like you're stripping away all my defenses." I shake my head and laugh under my breath. "I knew I was irrevocably bound to him, for better or for worse. He'd be my shield, my savior... and perhaps, in the end, my greatest downfall."

His breath tangles with mine. "I don't recognize this quote."

"Because it's yet to be written." I let go of the last of my inhibitions and crush my lips into his.

The tension I break between us ignites me into a blaze, but he doesn't move. His lips, as cold as the dead, don't reciprocate the kiss. I wait for him to make any gesture of acknowledgement or acceptance, even of rejection, but he doesn't. He's rigid, holding his breath, the green eyes that have once burned with such fierce intensity now shuttered and guarded. Then, suddenly, hell breaks loose in them. "What the fuck?"

My pride shatters with the sting of rejection. "I…I'm sorry. Jeez, I…I'm drunk. I'm so sorry."

"What the fuck was that, Birdie?"

"A kiss, Tristan. That was just a kiss." The realization that I've misread the intensity of the bond between us is a bitter pill to swallow. I've bared my soul to him, laid my vulnerabilities right in front of him, only so he can reject me. "A mistake, obviously, that won't happen again."

"Just a kiss? A mistake? This…this…" he hisses, bristling with something so dark I can't begin to fathom. "Don't you dare try to manipulate me, Birdie. That kiss is a knock on hell's door. And when you knock on hell's door, who do you think will open?"

CHAPTER 24

Birdie

orning light stabs into my throbbing skull like a thousand tiny daggers. I squeeze my eyes shut, trying in vain to block out the brightness assaulting me. A wave of nausea rolls over me. A foul taste settles dry on my tongue, and fractured memories from last night flood my brain.

Dread fissures inside me. I kissed my bodyguard, and he rejected me. I ruined everything between me and the only person in my corner. How could I be so stupid? I can't afford to lose Tristan, not when my enraged husband is determined to force me back into our violent marriage and there's a stalker killing in my name to make me his.

Cracking one eye open, I take in my room.

Yes, this is my bedroom, but why are the curtains open? I never leave them o—

"Morning. Coffee?"

I bolt upright when I see Tristan's face. He's standing on the other side of the room next to the terrace, holding my coffee cup. I drag the sheets to cover myself, hyperaware I'm in silk pajamas with no bra—and my hair must look like a bird's nest that has been through a tornado, hurricane and locust swarm all at once. "What are you doing here?"

"Hi, I'm Tristan Morra, your live-in security detail, aka your bodyguard."

Just like that every ounce of guilt I've felt for my foolish impulses crumbles into ash before turning into fury. "I know who you are. I neither have amnesia nor appreciate sarcasm that early in the day. What are you doing in my room, while I'm sleeping?"

"Rounds," he says as if stating the obvious. "The house and its rooms are checked every hour around the clock. Exceptions follow the client's slumber habits, but normally they're checked on after eight hours from the time of going to bed or four hours if they're taking a nap. It's in the—"

"Job description. I get it."

"I was gonna say the contracts. Monarca protocol is explained in full in them." He smirks.

God help me, sometimes I want to kill Tristan myself. "It wouldn't hurt to knock, though."

"I did." He saunters toward me, like he owns the place. "How is the hand?"

The pain in my palm throbs out of nowhere at the mention. "It's nothing."

He hands me the coffee. "Drink it with the pills I left you on the nightstand. Trust me, you need them."

"For my hand?"

"And the hangover." Here it is, the reminder of my shame glinting in his gaze. Is he going to talk about the kiss or is he just going to spark back the guilt and watch me burn with it?

What the fuck was I thinking, getting drunk and kissing my bodyguard on the first day of the job?

When I don't take the cup right away, he puts it next to the Tylenol. The scent of deodorant and his sweat fills my nostrils as he leans in. He's not wearing his regular dress shirts and pants. A black t-shirt clings to his torso, the sweat showing the definition of the rippling muscles underneath, and workout shorts that compliment it.

I hate how good-looking he is, how he smells of intoxicating masculinity when he seems to have just finished working out, and I hate the way it's drawing me in and halting any professionalism I have in me. I look away to avoid any impropriety I might end up in. "You need a shower."

"Next thing on my to-do list. What do you like for breakfast?"

It looks like I'm wrong about how he's going to behave. He's ignoring what happened last night and is back to being not only professional but also friendly. "That's not in the job description or the contracts."

"No, but I'm setting a new rule. Any phone or online purchases will be placed through the team's monitored phones and computers. That way we'll find out if they're intercepted or compromised. And if that doesn't work, all orders will be picked up on site by the team. No more deliveries."

I let that sink in as the fog of sleep lifts off. "Wait a second, Gia placed the call yesterday. Are you saying her phone is bugged?"

"I already checked. It was clean. That means the stalker used his time in your house and the valuable information he must have gathered through the cameras to know your habits, like the restaurants you like to order your food from. Then he found a way to track the restaurant calls. As soon as he got a hit, he swooped in."

This is disturbing on so many levels.

"Don't worry. We'll get him," he reassures

me with his usual conviction. "I'll go hit the shower. Let me know what you're having for breakfast."

He bestows me with the sight of his behind, and I ogle him like a horny virgin who hasn't seen a man before. Well, despite marrying two men who are physically very attractive and in great shape, I haven't seen a man's ass so delicious like Tristan's. *Stop it. What the hell is wrong with you? Be grateful the man is still here after what you've done and don't you dare ruin things any further.*

"Tristan, about last night… I'm sorry for…" For being completely unprofessional and for violating his trust. Not only is he my bodyguard and former student, but he clearly said he didn't like to be touched, and I kissed him with no regard to his boundaries. I don't know what made me think he wouldn't mind. Perhaps it was the way he carried me or the way I thought he looked at me. Still, I had no right to do it. The way he reacted was past rejection, extreme even. Touching him messed him up in a way I didn't expect or understand. I should have respected his limits.

"You were distraught and got heavily intoxicated. You hurt your hand, and I patched you up. Then you went to sleep. There's nothing to apologize for." He slides out of the door. "See you downstairs."

CHAPTER 25

Tristan

Birdie Able is a liar. A masterful artist of a special kind of deceit that distracts long enough to slip past the guardedness and defenses, to access something raw and vulnerable within.

I've always believed her lies. I've long fallen for them before I set foot in this house. Every tale, every word, every ache, I've felt them so deeply they hurt, marking me their own. How can I not when she designs them so carefully to lure you in with no intention of ever letting go? Once she catches you in her web, once you believe her lies, you're hers to do with as she pleases. And you? You won't run. You won't fight. You'll only ask for more.

In countless books she's written, her kiss silences his demons, the only thing that can. It turns out it's the cruelest lie of them all. Her kiss doesn't silence demons. It awakens them. It leaves them starving in an insatiable hunger only she can satisfy.

My fingers brush over my mouth where the imprint of her kiss lingers, as if I need the reminder, as if the warm softness of her lips that molded perfectly against mine, inducing a slow burn that has scorched me harder than war flames, hasn't carved a pathway straight to my heart, as if the intoxicating taste hasn't nudged awake the darkest recesses of my psyche I've been fighting to ignore and yet reminded me that things other than the darkness that haunts me do exist.

A tightness spreads in my chest until I'm choking with memories best forgotten. In all my years as a soldier and as a security detail, I've never allowed myself to get emotionally involved with the people under my protection. That's how I've kept my unit and clients safe. But with Birdie it's different.

Our connection started the day we met, developed since I saw her crying in the school pantry, and was cemented after I read her first book and never stopped. I've always related to her, to her own brand of pain and sadness.

You're not here to relate to her. You're here to guard her. Keep your head clear or you'll get you both killed.

Lusting after a client can only end in disaster. When that client is Birdie Abel, the woman who has shaped all my forbidden fantasies and taught me, without knowing, everything I've ever learned about romance and desire, it's absolute ruin.

I whisk the eggs so hard they splatter on the counter, hoping that making breakfast for the whole team will distract me when a strenuous workout and two cold showers have failed.

Then she appears at the top of the stairs, and all I can think of is the moment when there was only us and the ghosts of our pasts, when she opened up to me, and I wanted nothing more than to erase the pain shrink-wrapped around her like a cocoon she can't break out of, when she cursed me to hell and beyond with *just a kiss.*

Marcus behind her, she climbs down the stairs in jeans and a T-shirt, her wet hair tied back and no makeup on her face, and I don't think I've ever seen her more beautiful. I force my gaze back on the bowl. No matter how pretty or sad she looks, I can't allow myself to think of her like that. Why am I doing this to myself?

Because from her deft lies spring revelations that jolt you into seeing yourself for who you really are. They hold a mirror that exposes your hidden truths, which you can never understand on your own, not until it shows them to you. Because in her imagined triumphs and flaws, she makes you see the unnoticed shades of your buried struggles, fears and deepest yearnings; she is telling you the truth, revealing you to you.

She enters the kitchen and sweeps the counter with her gaze. "When I hired you, I didn't know I'd get myself a personal chef, too." She arches a brow at me. "Or is that another part of the protocol I've missed in the contracts?"

It seems she's sobered up and got her sass back. "No, ma'am. That's just me, making breakfast." The eggs sizzle as I pour them in the pan. "But don't get used to it. This live show is for one day only."

She hops and settles on the counter, her eyes roaming subtly over my body. "I might as well sit back and enjoy it."

My cock stirs in my pants at her mere gaze. Damnit. I clear my throat and steal a swift glance at her face. She's smirking, her unwavering eyes on me. She knows she's making me nervous, and she likes it. "What do you like for breakfast?" I ask, but it sounds like a warning.

"Tristan makes a mean Spanish omelet and French toast," Marcus says, oblivious to the fire smoldering between me and Birdie.

Her smirk turns into an innocent smile. "Does he?"

"Yes, ma'am. He's an excellent cook. Back in the army, we knew we'd never go hungry if Tristan was in the unit. He knows his way with food."

"Oh, wait a minute. Was that his position in the army? Please don't tell me I'm paying a military cook top dollar to be my bodyguard."

Marcus snorts a laugh, and I glare at them both. He presses his lips to control himself before he says, "No, ma'am, he wasn't a cook. Tristan is the best sharpshooter I've ever seen. Simo Hayha of his time."

"Should I know who that is?"

"Hayha was the number one deadliest sniper in history," I say, a little proud.

Unimpressed, she just nods, keeping her gaze on Marcus. I don't know why it irritates me or why I'm trying to impress her in the first place—or why I don't like that she's engaged in more than a two-word conversation with Marcus.

"But Tristan possesses great direct combat skills, too," Marcus adds. "You should have seen him back then. He's every enemy's worst nightmare."

"Why is that?"

"You never see him coming."

She stills for a moment before her pensive gaze drops to the floor. "I hope that's true and his skills in combat are better than in the kitchen," she slides off the counter, "because these eggs are burning."

As if on cue, smoke flies into my nostrils. I swear as I turn off the burner, and she chuckles, leaving. "I'm going to my office to work. I don't do breakfast anyway."

"I do." Marcus winks at me. "Since you're taking orders, I'll take that Spanish omelet with a side of French toast, please."

I toss the pan on his side of the counter. "You're having burned eggs." Then I wipe my hands and follow Birdie to her office.

"You don't have to come with me, Tristan. My office is literally down the hall opposite to the control room where you can keep watch all you want," she opens the door and enters without letting me inspect the room first, and then she twirls and smiles at me, "unless the real reason you're following me around is that you can't stop ogling my behind."

My mouth opens, but I can't find anything to say, not even a protest or an attempt at denial—I might have looked, once or twice. The woman has curves that are hard to go unappreciated.

"Yeah, I didn't think so." She shuts the door in my face.

I rub the heat radiating from the back of my neck, looking right and left to see if anyone has witnessed my embarrassment. Marcus gives me a knowing grin from the kitchen as he gobbles burned eggs straight from the pan.

Concha de la lora. He waves at me like an idiot. If he has been oblivious to the tension between me and *our client*, he is fully aware of it now.

I grit my teeth at the door and open it with enough force to knock it down. "You listen to me. You hired me to keep you safe, nothing more nothing less, and for that to happen, you do as I say and follow protocol." I stride to her desk and place both of my palms on the surface. "You never enter a closed room, not even in your own house, without me or someone from the team securing it first, do you understand?"

She takes her time before she peers at me over her glasses. "Noted."

That's it? "You're a goddamn pain in the ass proud woman, too proud for your own good," I mumble through my teeth.

"Excuse me?"

"You're giving me shit because you think I rejected you."

She removes her glasses, inspects them for smudges and puts them back on. Then she laughs.

"There's nothing funny about what I'm saying," I fume, her coldness driving me insane.

"To me, you're hilarious. I'm a writer, Tristan, rejection is a brutal yet familiar territory I've learned to walk every day without so much of a flinch," she says, typing something on her laptop. "Do you know how many rejection letters I've accumulated before I signed with Martha? Do you know how many one-star reviews I get every day rejecting not only my words and storytelling chops but also me as a person? I won't last a day in this profession if rejection bothers me. But do you know what irks a writer more than a form rejection or a bad review?" Her eyes suddenly shot at me, so sharp, a blue inferno ready to devour anyone in the way. "The lack of thereof."

Rejection she can handle, being ignored is what she can't stand. I can imagine how it must feel to pour her heart out in a story, all hopeful the world will get to read and appreciate, but then silence is what she receives. The story isn't good enough to be loved or noticed or induce any kind of urge in someone to leave a single word of opinion positive or otherwise.

Last night, the story was her, her reality, feelings and vulnerabilities, and today, I was the silence.

"I've never, ever, meant to hurt you. I was only trying to do the right thing," I confess.

"I get it. Believe me, I do. You're doing your job. You're saving me, Tristan, every day, from Blake, from the stalker…from myself. You wouldn't let me make that mistake, and when I woke up, I had nothing toward you but grati-tude."

I lean back from her desk and lower my

gaze. "Then I treated that moment like it never existed."

"You wouldn't even let me apologize to move on."

"Apologize for what?"

"Disregarding your triggers. I should have never done that, drunk or not, but it looks like you choose to treat them like they don't exist, either."

Fire scorches my veins, searing me from the inside out. "You don't know the first thing about what triggers me and what I have to do to deal with it."

"Then tell me. What's the *real* reason you don't like to be touched?" She takes her glasses off and studies me. "How did you get the scar on your face, Tristan?"

My hands ball into fists as my eyes snap shut to contain the wrath spreading in my chest at the unholy memories. "I'll leave you to work."

"Yes, run, Tristan, but it doesn't make it any less real, what I said, what I felt, what I did, it's all real… Same goes for you," she says as I storm out.

"Tristan," she calls out, and I stop in my tracks at the door, my heart violent against my chest, "it goes without saying the next time you think you can barge in and talk to me the way you did, you will be fired."

CHAPTER 26

Birdie

Marcus's shadow moves behind the office door. After Tristan stormed out, the second in command has been standing guard for hours. My fingers halt on the keyboard as Marcus mumbles something I can't hear clearly yet loud enough to interrupt my flow. I stare at the header of the chapter I'm writing, *Butterfly Man*, and give it two middle fingers. If it weren't for him, I wouldn't need that circus in my house.

Marcus knocks. "Mrs. Abel, can I come in?"

"I said no interruptions," I say, doing my best not to sound angry. He is just doing his job.

"I'm sorry, but there's a Detective Torrance for you at the front door. Should we let him in?"

My heart dips. What does Torrance want from me again? Why is he here? A regular follow up or…

"Mrs. Abel?" Marcus repeats.

I smooth my hands over my jeans as I get off my seat, and then I open the door. "Did he say what this is about?"

"No, ma'am."

Cold sweat breaks out down the back of my neck at the possibility Torrance has connected Saldana's death to Butterfly Man. No, he can't. I have the book on safekeeping, and from what I've witnessed Butterfly Man is smart enough to cover his tracks well. I clear my throat. "Is Tristan here?"

"Performing regular premises checks. Do you want me to radio him in?"

Yes. Despite the recent tension between us, I'd feel much safer with him in the room when I meet Torrance. "No need. You're here."

He smiles. "Always at your disposal, ma'am. Should I tell them to let the detective in?"

"Of course. No need to be rude."

Drawing in a steadying breath, I return to my seat. Marcus ushers Torrance inside my office, closes the door and stands within my reach.

"Good afternoon, Mrs. Abel," Torrance says, hulking over my bodyguard. I can't get used to how tall and big this man is. His steely gaze travels between me and Marcus. "Quite the security team you have here."

I force my lips into a welcoming smile and gesture to one of the chairs across from mine. "Detective Torrance, we meet again."

He takes in the room, subtly inspecting every corner under a false mask of admiration, and then he sits. "Yes, we do, Mrs. Abel."

"Would you like something to drink? My assistant isn't in today, so the choices might be limited."

"Thank you. I'm only here to ask you a few questions, if you don't mind."

"About?"

His eyes, those of someone who has seen too much darkness in the world, pin me in place. "The murder of Katie Saldana."

Every crime has a motive. Every goal needs an obstacle. Be the obstacle not the victim. I feign confusion. "Murder? Is this some kind of joke? Saldana killed herself."

"Based on the evidence we found, we have reason to believe Mrs. Saldana was murdered."

"That's…shocking." How could Butterfly Man leave incriminating evidence behind? That's completely out of character. "Why would anyone want to murder her?"

"For starters, she's a thief. She plagiarized your work, didn't she?"

I arch a brow at him, fighting the urge to snort at what he's trying to imply. "That doesn't mean she deserves to die for it, Detective."

He tilts his head, taking his time studying my face, and then he smiles. "Of course."

"If I may ask, why are you investigating her case? You're not Boston PD. You said you were with Oak Bluffs."

He scrutinizes my expression again, and irritation surges through me. "Where were you yesterday between eleven a.m. and six p.m.?"

"Excuse me," Marcus interrupts, "is this a formal interview? Is Mrs. Abel under investigation?"

Torrance shoots a sharp stare at him. "We'd be doing this at the station if she was. These are normal questions we ask every person that knows the victim to vet them out. Are you her lawyer, too?"

"No, which reminds you, Mrs. Abel has only allowed this meeting as a courtesy, and she is under no obligation to answer your questions without the presence of an attorney."

Torrance sneers at me. "Do you need a lawyer, Mrs. Abel?"

I chuckle. "Thank you for having my back, Marcus. It's much appreciated." I direct my gaze at the detective. "But I have nothing to hide. I was here all day yesterday. In fact, I haven't been out since we met at the café, Detective." I gesture at Marcus. "There are multiple witnesses that can confirm my alibi, obviously."

Torrance brings out a notepad from his pocket and scribbles something, ignoring my sarcasm as he's ignored my question earlier. "Did she call you yesterday or initiate any kind of contact?"

I shake my head. "One minute, my assistant was showing me Saldana's confession video, and the next, she's showing me the car crash photos. It all happened so fast. I don't think Saldana had any intention of reaching out to me before or after the video."

"Except her car crashed in Oak Bluffs, heading in the direction of Vineyard Haven, and your address was the last on her GPS."

We have just lost cabin pressure. "What?"

He leans forward, a predator poised to strike the moment I let my guard down. "You didn't know?"

That Butterfly Man killed her a few miles from my house and put my address on her GPS so that a detective, who knows about my having a murderous stalker targeting my enemies, ends up investigating her potential murder and linking the evidence back to me? "No. I wouldn't ask you why you were on the case if I knew it happened in your jurisdiction."

His gaze inspects my wounded palm. "What happened to your hand, Mrs. Abel?"

"I broke a glass and cut myself last night. Again, I have witnesses."

"Why do you think Saldana was speeding to you? To apologize in person?"

"She wouldn't have just come to my house. We, writers, don't do that. She'd have emailed, maybe, but after that video, the only correspondence between us would have been through our lawyers. What you're saying doesn't make any sense. With all due respect, none of this makes any sense. The video has Boston as the location tag. It's shot in her home office; it's the same setting she had in multiple other videos on her social media. How could she post that video from Boston, and within the next hour she's driving her car into a tree in Oak Bluffs?"

"She was on drugs and speeding."

"She wasn't driving a jet. It's a two-hour drive to the ferry alone on a good day. Assuming she had tickets in advance, add another forty-five minutes to that trip."

"Unless she shot the video earlier and posted it while she was driving to you without changing the location tag. Or maybe she didn't shoot it in Boston at all. How do you know it's not a deep fake backdrop that makes it look like it's shot in her home office, but she wasn't there in the first place?"

"That…" *could be exactly what Butterfly Man did,* "…is far-fetched."

"Is it?" He dips his hand inside his suit jacket pocket, gets out a bunch of photos and slips one my way. "Do you know this man?"

I peer at Saldana's photo in a car and the back of some guy's head. He looks like he's kissing her. "His face doesn't show in the photo, but judging by the intimacy, that's probably her husband."

"He's not."

My heart dips. Oh my God. Could this man be him, my Butterfly Man? Am I looking at my stalker? My hands clench on the arms of my chair. I risk a glance at Marcus, and his face echoes my thoughts; Tristan should have been here. "Well, you said it yourself. She was a thief. I wouldn't be surprised if she was a cheat, too."

"This photo was pulled from her security camera footage. That man was in her car with her in Boston exactly two hours and forty-eight minutes before the video was posted." He shows me another photo of the same car but from a different angle. Saldana and the man are still in it. His face remains unclear, carefully masked by the hoodie, cap and sunglasses he's wearing. "This one is from the CCTV as they drive in Oak Bluffs, twenty-one minutes before the post. What makes a woman like Katie Saldana post a condemning video that could end her career twenty-one minutes after having been on an intimate ride from Boston to Oak

Bluffs with her alleged boyfriend?"

Because that's not her boyfriend. It's my stalker who somehow coerced her to ride with him to Oak Bluffs while he drove her own car. Then he forced her to post the video, pumped her veins with drugs, crashed her car with her in it an hour later to make it look like suicide and failed. "Because he was a disappointing lay?"

Marcus snorts a laugh he quickly swallows, but humor doesn't touch Torrance.

"I don't know, Detective," I shrug, "neither do I know why you're asking *me* that question."

"You know what I think? Saldana didn't post that video willingly." His index finger tabs the man's face in the photo. "This man forced her to do it. You know what else I think? He killed Saldana and dressed it like a suicidal guilt trip."

The detective has figured it all out, but does he have the evidence that proves it? "Every crime needs a motive, Detective. Your theory misses the why."

His jaw sets in a hard line, the muscle feathering with tension. His eyes bore into me, all warmth stripped away by years of interrogating criminals, leaving only an intense scrutiny that studies my every micro-expression and pierces through the lies. "Perhaps he's a dedicated fan with violent tendencies who found out she was plagiarizing your books."

I feel utterly exposed under that goddamn stare, all my secrets laid bare. Can he sense my cracking facade, the doubt and fear gnawing at me? He isn't here to ask routine questions to cross me off a list of suspects. He's vivisecting my soul for that entrance point where he can slip the knife and let the truth hemorrhage out. Torrance has me cornered, going in for the kill. One wrong move, one stray tell, and his jaws will clamp around my throat.

Stay calm. Be the obstacle not the victim. Never the victim.

"This meeting is taking longer than anticipated, and Mrs. Abel has a full schedule today." Marcus moves and stands next to Torrance. "I'm sorry, Detective, but she has to cut it short."

Torrance lets out a soft grunt, unconvinced. His gaze lingers on me one second too long, but, finally, he rises to his feet. "Of course. Thank you for your time, Mrs. Abel."

"You know what *I* think?" I say as Marcus escorts Torrance toward the door, and my bodyguard's eyes scold me for not taking the save. Torrance spins, and his expression lights with attention. I push my glasses up my nose and look him in the eye. "She wasn't having an affair. She was just a drug addict, and I think the man in the photos is her drug dealer. He figured out she was famous and thought to blackmail her for sex or else he'd expose her drug addiction to the public.

"They hooked up far away from home so that her husband wouldn't find out. She got her fix and dropped the man off. The drugs kicked in and made her think it was a good idea to clear her conscience and post that drafted video she'd saved long ago on her phone. Then she figured she was close to my house. Why not apologize in person or fish for an opportunity to make me look bad when I don't accept her apology?

"She put my address on her GPS, but then she saw the influx of negative comments and reviews. She watched as her followers dropped by the thousands and realized her career was over. She sent her husband her suicide note over a text, another drug-induced brilliant idea, and crashed her car into a tree."

He pauses, but then he lets out a humorless laugh. He throws a glance at Marcus, "She's good," and then at me, "you're good. So quick with making up stories."

"It's my job. I hope you do yours."

His jaw clenches. "Your story is good to be in some fiction that entertains bored housewives and makes you a little richer than you already are, but in reality, that's…far-fetched," he deadpans.

"In my humble yet professional opinion,

my story is more palpable than the one you're trying to craft about Saldana being murdered. But at the end of the day, they're both stories, fiction like you said, backed with no real evidence except imagination. Now, would you care telling me what evidence proves Saldana was murdered because nothing you said or showed me does?"

"You're the wife of a police officer, Mrs. Abel. I'm sure you understand I can't reveal evidence pertaining to an active investigation. Is he around? I'd like to ask him a few questions as well."

My lips twist as I stifle down the wave of rage the mere mention of Blake sends rippling through me. "No, he isn't, and he won't be, hopefully ever again. I filed for divorce."

"Oh, I'm so sorry you're going through this. It must be incredibly difficult," he mocks.

I roll my eyes back to the laptop monitor. "Thank you for stopping by, Detective."

His footsteps stop abruptly, and he leans against the doorframe. "One last question, did your stalker send any more notes recently, let's say…yesterday?"

I freeze, his final strike to expose my guilt for all to see getting to me. I pretend to type to hide the shaking of my hands and force a taunting smile on my lips. "What stalker? It was nothing but a publicity stunt, remember?"

CHAPTER 27

Tristan

"Do you know anything about cars?" Birdie's voice streams from her office as I exit the control room.

"A thing or two, ma'am," Marcus says.

Keys rattle. "Excellent. These are my car keys. It's in the garage, but I haven't used it in a while," she says, standing behind her desk when I lean against the doorframe. "Can you check if it's running? I'd like to take it for a spin."

I fold my arms across my chest. "Where are you going?"

She hands Marcus the keys without so much of a glance my way. "Tristan, nice of you to finally join us."

Great. She's more upset than when I left her this morning, as she should. I wasn't there when that detective showed up unannounced and grilled her about Saldana. "Where are you going?" I repeat.

"Please let me know when it's ready. I'll go get dressed." She smiles at Marcus and taps his shoulder on her way out. Then she flashes her teeth at me. "I like him. He should be my number one."

A tightness grips my chest at the way her hand has lingered on his arm, at the stabbing words that followed. She's messing with me, punishing me still, but I can't shake that irrational surge of...possessiveness over her.

"Give me those keys," I glare at Marcus, my voice a gritty growl, "now."

"I said Marcus, not you," she says in warning, sashaying away.

My hands curl into fists as I dart after her. She ups her pace, as if racing me to her room. "Seriously?"

She lifts her chin defiantly and runs up the stairs. I roll my eyes and climb after her. My feet gain on hers easily; I'm a foot taller than she is. Then I cut her path in the hallway. "What did I say this morning? You never—"

"Enter a closed room, not even in your own house, without me or someone from the team securing it first," she finishes the sentence for me.

"Good, because I don't like to repeat myself. Follow me."

I slam open her bedroom door, and after inspection, I say, "Clear."

She saunters inside and then gestures for me to leave with a dismissive wave.

I stride to the door but only to close it. "You can't just decide to go for a drive. There are different security arrangements for vehicles. While we secure you, another team should be following to secure the car. With the current situation, we need every man inside the house. If you just wait until tomorrow, I can bring more men in to—"

"I'm only taking it for a spin. I don't need a parade for that. Marcus will suffice. Now, if you'll excuse me, I'd like to change."

That woman is going to be the death of me. "We need to talk about that detective."

"Do we? You can review the meeting in the control room, if you haven't already. You'll see that Marcus got my back. He was amazing in there."

Inexplicable jealousy simmers beneath the surface at the thought of her newly forming admiration. The irrational need to keep her close, to reestablish my place, overshadows any rationality. I'm losing my grip, and I must regain control before it's too late. "Stop pushing me, Birdie. This won't end well for any of us."

She walks toward me, every step quickening my heartbeat, and stops only when she's one breath away from shattering my composure. Then her brows knit in confusion. "I don't understand why you're so worked up. Marcus is one of my bodyguards, the man in charge when you're not here. I only asked him to start up my car, make sure it was running after being untouched for so long. Per Monarca protocol, I must choose one of the team to come with me as I take it for a drive, and I choose Marcus to accompany me while we get some air and… enjoy the ride."

I can't stand the idea of her being with another man, even if it's one of the security team like Marcus, just driving in a car alone together. *Mine.* The word slithers through me. "Birdie," I growl instead.

She peers up at me intently, a sickly-sweet smile on her lips. "Wait a second. Are you… jealous?"

Unmistakably. "Stop," I hiss. "You don't understand."

"What do I not understand, Tristan?"

"I had to ignore it. Last night… That voice… I can't listen. And you…" *Goddamn you for waking it.* "You have to stop pushing me, Birdie."

"And if I don't, what are you going to do about it?"

It takes every ounce of willpower to fight the urge to pull her into my arms, fist a hand in her hair and crush my mouth against hers in a harsh, branding kiss like I've been wanting, needing to, since her lips feathered on mine. A shudder runs through her as she seems to sense the dark possessiveness rolling off me in waves. I wait for her to recoil but she doesn't. Am I at the crossroads or have I already chosen the path? "Trust me. You don't wanna know."

CHAPTER 20

Tristan

"You must be kidding me," Birdie grumbles when she comes out of the house with Marcus and sees me in the driver's seat of her Lexus.

She narrows her eyes at Marcus, and he shrugs sheepishly. "He's my boss, ma'am."

"And I'm his."

"You're my client, not my boss, and as your head of security, I decided it was best to escort you on this impulsive drive you chose to take with no prior notice or a specified itinerary," I say, looking straight through the windshield.

"I'm driving this car, Tristan. Get the hell out."

I tilt my head and glance at the gauze on her hand. "When was the last time you drove?"

Her gaze spits fire at me. "Seven years ago, not that it matters or it's any of your business."

"For the safety of the passengers and yours I must insist that you shouldn't be driving with an injured hand and let—"

"Get out of my car, Tristan, or I'm calling an Uber."

"As your head of security, I can't let you do that either, especially with the escalating stalker situation."

She growls half a curse, clawing at the air between us, as if she's going to strangle me. Then she squares her shoulders and darts a glance between me and Marcus. "Listen to me, both of you, I didn't summon the courage to divorce the man that dictated every move I've made for the past seven years to let you or another psycho control my life again.

"You are not here to treat me as a prisoner under the guise of keeping me safe. If that was what I wanted, I'd just call Blake. So, you'll get out of my car, which I didn't even get to choose when Blake bought it on my behalf, and I will take it for a goddamn spin now and whenever I want."

Taking a deep breath, I level my eyes with hers. The fierceness in her expression tells me she's expecting resistance. What she doesn't know is that her words have struck a chord deep within me, reminding me of the former shell I was trapped in and my own reasons for summoning the courage to break free from a past prison as cruel as hers, maybe even worse.

Gently opening the door, giving her time to move, I climb out of the car. "You're right. You're more than capable of taking control of your life," I gesture at the driver's seat, "so take it."

She blinks at me, taken aback for a second, as if she hasn't expected me to give in that easily, or maybe she didn't want me to. But then she slides in and smiles at the steering wheel.

I close the door for her and glare at Marcus while I march to the other side of the car. "Shotgun."

He snorts as he climbs into the backseat. "Very mature, boss," he says when I'm in the passenger seat.

Birdie's eyes tighten with protest, so I hold up a placating hand. "While I admire your fiery spirit and determination to take back control of your life, you have to admit, driving with an injured hand isn't the smartest idea. How about you drive us around the block, and I just sit here, a safety net, no orders, no attempts to take over, only because I'm genuinely worried about your driving with that hand?"

Her face doesn't ease up. "That's the *only* reason?"

In the rear mirror, Marcus is giving me his

shit-eating grin again. I shake my head. Yes, I've let jealousy interfere with my decisions; it's wrong, it's stupid, but I can't help myself. That woman has no clue what she means to me, what being that close to her does to me or what war her touch can start inside me. And the thought of any other man having the tiniest chance to get to taste the fire of her touch…

"Maybe not, but right now, it's the main reason. How is the pain?"

"It's fine. I told you it's nothing but thank you for asking." She sets the car in gear and adjusts the mirrors. Then she pauses longer than anticipated, eyeing the road, her foot frozen on the gas pedal. My chest tightens when I spy the internal battle raging behind her gaze. After years of having every decision made for her, that first taste of freedom can be daunting. But I know she's stronger than she realizes.

She points at the glove compartment. "I forgot my sunglasses. There should be a pair in there."

I check but can't find any.

"I'll go get one from my room," she says, her hand already on the door handle.

"Hey," I give her my shades, "use mine."

Her chin wobbles for a second, but she lowers her head, putting on the mask she hides all feelings behind before they strike. "You sure?"

"Hundred percent."

She gives me a curt nod and puts them on.

"Thank you…for everything." And she hits the gas and drives us down the street.

Good girl. My lips curve into a reassuring smile. "They look good on you." I wonder what other clothes of mine she'll look good in. My jaw ticks as I watch her delicate hands grasp the steering wheel. Those same hands that have haunted my dreams, leaving phantom trails of fire over my skin. I've imagined them exploring every plane of my body more times than I can count.

Every time she switches gear, our arms are nearly brushing. She's so close I can feel the heat radiating off her. It would be so easy to reach out, to finally know the softness of her curves under my calloused palms. To pull her against me and drink in the sweetness of her lips...

I tear my gaze away and focus on the road. *You're her bodyguard. You're supposed to protect her, and she'll never be yours. Wake up.* The road unwinds, and she doesn't circle back; she follows. "Birdie, that's not just a spin around the block. Where are you going?"

Her fingers ease on the wheel, and her face softens. "I was thinking the beach, before it gets dark and unbearably cold." She glances at me and then at Marcus in the mirror. "Have you been to the island before you came here to take the job?"

"No, ma'am," Marcus says, and I shake my

head.

"Okay, then you must see the lighthouses. The island has five. The most famous one is Gay Head by Aquinnah Cliffs, but my favorite is the one in Edgartown. There's a nice bookstore slash bistro there, too, where we can eat. It's my second favorite after Sweet Home in—"

"Oak Bluffs. Your favorite hangout. Yeah, I did my homework." I pull out my phone and search Edgartown Lighthouse. "It's a twenty-minute drive from here to the beach. Then it's a ten-minute walk to the lighthouse itself. It says you can't see inside it off-season, though, so it's pointless. Let's just go back."

"Don't worry. I know the guy who works there. He'll let us in."

"How about we don't? That's not what we agreed on. I've explained to you that we need another team behind us to secure the vehicle. Besides, a spontaneous stroll on a public beach is a security nightmare, let alone securing a lighthouse."

She grunts. "Marcus, can you remind me what Tristan promised so I'd let him tag along with us?"

"He said no orders or attempts to take over. He was here as a safety net *only* because he was genuinely—"

"Jesus Christ." I throw my hands in the air, glaring at him. "You're a pain in the ass."

Birdie chuckles and lifts her injured hand

above her head, palm in Marcus's direction. He leans in and gives her a gentle high-five.

"Seriously?" I mumble, blood simmering. This rapid bond they've seemed to form in the past few hours is eating me up.

She shrugs. "What? I told you I liked him."

"Thank you, Birdie," Marcus says, and I contemplate smashing his jaw. *Birdie? She lets him call her Birdie, too?*

I call Brandon and tell him to take another detail and follow us to the destination. Birdie rolls her eyes at me and sighs in disapproval. I don't care. "We need music." My fingers stab the radio screen multiple times, but it doesn't start any channels.

"Easy tiger. I get to pick the music." Her hand grazes mine as she fiddles with the chan-nel settings, sending an electric jolt through my body. "My car, my…"

Impulsively, compulsively, I envelope her fingers with mine.

Birdie quivers, her eyes widening behind the sunglasses. "…rules."

My heart pounds in my ears as I drink in the softness of her skin against mine. I've imagined this moment countless times, but re-ality is more intoxicating than any fantasy.

In the rearview mirror, Marcus's eyes nar-row with concern. He clears his throat, but I can't let go. Not yet. Hers is the only hand I never want to escape from, grounding me rather than making my skin crawl. It defies all logic and experience, but Birdie has become the sole exception to my rules. While anyone else's touch makes me want to shut down or kill, hers simply makes me feel alive. Safe. Wanted. Like I can exist peacefully in my own skin for those fleeting moments. That feeling surpasses any shame or guilt.

And, appropriate or not, he needs to know she's mine. Even if I can't have her, no one else can.

"Tristan," Birdie whispers, her gaze torn between the road and Marcus, "what are you doing?"

I realize how far over the line I've stepped. One foolish moment, and I may have ruined everything and lost her forever. But I've warned her, and she didn't listen. "I said stop pushing me, Birdie," I whisper back.

She swallows, trying to take her hand out of mine. My grip tightens in warning. When she stops resisting, I cradle her hand in my palm and pretend to be inspecting the gauze. "It's… falling off. Maybe we should stop by a drugstore and change it."

"No, it's fine. It'll hold until we go back home." She slides her hand out of mine and doesn't speak for the rest of the drive.

CHAPTER 29

Tristan

irdie expertly maneuvers into a parking spot. Unlike what I've expected, considering she hasn't been behind a wheel in years, she's a skilled driver, even with one good hand.

She catches me staring at her as she cuts the engine. "What?"

"What kind of car would you have bought?"

"I'm not following, Tristan."

"You said your husband bought this car for you and you didn't have a say in it. Which car would you have chosen?"

Pensively, she regards the beach ahead of us and follows the stark white lighthouse up with her gaze. "None. I'd have chosen a motorcycle."

I can't help the smile on my face. "You ride?"

"I used to be a biker's old lady. Of course I do."

Of course she does. I nod for Marcus to secure the perimeter. When Birdie and I are alone, I explain to her the security protocol for open spaces. Has it killed the silent tension between us and distracted me from picturing my hand squeezing gently around her throat while I'm devouring her lips? Debatable.

"The beach isn't that crowded. Can we just get out of the car now?" she says.

"Not until Marcus radios it's clear."

She purses her lips and nods, but nothing about her seems agreeable. "So when I kiss you, you run for the hills like you've been bitten by a snake, but you can touch me without permission, and I'm not allowed to run?"

"I was…only making sure your hand wouldn't compromise your driving for your safety and ours."

"You were marking your territory," she scoffs.

You knocked on hell's door, Birdie, and that part of me you unlocked wants nothing more than to pin you against this car and claim you in front of the whole world to let it know you're mine. You're lucky I only held your hand. My shoulder lifts with a shrug.

She yanks my shades off her face. "I'm not a territory to be marked, Tristan."

"You think I don't know that? I'm not Blake Abel." I hold her fiery gaze, pleading for her to see the war she's waged inside me. "I'm not here to imprison you, if anything I'll protect the freedom you've fought so hard for. And as much as I want to make you understand that you belong to me, as much as it tears me apart I can never truly have you, I lock away every need to brand every inch of your body mine because acting on those feelings would be catastrophic. But when you push me like that, I can't control it."

She leans in, closer, and closer until my chest is heaving with flames she stokes in me with just her breath on my face. "Why? Why can you not control it?"

My body grows rigid as I fight every primal urge, every fantasy proximity bids alive. "Because to me, you're not a territory, Birdie. You're the whole world."

She searches my face, brows knit, wrestling with my confession. The heat between us charged like lightning before a storm. "Tristan, I—"

"When you push, I'll push back." I'm not afraid to show her how utterly powerless I could be against her or the hold she has over me, but I won't let her take advantage of it.

"You'll bend, and I'll break."

"What happens when you break?" she whispers.

The question hangs heavy in the confined space of the car, the weight of the impending answer threatening to shatter us both. It won't be slanting my mouth over hers in a heated clash as I mold her body flush against mine. It won't be drinking in her surprised gasp or swallowing every sweet whimper as I stake my claim. It won't be my calloused hands roaming her soft curves to finally satiate the possessive hunger burning in my veins for her. It won't be letting my desire for her pour out unchecked after holding back for so excruciatingly long.

It will be chaos, ruin and blood.

"Tell me, Tristan, what happens when you break?"

I suck in a ragged breath. "Hell's doors open wide."

Her lashes flutter, and she finally leans back, leaving me gulping for air.

"All clear. Ready to move," Marcus's voice streams in my earpiece, saving us.

"The beach is clear, but we'll wait for Brandon to—"

She unlocks the car and climbs out, jamming the shades onto her face.

"Hey!" I scramble out and block her way. "You don't do that. Ever." The scent of the ocean fills my nostrils as they flare. The roar of the waves clashes with the wind, echoing my heartbeat.

She plays with a strand of her hair, an impish smile on her lips. "Sorry, daddy. I promise next time I'll be a good girl."

Hijo de puta.

Her head tilts as she gives me a onceover glance, and then her smile grows into a grin. "Oh, he blushes."

"No, I don't. I'm…angry. You're gonna give me an aneurysm."

"If you say so, daddy."

My dick pulses in my pants. "Walk. Just walk."

With a giggle, she spins and starts down the walkway. "Shall we go to the lighthouse we're all so excited to see?" she taunts, when Marcus meets us at the start of the beach trail, as if nothing happened. Hell is about to break loose in me, and she treats it like nothing; she's giving me a taste of my own medicine, and it stings.

Strolling down the beach, she's on her phone, and we're behind her. Before the man in me indulges in the sight of her curves, I drag my stare away and decide to pour all my focus on my job. I must treat Birdie as nothing more than a client before I go crazy and jeopardize both our careers, reputations and even lives.

I sweep the place with my gaze. There are

a few families sitting on the sand, children are playing, and three separate seniors are enjoying the view. None of them is a possible threat. The next few minutes on the job will be easy if I ignore Marcus's suspicious side eye and my client's gorgeous ass.

"Gia is still not picking up," Birdie says. She's been trying to reach her all day and all the way to Edgartown. Her assistant has the light-house keeper's number, who will let us inside without filling out the necessary forms to visit off-season.

"Should we be worried?" Marcus asks.

"It's not like her to miss work and not re-turn my calls, but we kind of had a fight last night…and the day before. I guess she doesn't want to put up with my crazy today." She frowns and lowers her eyes back on the phone. "Anyway, she keeps all numbers and addresses in a shared document I can access," her fin-gers work fast on the screen, "here. I found his number."

She makes the call, and *Spencer* is gonna let us in.

I exchange a glance with Marcus before I ask her, "You're on a first name basis with the lighthouse keeper?"

"I guess I am. I come here a lot." She con-tinues down the trail.

"We're going to need that list of numbers

and addresses, ma'am," Marcus says, reading my mind.

Her hair whips over her face as she glances at him over her shoulder. "Why?"

"We were under the impression that your public interactions were limited and mostly done through your assistant and former manager. Apparently, that's not the case." Marcus exchanges another glance with me. "If you're friendly with a man like the lighthouse keeper, I bet you are with others, too, and one of them might have mistaken your kindness for something else…"

"Your stalker could be one of those people on the list, Birdie," I finish.

CHAPTER 30

Birdie

I stop dead in my tracks. One of the people that I've known for years could be my stalker? "That's…" I work a swallow, but my mouth is too dry. "Are you telling me Benson from the bakery could be the man terrorizing me for months? Or that seventeen-year-old waiter at Sweet Home? Or Travis, the local bookstore owner's husband?"

"All it takes is one person misreading the situation, fixating on you in an unhealthy way. We can't eliminate anyone or assume your stalker is a complete stranger," Tristan says firmly. "Think about it. He had access to your house. He never broke in."

"Which made me fire all the help even though they were all females and changed the locks, leaving only me, Gia and Blake with keys to the house. Still, it didn't stop him from reentering it."

"Then he must have had access to those keys from one of you and made his own set, and who is more likely to do so other than the people you interact with on a daily basis like those on that list?"

A shudder runs through me. What if what he's saying is true? Butterfly Man isn't a random fan I've never met before. He's someone I know, closer to me than I think. The threat isn't coming from a stranger. It's from someone I trust.

"Hey." Tristan's voice is gentler now as he falls into step beside me. "I'm not trying to frighten you, just preparing for all contingencies. We'll get to the bottom of this."

I take in his face, that strong profile, that firm set jaw, and a flicker of reassurance buds in me. Despite our...complicated interactions, he's always looking out for me. I'm no longer facing dangers alone. I know in my heart he'll do everything in his power to protect me. "You're right. No one can be trusted. Everybody is a suspect." I give Tristan access to the document.

"It's best if we head back, Birdie," Marcus says this time. "Until we vet everyone on the list."

"No. I didn't come all the way just to head back. You can relax. Spencer can't be the stalker." I continue down the path to the lighthouse.

"How could you be so sure?"

"Because if he has any obsessive tendencies, they'll fixate on someone who looks like you."

Spencer is waiting at the bottom of the lighthouse when we arrive. He is a bald, lanky man with strawberry blond facial hair and acne that hasn't seemed to heal over the seven years I've known him. He grins when he sees me. "If it isn't our local celebrity writer… Long time no see."

A little over a year. "Spencer, my man. How are you, and how is Aedan?"

"Glorious. He'll freak when he knows I met you today. He's a big fan, and I brag to him all the time that I know you, but he doesn't believe me. I know you don't allow photos, but—"

"Could you open the entrance please?" Tristan interrupts. "We'd like to conduct a swift security check before Mrs. Abel goes in."

Spencer's grin vanishes. Confusion dulls his expression, perhaps fear, too. Tristan can be very intimidating. Add Marcus to the equation, and I bet they can make grown men piss their pants just by staring at them. Poor Spencer blinks at me. "Are these gentlemen your friends?"

"Bodyguards. After the last book, things got a little…you know…"

"Oh, of course! *Twisted Obsession* is epic. I can imagine fans lining up at your door." He lightens up, but when his stare collides with Tristan's he recoils. "Where is Mr. Abel?"

"It's just me now, Spencer."

"What? But you were the most adorable couple… Those wedding photos…" He looks like he's about to cry. "If you split up, what hope do people like us have?"

"The doors to the entrance, please," Tristan repeats, and I can practically hear his teeth clenching.

"Yeah. Sure." Spencer lets us in, but Tristan tells me to stay with Marcus until he secures the lighthouse. I thought he'd assign Marcus the task and he'd be the one staying with me, but jealousy doesn't have room in his repertoire when it comes to my safety. He'll always step up to ensure the job is done properly and to his standards. A smile crawls on my face despite the emotional turmoil I've been through.

A few minutes later, filled with Spencer's babbling about how Aedan could be the one, Marcus gets the go-ahead from Tristan, and we start climbing.

"Thank you, Spencer, for doing this," I tell him over my shoulder, catching him staring at Marcus's behind, "I'll send Aedan a signed book."

His cheeks turn redder than his beard, and he yanks his gaze away. "Anytime. Thank *you* so much!"

Yeah, Aedan is definitely the one. I do a mental snort.

Pale light filters down through the narrow windows, casting eerie streaks across the spiral steps as Marcus and I ascend the winding staircase inside the lighthouse. I take off Tristan's sunglasses for better optics.

"You'd think after all these years, they'd have installed some better lighting in here," Marcus huffs from behind me. His footfalls echo with every upward revolution of the staircase.

Did he not say he'd never been on the island or to any of the lighthouses on it before he moved in for the job? The thick stone walls press in all of a sudden, the air thick with the scents of aged brick and marine brine. I slow down and run my hand along the cylindrical wall to guide myself.

"You okay?" Marcus's voice echoes, laced with concern.

My heat hammers against my chest. Should I confront him or pretend I've never heard him make that casual complaint about the lighting as if he was familiar with the layout? Swallowing, I look up. If I yell for Tristan, can he hear me?

"Birdie?"

No one can be trusted. Everyone is a suspect. Be

the obstacle, not the victim. If I'm going to confront him, if my suspicions turn out to be true, it's best I'm not alone in a dark, confined place with him, without having Tristan close enough to protect me. I plaster the smile I give my fans on my face. "Yeah, just...it's steeper than I remember. Not as young as I used to be when I last climbed these stairs."

Marcus lets out a small chuckle. "Don't sell yourself short. We're almost at the top."

We're not. Is it another lie to cover the first? Has he sensed my suspicions? Is he trying to convince me he hasn't been here before? What if Marcus is hiding something?

What if he, of all people, is Butterfly Man and he knows I'm on to him?

"Go ahead." I shouldn't be alone with Marcus any second longer. "I just need a second to catch my breath." Pulling my phone out of my pocket, all I can think of is that I need Tristan. Subtly, I try to call him, but there's no reception.

"I can't leave you, Birdie. You know better."

Something in his voice sends a chill down my spine, and my mind spirals. Am I staring at one of the people I've entrusted with my safety or has Butterfly Man's mask finally slipped off, revealing the face lurking underneath?

CHAPTER 31

Tristan

Spencer's watch room is empty, and the lighthouse gallery is completely devoid of visitors at this time of the year. Birdie is right. The place is safe after all. My gaze drifts with the crisp wind whipping through the golden beach grass. Today should be a lesson learned. I am being overprotective of her, and not in a good way.

As I wait for Birdie and Marcus, I step back inside the chamber that houses the beacon light. It has slanted windows running along the circumference, framing a vista of ocean meeting horizon from all directions, allowing me a comprehensive visual of the perimeter. Also, I can hear them better from here as they approach.

What's taking them so long, though?

"Marcus, do you copy? Is everything all right?" I speak into the mic.

When he doesn't answer, I repeat, "Marcus, do you copy?"

Two more seconds pass, and nothing comes in. Shit.

I pull my gun and sprint back towards the winding staircase entrance. My footsteps thunder against the old stone floors. "Marcus, status report now."

Static answers me. Either he's not receiving my transmissions...or he's choosing not to respond. What the hell is going on? My blood runs cold at the thought of Birdie being harmed in any way. If anything happens to her, I swear to God…

"Birdie! Birdie, can you hear me?!" I fly down the stairs. The only sounds I'm getting are the hollow reverberations of my own voice bouncing back at me. I redouble my pace, practically flinging myself around each dizzying curve of the stairs. "Someone answer me, Goddammit!"

"Tristan, you might wanna come down here," Marcus says at last.

I take the remaining stairs three at a time, using every ounce of speed and strength I possess. I have a glimpse of her face, pale and hard, but she's there in one piece. Thank

God. I even my breath, willing my heartbeat to slow down the frantic rhythm. "Birdie, are you okay?"

She glances up at me, holding on to the wall as if she's going to fall, Marcus in front of her. "Y-yes. Yes, I'm fine."

"You don't look fine. What happened here?" I climb down the last of the steps to them and scowl at Marcus. "And why aren't you answering? I radioed three times."

"She said she was having trouble breathing, and she wouldn't climb any higher. I was trying to help her. Birdie, be honest, are you afraid of heights?"

She squints at him incredulously. "What? No."

"Claustrophobic?"

"No, Marcus. I've climbed to the top of this lighthouse so many times before."

"Then what is it?" I ask firmly, holstering my gun. Something is happening, and neither of them is telling me the truth.

"Nothing. It's just… Every time I came here, Blake was with me. This place is where we had our wedding photoshoot. It holds a lot of memories, and it overwhelmed me. That's all." Her eyes want to tell me something more, different from the lie she's just spawned.

"Do you want to go home?"

She shakes her head. "I need some air. Let's

go straight to the balcony."

"You mean the gallery, ma'am," Marcus corrects.

My eyes narrow at him with a glare. Our client looks like she's just come back from a panic attack—maybe because of something he did—and he cares about terminology. "Go down and secure the lighthouse entrance, Marcus." I usher Birdie up the stairs. "And maintain comms protocol. Don't go radio silent again, understood?"

"Yes. Sorry, boss."

When Birdie and I reach the gallery, she looks like she's about to cry.

I want to give her a moment to calm down, but I need to know what is wrong. "What the hell happened down there? Are you okay? Did Marcus do something to you?"

Her sunken stare alarms me. She points at the mic in my sleeve. "Can he hear us?"

"Not unless I want him to. Birdie, please, tell me what happened."

"He lied to us. In the car, he said he'd never been here before, but as we were coming up, he said you'd think after all these years, they'd have installed some better lighting in here. He was here years ago, Tristan."

I wait for the rest of the story, but she seems finished. "That's it?"

"What do you mean that's it? I'm telling you

he lied about never being on the island. Does that not raise any suspicions in you?"

My hands rest on my hips while I sigh in relief. "No, Birdie, because Marcus isn't lying."

"Did you hear a word I said?"

"Every single one, loud and clear. But what you don't know is that Marcus was a Coast Guard officer before he joined the Marine Corps. He's been inside countless lighthouses, and he's always complained about how boring they are because they all look the same on the inside. That comment was just his general impression of old structures like these."

Her lips twist as she seems to be mulling it over. Then she rests her arms on the railing and lowers her head. "A Coast Guard officer. Is that why he was giving me a lesson in lighthouse vocabulary?"

"Yes, ma'am."

"God, I'm going crazy. For a hot minute there, I thought…"

"You thought he was the stalker?"

She nods with a scoff.

"You're under a lot of stress, and today didn't make it easier. *I* didn't make it easier. With everything that's happened between us, and then I go and make you suspect literally every person you know."

"We get into each other's heads, Tristan," she pins me with a stare, "in the worst ways possible."

It's unfortunate but true. "We can't let that happen anymore."

"How do you propose we accomplish that?"

I must start treating Birdie like any other client, no more crossing lines, no more breaking rules or letting emotions get in the way. "I'll step back and make Marcus your number one like you asked." My heart squeezes as those words fall out of my mouth, but it's the only way to keep her safe.

She purses her lips as the blue of the ocean drowns in her gaze. "I used to find such solace in this place, in the comforting rhythms of the waves and seabirds. Now it all feels tainted, unsafe."

"I'm sorry."

"It's not your fault. It was ruined long before we came today. What I said about my wedding photoshoot and coming here with Blake was true. I loved this lighthouse so much, but after what he did to me last year, I just… I thought coming here today, driving my own car, knowing I'm this close to getting him out of my life, would make me see this place as I once did. I was wrong. It's funny how one person can ruin your favorite places and memories forever."

"Then make new memories, ones neither he

nor anyone else can ruin, and then the places will become favorites again.”

Her head bobs up and down, and then a smile tugs on the corner of her mouth. “Okay. Let’s try it your way.” She hands me her phone. “Take my picture, and every time I’ll look at it, I won’t see the pain that led to it. Instead, I’ll choose to see the day I broke free from Blake’s cage…and the moment I realized Marcus wasn’t Butterfly Man.”

She poses, and I capture the photo. Then I give her the phone, aching to let our fingers twine, to caress her face and taste her smile. I shove my fists in my pockets instead. “Good choice.”

Her fingertips zoom in on the photo, and her smile vanishes. “Wait, is this…” She spins and peers at the railing. “Oh, for God’s sake. Can you just give me a break?”

I track the spot she’s yelling at, and my stare collides with a butterfly. “That’s weird.”

“No, it’s not, not with my luck. If it’s not Blake ruining my life, it’s my freaking stalker or the reminders of him.”

“I understand your frustration, but I mean it’s weird for this butterfly species to be in this part of the country.”

“It’s a monarch, Tristan. It’s everywhere.”

“Actually, that’s a queen butterfly. See how the wings have a rich brown color with white spots along the edges? Monarchs have more of an orange-brown color with black lines forming a distinct pattern. It's very rare to find a queen here."

"Why?"

"They're tropical insects, mostly found in the south like in Texas or Florida. They don't like the cold."

"Well, like I said, it's just my luck. A rare insect makes its way into the one photo I take to christen my new life to remind me of my worst nightmare, as if I can ever forget."

I stretch a hand between us. "Let me take another photo."

"No." She slides the phone in her pocket. "It won't make any difference, not until Butterfly Man is gone."

"I really wish you stopped calling him that."

She shrugs with a snort. "How do you know so much about butterflies?"

I step back, inching up a brow. "She asks warily."

"No. We've already been there, and like with Marcus, we've established that you are not my stalker. Besides, you're with me twenty-four seven, busy being annoying and anal. You don't have the time to be Butterfly Man. It was a genuine question."

"Well, here's a genuine answer. My mother." I lean my arms on the railing, distracting the memories with the sight of the ocean. "She loved them. Her father owned a butterfly farm in Argentina. He died before I was born, but he taught her everything, and she taught me. It was our thing."

"Monarca," she says slowly, as if she's just made the connection between my firm name and the reason behind it. "That's monarch in Spanish, isn't it?"

"And my mother's name."

"You loved her that much, didn't you?"

"More than anything. She was the kindest person I've ever met."

"I'm so sorry for your loss." She reaches a hand to my shoulder but retracts it immediately, thinking I'd mind. And I don't tell her I need nothing more than her comforting touch now. "What about your father?"

My fists squeeze the cold metal until my knuckles turn white. "Do you like butterflies? I mean…before the notes."

She regards my face for a few moments. I can't tell if she's considering my question or wondering why I've evaded hers. A long sigh seeps from her lips as she shakes her head. "Not really. I mean, they look so mighty, so graceful, those beautiful colors, those strong wings, and yet…none of it is real. You capture a butterfly, pluck its wings, then what is left?"

"What?"

She holds my gaze. "An ugly bug to crush."

That's…disturbing, even for me—especially for me. "An ugly bug to crush? You're evil."

"I'm sorry to dump a hint of my darkness on you like that, but you asked."

"Oh I'm used to more than a hint of your darkness. I've read it all. But don't take it out on the butterflies," I say, and she chuckles. I wish I could laugh with her, but one memory assaults my humor.

Once, I said something similar to my father, except I wasn't joking. I was begging. I grip the railing tighter. The pain helps ground me, forcing the images down. My father's sneering face, his cruel taunts about my failure to live up to his vision of masculinity. The way he crushed everything I cherished as easily as one might stomp on an insect.

I focus on the rhythmic crash of the waves before more memories threaten to resurface. "They're supposed to be a symbol of hope, rebirth and freedom. How can someone like you not relate to that struggle, to emerge from the confining chrysalis, this quest to become something more, to spread your wings and finally take flight?" *I know I do.*

"Look, I get it. You bonded with your mother over them, and that makes them special for you. I totally respect that, but I see them differently. Those creatures are so fragile they won't survive a second without their camouflage. What they really symbolize is…deceit."

"Deceit is the ugly bug's only defense against the cruel world. Can you really blame it for trying to survive?"

She averts her gaze toward the sky. "It's going to get dark soon. I'm ready to go home."

When we exit the lighthouse, Marcus isn't the only one waiting for us. Brandon and the team that has come to secure the car are there, too.

Birdie takes one look at their faces, and her shoulders slump. "For God's sake, what now?"

"When we arrived at the parking lot, this was on the windshield of Mrs. Abel's car." Brandon's gloved hands hold a yellow envelope. It has a butterfly drawing on it.

CHAPTER 32

Birdie

The envelope doesn't hold a note. No quotes, no vows, no words, just photos. Six to be exact.

They say a picture is worth a thousand words. Each one of these is a thousand daggers in my back. I lean back in my chair behind my desk and close my eyes for a moment's reprieve, as if I can ever get those images out of my mind.

"Birdie, you have to say something. Anything," Tristan says, and it sounds like a plea.

I've lost track of how long I've been sitting there staring at the photos. I must have looked at them a hundred times. I don't know what I expect to change every time I take in Blake and Gia, both butt-naked in her bed, from six different angles.

"I've always suspected Gia has a thing for my husband, but I've never thought he'd go for her. She's not his type." I shrug. "I don't understand."

"You're shocked. You're angry. Whatever it is that makes you think you must hide your feelings, whoever convinced you that you'll be punished for your tears, they're not here. You're free. Let it all out. Don't let that shit eat you up."

How can he say one thing and the complete opposite in the same phrase? How does he understand the aches that have shaped what I've become to the core without my telling him the stories behind them, and, at the same time, expect me to cry, my eyes open and bask in the immortalized betrayal, looking for the tears I'm supposed to shed, *over this?*

"Your husband and your friend betrayed you in the worst way possible. You can't pretend that you feel numb. No matter how much you hate him, it still hurts. No matter how much you love her, it's unforgivable."

I rub my fingers over a sigh. "When someone recommends a romance book, even one that is pitch black, do you know the first question readers would ask to determine whether they'd read it or not?"

He crouches by my side and stares at me with both curiosity and concern.

"Is there cheating?" A humorless laugh slips

its way under my breath. "Can you believe this? They don't care if the main character is a sick murderer who takes lives. They don't care if he kidnaps her and forces her to become his. They don't care if he's so violent he physically hurts her. Heck, they don't even care if he rapes her bloody, so long he doesn't cheat on her.

"In the world of romance, Tristan, the only sin a woman can't forgive is betrayal. Don't think for one second what I feel now is numbness."

"Then lash out, scream, free those trapped tears."

"Screams and tears?" I lean forward until my mouth is an inch apart from his ear. "Do you know the first thought that crossed my mind when I found Butterfly Man's note on my pillow, before morality, rage and disgust roiled in?"

"No."

"I thought that psycho was the answer to my prayers."

His head jerks, and his eyes widen at me, as if in shock, as if he didn't know, as if he's never whispered the same prayers at a different place and different time, as if he never wished for his own Butterfly Man. "Birdie, you know why he sent these photos. Gia is already MIA. She's not answering her phone, and Brandon just came back from her apartment and didn't find her. You know what's gonna happen to her and Blake after."

"When Saldana happened, I wondered why start with her when the monster that matters the most is still out there spitting venom on what's left of me," I continue whispering in his ear. "Then he sends me these photos, and it's no longer screams and tears I'm hiding, Tristan. It's the biggest grin I can muster."

"You can't think like that."

I can't think like that? Drawing back, I point at the pictures. "Do you see the bed in the photos? That used to be Gia's bed when she had to stay over in what now is the control room. Take a look at the timestamp."

He rises to his feet and glances at the little numbers. "What about it?"

"That's two days after I got out of the hospital last year."

A grimace contorts his face. "What?"

"She wished me goodnight and went downstairs to fuck my husband in my own house two days after he beat the hell out of me and left me for dead. Don't you dare tell me *I can't think like that.*"

CHAPTER 33

Birdie

Cold wind lashes at my skin as I step into the garden. My arms circle around me reflexively, but I have enough fire underneath to burn the world down. I focus on the distant sound of the waves and hum with them before I go crazy. Everything Blake has done to me was in the name of his brand of love—possessive, obsessive, violent and toxic, but reserved only for me. At least, that's what I thought, what I led myself to believe to justify the pain.

Have I been that blind? Has it always been the money he's after and nothing else? If that is so, why Gia? Why not someone wealthier? Why not another young, blonde, with mommy and daddy issues, that is to break?

Tristan opens the French doors that lead to the garden and marches toward me, his strides wide and angry. "Birdie, we need to talk. There's something you need to see."

I cross my arms over my chest and gaze at the darkening sky as it connects with the sea. "I understand you're a man of honor, wired to protect, and I'm sorry to have dragged you into my morally grey world, but there's nothing you can say that's going to change my mind and call the police. If you want to call them yourself, I can't stop you, but know that I'll burn all evidence Butterfly Man existed. As for Gia, she texted later today from a new number." *One I'm buying.* "She was a little under the weather and slept in. By the time she woke up she realized she'd misplaced her phone and couldn't reach me or get my messages. She deeply apologized for the inconvenience, and I told her to take all the time she needed to feel better before she came back to work."

"Birdie, that's—"

"I'm not risking anything for those two, not after the things Detective Torrance said. Butterfly Man might have returned the book, but he's purposely leaving breadcrumbs in his scenes that can lead to me. I'm not stupid. I know what he's planning. If he doesn't win me with the murders, he plans to use them as leverage. Either I become his or he'll frame me for them. I can't let that happen."

He invades my space, and the folder in his hands comes into sight. "That's why you need to look at this, but first do you have the stalker's older notes?"

"Blake has them in his office. Why?"

"We need to compare them with these." He takes out Butterfly Man's carefully bagged notes and the latest envelope and places them next to each other on one of the benches. "Look at the drawings." His voice drops an octave. "Look at the wings."

The second my stare zeroes in on the butterflies, Tristan's earlier words echo in my head. *See how the wings have a rich brown color with white spots along the edges?* "They all look like the one we saw at the lighthouse. They're all queens."

"If the old notes have the same drawings, it means it's intentional."

"I can't remember the exact species the butterflies are in those, but I remember one detail. Unlike in the recent ominous notes, they were all blue."

"Why blue?"

"Everybody thinks that's my favorite color, even Husband Dearest. I thought maybe as a fan, he thought so as well." I shrug, examining the illustrations before me again. "The old notes don't matter, though. We don't need them for confirmation. He drew the exact same butterfly four times. One is nothing, two is a coincidence, three is a pattern, but four..."

"Four is a message."

My heart skips a beat because I know exactly what the message is.

"It's a symbol of your name." Tristan locks his gaze with mine, swallowing, and I realize he, too, gets the clue. "Your real name. The stalker knows who you really are…Reagan."

CHAPTER 34

Butterfly Man

I was hunched over my sketchpad, pencil flying across the page as I tried to capture the angular depths of the barista's face, unaware of the bustling coffee shop around me until...

"One Americano to go, please."

Her voice, calm and raspy, cut through the dull roar of the world. My hand stilled, and I had to look up, to put a face to that voice.

From where I sat, I could only see her from behind. Her blond hair cascaded down her back in gentle waves, the color striking against her leather jacket. Her dress was sunset orange, and she wore black boots. The barista asked for the name to write on the cup, and she said, "Reagan."

"Reagan," I whispered to myself, a sweet secret lingering on my tongue, a taste I'd longed to savor.

Then her face turned in my direction as she opened her purse. One gaze at that shade of blue of her eyes and everything I'd ever known fell into insignificance. All at once, she became the entire world—the only thing that existed or mattered. I drank in the slight crease between her eyes as she concentrated on retrieving her wallet. The way her slender fingers wrapped around it. The subtle flicker of her eyelashes as she blinked. The effortless tuck of hair behind her ear. The slight uptick at the corners of her mouth when she gave the barista her card to pay. Each minuscule shift in her expression etched itself into my memory, pulling me in like ivy, choking every part of me, piece by piece, until I lost my whole being to her.

Reagan. The queen. My queen.

When she stepped away from the counter, her eyes found me. *Look away before she notices you've been staring. Fuck, what if she has already?* My heart pounded out a frenzied staccato, but I didn't dare take my gaze off her. I couldn't.

There was no flicker of recognition or guarded assessment in her expression. Stranger meeting stranger with no intention of crossing paths again, unaware of the havoc she left in her wake. *Does she even see me? Does she feel the in-*

escapable spark that will burn our souls into one?

To my relief and ruin, she answered me; Reagan's lips curved in the ghosting of a smile towards me. An unmistakable acknowledgment, the opening chapter in the rewrite of both our fates. In that moment, I became eternally, unshakably bound to her.

I tried to return the smile, but my lips were heavy with unspoken promises I intended to keep no matter how long I had to wait. *She will be mine, and I will be hers.*

"Good morning, Ms. Fletcher!" A tall boy, muscles bulging under his jersey, approached her.

Her body stiffened in his presence, and her smile vanished. "Morning, Aaron."

"Fancy seeing you here, alive and well."

"Excuse me?"

"When you didn't show up yesterday, I thought something happened to you." He took a step too close to her, invading her personal space, and his eyes roamed over her body like she was a piece of meat. "You got me so worried I was this close to stop by your place to check on you myself."

Reagan recoiled, revulsion clear on her features as his tongue swept out to crudely lick his lips before giving her an obnoxious smirk. She strode back to the counter and asked if her coffee was ready.

Rage blazed through me at the nauseating display. How dare this oaf make her feel violated and unsafe?

Reagan collected her coffee and swept out the door, the bell jangling at her abrupt exit. Part of me ached to go after her, to apologize on behalf of my entire gender for that vile pig's behavior. But the stronger instinct urged me to deal with the source of her distress in a more...permanent way.

Aaron turned to me, as if he sensed the scorching weight of my glare, that insufferable smirk begging to be knocked out of his face. "Hey, asshole, what are you looking at?"

An arrogant jock overcompensating for his tiny dick. I looked away, refusing to be baited.

But he puffed out his chest like a territorial ape as he advanced a step. "You got a problem?"

I took a steady breath and held my ground, meeting his glare with an unflinching stare. *The only problem here is the likes of you making the world a sorry place.*

With a guttural growl, Aaron lunged, only to be swiftly intercepted by the burly barista, who inserted himself between us. "Take it outside if you two wanna scrap. I'm not having that mess in my café."

Chest heaving, Aaron shrugged off the restraining hand. "Whatever man, he's not worth the charges anyway." He shoved past me, offering one last parting sneer. "It's okay. You're not the only prick who wants a piece of that ass. Every mother fucker at school is hot for teach." He bent to whisper in my ear. "But that piece of ass is *mine*. They can't have her, and neither can you, not until I'm done with her. Only then, you can have what's left."

I watched in seething silence as he swaggered out. As if in trance, I grabbed my sketchpad, the barista's face long abandoned, and Reagan's materialized on the page almost of its own accord.

A silent vow stitched itself into every stroke, every captured piece of her essence. No matter the role I was destined to play, I would shield Reagan's light from the creeping shadows that threatened to extinguish it. She'd consumed and shaped my entire existence in a handful of seared moments. And I would live and die to safeguard her, no matter how darkness tried to intervene.

Reagan Fletcher, you will be mine.

CHAPTER 35

Tristan

"You're shivering." I take off my suit jacket and drape it over Birdie's shoulders.

She clutches the jacket tightly. Her eyes, sunken in fear, look up at me. "Thank you."

It tears at my heart to see her this way. Those beautiful eyes should never be overwhelmed with dread. My throat tightens as I fight back the urge to pull her into my arms and chase away her fears with my embrace. But I can't. We promised. Loosening the boundaries of our roles has gotten us into too much trouble. We need our heads to be clear to face the danger running our way. Right now, I'm her bodyguard, her protector—nothing more, no matter how much I want to.

"I won't let anything happen to you. You're

safe with me," I say, conviction ringing in every syllable. Protecting her is my purpose, and I'll do whatever it takes to ensure her safety and peace of mind. "I'll go get a piece of paper, and I want you to write down every person in this state you think might know your real identity. We'll investigate every single one of them until we get him, I promise."

She calls out my name as I hurry toward her office. "No need. The list isn't that long to write down. See, when I decided to leave Florida, I changed my name officially. Birdie Abel is the name I have on every contract, every bank account, even on my marriage certificate. My agent, my publisher, Gia and everyone in my network here knows absolutely nothing about who I was in Florida. As far as I know, there are only two men in this state that know the name Reagan Fletcher."

"Only two men?" Adrenaline spikes in my body as I turn on my heel to face her once more. "That narrows down the potential threats considerably. Who are they? Tell me everything you know about them."

She sits next to the notes on the bench and purses her lips. "The first is Blake."

I scamper toward her. "He can't be the stalker for obvious reasons. Not after those photos anyway. That means there's only left, and he must be that creep." My heart pounds.

I'm so close to finding out who she thinks he is. "Who is it, Birdie? Who is Butterfly Man?"

She locks her gaze on me, her eyes piercing, her face unreadable. "You."

CHAPTER 36

Birdie

Tristan barks something in his native language. I don't speak Spanish, but as a teacher for troubled boys in Miami, I had to learn cussing in several South American dialects or, at least, identify swear words even when I didn't know what they really meant. Tristan is definitely swearing.

"He's toying with us!" he snares, pacing the area like an angry animal. "He didn't draw the butterflies to tell you he knew who you really were. He did it so you'd doubt me, so you'd lose your trust in me, so you'd be alone with no protection, isolated, an easy target to dig his filthy claws in." Another curse flies out of his mouth.

I regard him, his body language, his anger.

Could I have been so blind to see the truth? Can the knight sworn to protect me be the monster that terrorizes me? Or is Butterfly Man playing another sick game to make me lose the one person that's standing between me and him?

All emotions aside, I review everything that has happened between Tristan and me. The facts. Tristan knows my real name. He's read all my books. He knows so much about butterflies. He is very good with technology, has access to high-tech gear, and he is capable of taking lives.

And, no matter how hard he wants to ignore it and not act upon it, he has…feelings… for me. I don't know how long he's had them, but I doubt he's developed such an intense crush in the span of the few days he's spent here. It may have started with the books. It may have started earlier; he wouldn't be the first student that was hot for teacher.

In a character bible, Tristan Morra would fit Butterfly Man's role perfectly.

Except, since the day Tristan and I met again, every time Butterfly Man has sent one of his notes, Tristan was with me. He couldn't be at two places at the same time. Even if he's found a way to deliver the notes via a proxy, why would he send this message when the conclusion I'd draw would expose him? Why lose access to me? He's not done killing the people that have hurt me. He hasn't earned me yet.

"You're eerily silent." He stops pacing and clasps his hands together under his chin. "Please don't tell me you'll let him mess with your head. Please, Birdie."

"I won't be still sitting here, wrapped in your clothes, if that's the case."

He sighs in relief and sits next to me. "Thank you."

"You're right. He's trying to isolate me to make me vulnerable so that I'll have no one else to trust but him, so that I'll have nothing to protect me from his darkness. I'm more than familiar with the tactic, thanks to Blake."

"I won't let him anywhere near you." He collects the notes and studies them again one by one. "I will find him, Birdie, I promise."

"How? Butterfly Man isn't a reader turned stalker or even a random guy from Massachu-setts like we've thought. He's someone from my past. He saw me in Florida, developed a dangerous obsession with me, and followed me all the way to this island. I don't even know if his obsession started in Miami or earlier in Jacksonville when I used to live with my par-ents. I don't even know if I've ever spoken to the guy or if he's been watching from afar all these years like the creep he is. It's impossible to narrow him down from a list. He could literally be anyone."

"He's been obsessed with you for so long. It's highly unlikely he's never interacted with you. The theory that he's one of the people on the document you shared with me at the lighthouse is more valid now than before. We'll do background checks on everyone on that list to find if they have any ties in Florida and take it from there." He gives me the notes. "But you know him, Birdie. You just need to find the hidden clues."

"You think I haven't tried? Ever since he broke into my house, I've been wracking my brain to find out who Butterfly Man is to no avail."

"He speaks to you in quotes. Each note is a chapter in a story meant for you, and only you, to read. But you're the storyteller, not him. Who is better than you to figure out the plot twist early on?" He points at the notes. "There must be something in here, something only you can discover that will give him away."

I take a deep breath. The cold air tightens my chest rather than easing the tension as I flip through the messages, reading between the lines, looking for hints or patterns I've missed before. Anything. "Let's see. Butterflies. I've never had any friends or classmates who are interested in them."

"What about boyfriends? Anybody who

might have called you a butterfly or queen as a pet name? Fleeting crushes? An unrequited love?"

I scoff. "No, none of the above. Never been kissed until Shane."

"What are you talking about?"

"I've never had any boyfriends before him. He was my first…everything. Who would have a crush on the nerd who dressed like a nun, let alone an unrequited love? Too smart for her own good. Too much of a prude. That's what they said about me. No one cared about the heart of the nerdy girl who was born to parents incapable of love, who was desperate to find it with someone else. No one realized the long sleeves were to hide the bruises."

He scowls, and his gaze drops to his shoes. "I'm so sorry."

"It's not your fault."

"Where is Shane now?"

"Where he belongs. Prison."

"For long I hope."

"Not long enough if you ask me. Sooner or later, they're going to let him out, and he's going to be another thorn in my back." I shrug with a sigh. "But we'll cross that bridge when we get there. We have a much bigger issue to deal with."

"Have you dated anyone after him? I mean before Blake?"

I shake my head. "Just the two. I sure know how to pick them."

"Jesus, Birdie. A woman like you doesn't deserve this. You've been through a lot of pain."

Tears clog my throat and threaten to spill from my eyes. I push them down. I don't have time for them. "It is what it is. Can we focus on the missing clues, please?"

His eyes trail on me. I pretend to read the notes in my hand because if I so much as glance at him, I'll break, and I can't do that. Not now.

"What about the handwriting?" he asks.

"I don't recognize it."

"It doesn't remind you of any of your friends' handwriting? Former bosses'? Teachers'?"

"Teachers? That's too sick, Tristan."

"The stalker is sick. We can't exclude your teachers because it's creepy. You said it yourself. It could be anyone."

I go through the shape of the letters one more time. "No. This handwriting doesn't belong to any of my friends, bosses or teachers."

"What about students? The school didn't only cater to kids with special needs and reading difficulties. You taught students with behavioral issues, too, at risk youth, right?"

Students with behavioral issues, to put it lightly. They were dysfunctional and disruptive. Society rejects. My skin crawls at the memory of one of them in particular.

"Birdie?"

His voice brings me back from one of the worst nights of my life. "Yes?"

"You remember something, don't you?"

How can I ever forget? "I…I've seen so much handwriting over my teaching years it starts to blend. Besides, it's been over eight years. I can't remember."

"Don't lie to me. Now is not the time to keep secrets. You remembered something. You have someone in mind. Who is it?"

It doesn't matter. It's not his handwriting, and it's not him. It can't be. "It's getting cold, and I'd like to rest. I'm heading back inside."

"No." He blocks my way. "You can't do that, not when we're this close. You have to tell me."

I squeeze my eyes shut, the images of the person that ruined my life flashing behind my eyelids. My nails dig into my palms as I try to push the memories away, but they only grow stronger, creeping up my skin as if happening now. The predatory stares in the classroom. His cornering me every time he found me alone. The things he said he wanted to do to me. The threats if I didn't submit to his desires. The whispers that followed me everywhere and the way my friends' eyes changed when they looked at me—all because of the lies he spread. The suffocating feeling of being trapped in a web of deceit I couldn't escape.

"Please, Birdie. Anything you know is gonna help us find him and end this nightmare."

I can't bring that name to life after all these years. I can't dig it up after the price I've paid to keep it buried. So I do what I do best. "How did you get the scar on your face, Tristan?"

His eyes widen, his stare a mix of blame, fury and a plea. I expect him to shut down or run as usual, and when silence stretches between us, I, too, turn to escape.

"It was my father," he confesses in a whisper that pierces the silence. The tremor in his voice belies the anguish he normally keeps so cautiously guarded.

My heart thrashes, and my feet halt at the threshold.

"He used to beat the crap out of me and my mother. I never stood up to him. I was too scared. Until one day I…"

Slowly, I spin to face him, apprehensive about betraying this unprecedented moment of vulnerability, but the solemn determination to open up in his expression encourages me to approach him. "Until one day, you said enough. Your fear turned into something else, something more sinister yet empowering. Finally, it gave you the courage to fight back."

"He fought too."

His pain infiltrates my soul. "Who won that day?"

"I'm not the one rotting in a grave."

A shudder ripples through me at the anguished admission. I hear him, what he's telling me. I see his *hidden clues* just like I see the truth of the man he is. Forged in violence and unspeakable suffering, forced to embrace the darkness just to stay alive, forever marred, carrying the mark of a survivor.

The urge to run my thumb over his scar, to show him he's whole and beautiful, to let him know he's understood and accepted, pulses through me, but I know better. "You're safe with me," I say instead, hoping it's enough.

He bends his forehead to mine, almost touching, his breath scorching my face. "So are you. You're not alone, Birdie. I know what it's like to have your life derailed by evil men. To be beaten down and commit unspeakable sins because you felt you had no other choice. So whatever hell you went through, pour it down on me."

My breath stalls in my lungs. Tristan has shattered through his walls. Now, it's my turn to make the same leap. Shaking, I rub my fingers over my mouth. The words choke in my throat.

"You promised if I trusted you enough to

tell you how I got my scar, you'd tell me about yours," he reminds me.

He's revealed the truth of his past so that I can share my own. If he could find the strength to bare open his most guarded wounds, then I owed him the same.

"His name was Aaron West," I begin.

CHAPTER 37

Birdie

aron West. Just saying his name aloud after so many years sends a chill down my spine. "From the first day, he was...disruptive. Troubled in a way that went beyond the typical behavioral issues I dealt with. He'd stare at me inappropriately during class. He'd find excuses to linger after the other students left, follow me everywhere and say things no student should ever say to their teacher.

"I tried to deal with the situation as professionally as possible. I didn't want to take it to the principal because Aaron had already been expelled from two schools before he came to mine. I wanted to give him a chance, so I talked to his therapist instead."

Tristan gives me an understanding nod to continue. "And?"

Bile rises to my throat, and I have to pause. "What did the therapist do about it?"

"He was very skeptical of my claims because Aaron had told him it was me who was trying to seduce my student. Aaron even showed him a very disturbing pornographic video I'd allegedly sent of the…things I'd have liked him to do to me."

"Son of a—" Tristan bites his lip. "I'm so sorry, Birdie. You must have been furious. How did you handle it?"

"I had no choice but to take it to the principal, but I got the same response. Aaron was one step ahead of me, telling them lies to cover his tracks. *I* received a formal warning while Aaron was patted on the shoulder. The only reason I kept my job was that they couldn't prove I sent that video."

Tristan swears again. "I can't believe this. I hate what they've done to you. There has to be something we can do to make them pay for it."

"It was his word against mine, and in situations like these, even with at-risk students, theirs carries more weight. Every time I tried to defend myself, it made me look more guilty. Every time I rejected Aaron and demanded he leave me alone, he fed more of my colleagues at the school the same lies. I was stuck in a nightmare I couldn't wake up from. There was nothing I could do, so I just kept going and tried to put it behind me."

"Why didn't you leave, find a job somewhere else?"

"Because I needed the money and pulling out of my contract like that would have confirmed the rumors, but mainly because I was scared of Aaron. He threatened if I left the school, he would…" I trail off, the words too vile to voice.

"He would what?" he urges gently, his voice a whisper.

"He'd ruin me and make sure I never worked anywhere else." I swallow hard, forcing the words past the lump in my throat. "He'd make everyone see me as the monster he painted me to be because he'd tell them I raped him."

Fury flashes in Tristan's eyes. His fists tighten, his knuckles turning white. "There has to be some kind of justice. He can't do this to you."

"I tried to reason with him, but he got a kick out of the power he thought he had over my life. That was when I realized I'd lost either way. If I'd left, he'd have told that horrific lie about me. If I'd stayed, what would have stopped him from flaunting the same threat down the line to force me to sleep with him. No matter how hard I fought, he'd still win. The only way to beat him was to take that power away."

"What did you do?"

"I was done being a victim. I told him to go ahead and say what he threatened to say about me. I'd leave the school, disappear and never have to endure his harassment again."

"What?"

"I already had plans to leave Miami because of Shane. Aaron gave me more reasons to follow through with them."

"If all of that happened right after Shane, it meant you didn't leave right away. You wouldn't have taught me or met Blake if you had. You stayed for a while. Why?"

"I couldn't believe it at first, but Aaron promised to behave and begged me to stay. What I said took him by surprise, and he realized how much damage he was causing me. I had my doubts it was another one of his games, another way to regain the power he'd lost, but he did behave. For months, he'd kept his promise, and I was convinced he'd come around and showed true remorse.

"But then I started seeing him everywhere I went again. The coffee shop, the park, the beach. He returned to corner me outside school, saying terrible things, until one day I saw him in his car outside my house.

"I decided to act before he could manipulate his way with more lies, so I took photos of him outside my house and yelled at him that I'd call the cops while I filmed the whole thing. He ran and stopped showing at my place. I was engaged to Blake then, and I believed it scared Aaron away. I thought it was over, but then I got weird messages on my socials from private profiles. There were phone calls in the middle of the night from screened numbers, and when I picked up, I only heard someone breathing. It was him. I knew it."

Tristan lets out a frustrated sigh, running a hand through his hair. "He stalked you, and now, after all these years, he's back."

"No, Tristan. Aaron can't be Butterfly Man."

"Why not? Because you still think he's redeemable after all the things he's done to you?"

"Because he's dead."

He blinks and then shakes his head slowly. "Dead? I don't understand. I thought…"

"You think I wouldn't tell you about being stalked before if I thought for one second they could be the same person? I told you revealing Aaron's story wouldn't make any difference now. He died nine days after I'd threatened to call the cops on him."

"What you've just told me isn't the whole

story, is it? There's more."

The memories of how Aaron ruined my life weigh down on me, so I sit. "I told Blake what happened, and he went to talk to Aaron. The next day, Aaron filed a report accusing Blake of harassment. He took that report to the school and asked to switch classes so that I'd no longer be his teacher. They granted him his wish and gave *me* another warning.

"One more, and I'd have been fired, perhaps even faced charges. I had to do something to stop him, so I asked Aaron to meet me away from the school and promised I'd come alone."

Tristan grimaces. "Why would you meet that sicko alone?"

"A trap to get him to confess, to get the truth out of him, while I recorded him. That would have been evidence strong enough to clear my reputation. It'd have been leverage to make him stop harassing me." My throat constricts with bitterness. "Except he never showed up, and the next morning he was found dead."

"Jesus Christ. I didn't know any of this. I don't even remember someone at school who died." He muses. "Wait, there was this one student who OD'd and was found dead in his car. Was that him?"

I nod once.

"I don't get it. If he was dead, why did

you leave Miami, change your name and come here? Why would you upend your life, excise it from one place and plant it in another as a different person?"

"Because even in death, he wouldn't leave me be. Aaron had one of those apps on his phone for daily check ins, as a part of his therapy program. He set it that if he missed a day, the app would send an email to his parents and his school therapist. When he died, the email went out."

"What did it say?"

My heart contracts, and a wave of nausea attacks me. "If I'm dead, it's because of what she did to me."

Tristan blanches. Even in the dark, under the moonlight, I can see the color rushing out of his face. All the time I've been telling him this story, he was angry and appalled but not shocked or disturbed. This part, the sick note…that's what got to him.

I rest my forehead on my clasped hands. "You can imagine what they thought after that email. The police confirmed Aaron OD'd, and I had nothing to do with it, but his parents wanted to sue me. They said he committed suicide because I abused him. Blake pulled some strings, though. His friends at the station covered the whole thing up and convinced the parents there wasn't evidence to back up the implied accusation in the email.

"The school covered it up as well, provided I resigned and never pursued a career in teaching again. As for Blake, he was suspended because he smashed the face of one of his colleagues after calling me a molester. Then he was forced to retire early." I glance up at him. "There, now you know the whole thing. Why I had to leave. Why I didn't want a former student of mine to be my bodyguard. Why I had to bury Reagan Fletcher and become Birdie Abel."

Sweat beads his forehead. "If I could dig that maggot food out and kill him again for what he did to you, I would."

"That's…"

"Dark and twisted and sick? Yeah, I know, but he deserves it."

"I was going to say sweet." I shrug. "Not that it'd have made any difference. God, I hate drugs and what they make people do. They turn them into monsters capable of evil atrocities that ruin others' lives and theirs. Aaron, Saldana, Blake…"

He pauses for a minute before he squints at me. "Did you say Aaron overdosed and was found dead in his car?"

CHAPTER 38

Tristan

irdie gasps. "I can't believe I've only now connected the dots. Aaron and Saldana died the same way."

I peer at the stalker's notes for the millionth time. "And we know Saldana didn't off herself."

"That means it's possible Aaron didn't accidentally kill himself over an OD either. His suicide could have been staged just like hers." Her jaw hangs low, and she shakes her head infinitesimally. "Oh my God. Saldana isn't Butterfly Man's first murder in my name. He killed for me before. Butterfly Man killed Aaron."

"Aaron hurt you. He took care of it, looking after you…or so he thought."

"But wh… What if the creepy calls and

messages were from Butterfly Man, not from Aaron? What if that was when it all started?"

I mull it over. "The timeline makes sense. He began watching you, got obsessed, stalked you and found out about Aaron."

"Yes, because if it started earlier, he would have known about Shane and taken my first husband out of the picture, too, but he didn't."

"This is very valuable information, Birdie. Now we know he lived in Miami, and he started stalking you after Shane but before Aaron's death. I'll pass it along to the team conducting the background checks for cross-referencing. This helps narrow it down immensely."

"I still can't wrap my mind around all of this." She stares at me in disbelief. "Could this be true?"

Has her stalker's obsession been twisting for years into an ever-darkening malignancy? Yes, it's true. I gaze back into her haunted eyes. She's terrified out of her own skin, as if the monster is here, manifested in the flesh, coiling his evil around her. "There is only one way to find out."

Her eyes turn into a question, and I point at the proof of infidelity photos. "He thinks he's taunting us, but I won't let him win. He's marked his next victims. All I have to do is watch them and wait for the bastard to make a mistake. One is nothing. Two is a coincidence."

"Three is a pattern," she murmurs.

"If either of them dies with a shit load of drugs in their system or in a car crash, we'll have our answer."

She gives a grim nod. "I'm scared of finding out."

I sit beside her. "As long as I'm here, I don't wanna hear that word from you. I'd die before anything dared touch you again. This is good, Birdie. You should feel safe because that's how we get him." I chase her eyes until I'm certain she can see the determination in mine. "That's how I end him."

Her breath shudders on her lips. "What if you can't? What if he kills Gia and Blake and you still haven't caught him? You know who will be next on his list."

The last line of defense that keeps him from claiming his prize. Me. "Let's get you inside before you catch a cold. I'm gonna head out for a while, and when I return, we'll have to fill Marcus in about the updates. He'll be your number one as you requested."

"What? No."

"Birdie, we agreed that solution would be for the best. We need clear heads to be at the top of our game to beat Butterfly Man. You can trust Marcus."

"I can't, not with this." Her gaze beseeches me. "Tristan, you can't just take a backseat, not after everything I've told you. Those secrets… They must stay between us. Please."

Her pleas bind me to her side despite every instinct screaming to put space between us. She trusts me, and only me, with her darkest secrets. I am the vault for the demons that haunt her past. How can I deny her my solace when she needs it the most?

I can't. Even when I'm hyper-aware of the scant distance between us but can't stop myself from tracing the delicate slope of her jawline, the facets of her face and the terrain of her lips. Even when every moment passes in her proximity, all my energy goes to fighting the urge to do something that could ruin everything between us.

"I'm imprisoned by the tangled impulses that war constantly within me. Protect you from the monsters outside, yet somehow keep you safe from the one I carry inside, stitched into the fabric of my very existence."

Her gaze holds me transfixed, imploring me to be there for her. "I don't need protection from you, Tristan."

I suffocate with everything I can't give voice to. I'm afraid if I part my lips, every ill-restrained need and unhallowed longing will come barreling out.

Holding my gaze, she flexes her fingers slowly next to mine, and her knuckles feather against my skin. A tremor goes through me, the ghost of a flinch before my body remembers it's her. The only human whose touch wields comfort instead of pain.

Her eyes drop to our hands, and when she realizes I haven't moved away, she searches my face for encouragement. I inhale deeply, leaning into the tendril of human connection grounding me, and twine my smallest digit with hers.

I bite my lip on the scorching wave of fire engulfing me at her touch. My heart bangs violently as her lips move with a flicker of a smile. I let my palm meet hers slowly, allowing her delicate fingers to weave between my calloused grip like a lifeline pulling me back from the precipice.

I squeeze her hand gently and carve the feeling on my soul. A memory that can last forever unlike this moment that has to end too soon. My eyes close as I wish to speak out my heart, but I mutter only what she can understand—her own words.

"In that breathless moment, I shored myself against the tide of my own damaged spirit. I would endure and weather any storm to be her sanctuary when the world grew too dark. Her protector, her source of courage in the madness."

CHAPTER 39
Birdie

I didn't think I'd be able to sleep last night, but I slept like a baby. There was this weight I've been dragging with me since Aaron's death aftermath, and Tristan helped me carry it when I let him in on the secret.

There is a heavier weight that has been pressing on my soul, rendering me breathless, lifeless, for so long. Blake.

The photos of his betrayal are a promise that weight, too, will be lifted off me. And when I got a text last night from *Gia, from a new number because she lost her phone*, I knew where Tristan was when he went out. He's no longer conflicted about what needs to be done, and he'll let Butterfly Man finish what he started before catching him.

My imagination runs to a violence-free life.

No more walking on eggshells. No more fear or hurt. Just me, my books and peace. And maybe a man with whom I can feel safe again, a man who cherishes, respects and loves me for me with no ulterior motives.

Tristan's face jumps in my head at the thought. I laugh at myself, dismissing the juvenile fantasy. We had a *moment* yesterday, but what he said after sentenced it to an end. He must avoid any distractions or temptations to gain the clarity he needs to catch my stalker, and I can't agree more.

He may be trustworthy, respectful, unabusive—and I bet he's going to blow my mind in bed after reading all my smut books—but I can't allow myself to think of him as anything more than my bodyguard. Even after he catches Butterfly Man and *neutralizes the threat*, the demons of our violent pasts will always be in the way of any future for us together.

I wash away the sleep and get dressed to go down to my office. Tristan and I can't have a thing, but the characters in my book can't care less about our boundaries, and they are begging me for some quality steamy time.

When I open the door, it's not Tristan or Marcus that's on guard. It's that young, blond man from the team whose name I can't remember.

"Good morning, Mrs. Abel," he says.

"It was, until you called me that. It's Birdie. Just Birdie. Do you think you can do that for me, um…?"

"Gatsby…Brandon Gatsby, ma'am."

"Can you do that for me, Brandon?"

He swallows, color rising to his cheeks. He's one of those people whose skin exposes them no matter how hard they try. "Yes. I'm sorry, Birdie, ma'am."

I'm making him uncomfortable—he's making me uncomfortable, too, because he looks a little bit like Shane—so I wrap our conversation short. "Where are Tristan and Marcus?"

"Marcus is doing sweeps, and Tristan is in his room. He said he'd take over in a few minutes. Are you going to your office, ma'am?"

I was. Not anymore. Not with you. "I'm sure you're more than capable of doing all the tasks you're assigned, but I'll wait for Tristan. No offense, but you remind me of someone I don't want to be reminded of."

His face blazes. "I'm sorry, ma'am."

"It's not your fault. It's his."

I even my breath and knock on Tristan's door. He's taken the room adjacent to mine, where Blake used to sleep after I came out of the hospital. The two opposite rooms are shared among the rest of the team.

When Tristan doesn't answer, I call out his name. Is he sleeping? As silence replies again, my hand drops to the knob. Brandon appears next to me in a split-second. "I must secure the room before you enter. It's protocol, ma'am."

Rolling my eyes, I step back. "By all means."

Brandon does his job and comes out. "All clear, ma'am. Tristan is in the bathroom, showering."

"Thank you." *For the unnecessary report and… visual.* I clear my throat and step inside the room. Brandon nods once and closes the door behind me when he exits.

I haven't been inside this room since Tristan moved in. Apart from a few rearranged chairs, it's pretty much the same, except it's meticulously kept. Blake used to make a mess worse than that of a pig. I've heard the Spanish profanities the housekeeping staff spat every time they came in to clean.

Tristan, on the other hand, is a neat freak. The surfaces are immaculate. The bed is made with military precision. There isn't an element that's out of place. Even the books on the nightstand are stacked too neatly, screaming untouched. If I didn't know he was a reader beforehand, I'd think those books were solely decor.

I run my fingers along the spines—classical philosophy and psychology texts mixed with my novels. *So he does have other interests beside smut.*

Sitting on the bed edge, I grab *The Nightin-*

gale's Whispers, Tristan's favorite book of mine. Does he annotate his reads or highlight the quotes? Dogear the pages or use bookmarks? Curiosity peaks through me as I flip through the pages and find the book as immaculate as the room.

"That's weird." Or not. Many readers like to keep their books in pristine condition. Given the cleanliness level of this room, it's normal he's one of those readers. Unexpected, when he has all those quotes learned by heart, but normal. I guess I'm just disappointed I've missed out on some secret insight into what he truly loves about my work.

I put the book back. My fingers glide up the sheets on the side where I think he sleeps, and a smile creeps to my face. Does he sleep fully clothed? In underwear? Nude?

My skin tingles as my author mind seeks all the details to build his character in depth. It's inevitable that one day I'll write Tristan in one of my books, if not in my current WIP. The woman in me, too, demands answers, for non-book related, NSFW purposes.

I direct my gaze toward the bathroom door, hyper-aware Tristan is fully naked in there right at this moment. A reckless part of me wants to sneak in, to get the full picture of what he has under his suits, to know what it means to be ravished by Mr. Morra, my off-limits bodyguard, especially when his scent has seeped from the sheets and lingered on my fingertips, and one whiff at them makes me throb in all the right places.

Heat rises to my cheeks. *Get a grip. This is your bodyguard, nothing more. He serves a purpose and goes on his way. He's not an option. Never was. Never will be.*

To distract myself, I picture Blake sleeping in this bed. God, I want to smash his face, break his bones to make him feel a shred of the agony he's been causing me. Did he bring Gia here, too, to fuck while I slept the pain off in the next room?

Rage ripples through me in waves. An image of Blake's face covered in blood in his car with a needle stuck in his arm flashes in my head. Nothing is going to extinguish the fire in my chest but his and Gia's death.

I jump to my feet, the need to leave this room urgent. My steps echo over the sound of the water running in the shower. I raise a fist to knock on the bathroom door but stop midway when Tristan groans in Spanish.

"Reagan… La tengo parada sólo per ti… Sí…ah… Chúpame la verga."

I freeze, my raised fist hanging in the air as Tristan's muffled voice carries through the door. His words flowing in a low, heated rumble. I can't make out exactly what he's saying, but the tone leaves little doubt as to the nature of his thoughts—and what his hand is doing—now.

I should leave and pretend I never heard a thing, but my feet remain rooted to the spot. Even my ears disobey me and strain to make out more words, more of that hoarse need in his voice that sends unbidden thoughts ricocheting through my mind.

There's power in standing here unwatched while he's indisposed, giving voice to his fantasies, the secrets he's been hiding from me. He moans my name over and over, Reagan, not Birdie, and it does something unholy to me. Hearing my real name groaned in the pain that chases after pleasure, in that sinful voice, adds more to the forbidden indulgence.

Reagan, the woman he's known before he became her protector, is the center of his madness. The fruit he would never taste. The sin for which he can't atone.

On their own accord, my fingers caress the doorknob. Bathroom lights spill from the cracks, and I realize all this time the door has been open. My heart skips a beat. Does he know I've been here listening to him?

He mumbles something in Spanish followed by my name and another moan, answering my question. He's too engrossed to notice my presence. Slowly, I open hell's door without so much of a knock.

I blow out a shaky breath and watch it dissipate in the humid air. My gaze is drawn to the shower stall itself. The glass is opaque with steam, but I can make out Tristan's silhouette, broad, powerful and dangerously beautiful, behind the haze.

He leans back his head, his behind pressing against the glass, allowing for a gorgeous, clear view of his toned, very naked ass. I've never seen so much of a full arm of his body. Other than that one time I saw him in gym shorts, he's always formally dressed around me. Now…

I marvel at the rippling muscles and throb with each groan he releases in need. His shoulder rocks as he works harder on himself. His panting accelerates against the streaming water. And I watch. I'm playing with fire, but I'll enjoy the burn.

Then, my name straining out of his lips, he turns.

Our gazes lock. He sees me, and I see everything. In that fractured moment, before his expression morphs from naked vulnerability to an inscrutable mask, I see the longing, the self-loathing, the warring hope and hopelessness swirling in those intense eyes. His unresolved demons.

He doesn't try to cover up. The hand that

has been rubbing pleasure out of him closes the water.

Tension and silence hum in equal measure between us. He takes one step back and squares his shoulders, his eyes, shameless, never leaving mine, as if he's saying, "Here I am. Look closer. See it all. Enjoy the view."

Images of him naked, on top of me, under me, behind me, crowd my brain until heat pools between my thighs. His eyes darken, as if he crawled inside my head and saw every dirty, forbidden scene playing about him. He pushes the door open, his hand leaving a print on the steamy glass, and comes out.

The thick air clears bit by bit, revealing the whole picture. I fill my fantasies about him with the missing details while he's standing a few feet away from me, staring right at me. The angry sinews that bulge out of his flesh. The scars of the wars in which he had to win. Too many to endure yet survived. Three visible tattoos. One on his chest right above his heart—*Monarca* wrapped in butterfly wings. Another on the side of his perfect abs—an open book on top of a cobweb, and *'One shattered rhythm. Two sides of a broken heart.'* written underneath. It's the same tattoo the protagonist in *The Nightingale's Whispers* has. The last one I see is on the plain surface above his erection.

His hardness demands my attention, distracting me from reading those inked letters, and while my eyes widen at the mischievous glint of the rings adorning the crown and the shaft, they're more eager to decipher that tattoo. It's in Spanish.

"You are the sin scorched onto my soul's darkest covenant." He translates for me, and it feels like a confession.

"When did you get that?"

"Right after I read it."

"That's from my first book, Tristan." It was published six years ago. "How long?" I rasp. "How long have you been doing this?"

"This?"

"Fucking your fist thinking about me."

He steps closer, and my heart thuds. "Long."

I swallow. "Since you started reading my books?"

He takes another step towards me and shakes his head.

"How long, Tristan?"

"When I'm baring myself and the truth naked before you, don't you dare lie to me. You already know how long, Reagan. At least, suspected."

He's been having forbidden fantasies about his teacher. Like Aaron. "This is sick."

"You of all people can't say that. Imagination isn't sick. There's no right or wrong when it comes to what goes on in our minds." His brows furrow. "I've never acted on my dark desires for you. I've never so much uttered a single word about them to you. Even now, when I'm desperately aching for you, when you're standing so close but never close enough, I keep my distance."

His voice drops. "But you're right. I am sick." He tilts his head and lets his male gaze sweep me from head to toe. "So are you."

"Me?"

"You're here, aren't you?" His hand wraps around his erection and tugs. "Standing in my bathroom, watching instead of leaving, fucking me in your head." His lower lip curls under his teeth as he starts rubbing himself. "Tell me you don't wanna watch me finish. Tell me you don't wanna hear your name on my lips when I break."

I do…and more. I want to know if his muscles are as firm as they look, how his skin tastes as I lick the water droplets that get to touch him while I don't, how rough his scars will be under my fingertips, how the rings of his piercings will feel inside of me, if they will rush my orgasm, if they will prolong the pleasure, what kind of sweet nothings he'll whisper, what other sounds he'll make when he *breaks*.

I'm thirty-four. He's twenty-seven.

He used to be my student. I was the teacher

he had dirty thoughts about.

I'm his client. He's my bodyguard.

It's wrong, but I can't stop staring at him touching himself in front of me.

Rugged breaths tear from him and mingle with mine in the shadowed space between our bodies. Reason is a distant, mocking whisper lost in the roars of our hearts. His eyes blaze with primal hunger, scorching me with a look that threatens to undo every stitch of restraint still binding me.

You're married, and Blake is still alive. If he finds out before Butterfly Man gets him…

Just like that the haze of temptation lifts off my brain, and I'm brutally yanked and thrown into the violence of reality. I drag myself to the door. "I have to go."

"Don't go. Please."

Staring at the door, I shake my head. "I can't, Tristan. What you said yesterday… That quote, it's about fighting and sacrifice, not succumbing to selfish desires."

"*This* is me trying to fight. I need to clear my head, to take out everything that's there other than protecting you. So please…help me."

"If Blake finds out and uses it against me—"

"He can't. He'll never find out. Besides, there's nothing he can use here. We're not doing anything wrong. *You* aren't doing anything wrong. You don't even have to look at me. Just tell me, if this was a scene in your book, how would you write it?"

The question unlocks something in me, a torrent of words and imagery clawing their way out of my head. I close my eyes and urge myself to walk out of here, but not one fiber of me is willing to obey.

"Please." His voice lowers in a prayer that asks for damnation. "Just this once. I'm begging you."

He was right. I knocked on hell's door, but it wasn't a demon that opened it for me. It was the devil himself.

I exhale a breath I've been holding for so long. "I want to wrench open the door and stride out of that inferno of tantalizing dangers, but the need in his plea chains my feet. Does he know I can't resist when a man begs? Is he telling me what I need to hear to get his way? Or is his beseeching genuine?"

"After my father's death, I promised myself I'd never beg anyone for anything again. Today, for you, I broke my promise. Only for you, I'd beg. Only for you, I'd go down on my knees."

Oh God. My head tilts back as I let out another heated breath. "He's driving me crazy with those words. I nibble on my bottom lip, unable to erase the image of him hard and straining behind me. His low and gruff moans as he touches himself are so delicious. Will he make the same sounds if it's my fingers that are wrapped around him? My lips? My arousal?"

He groans a curse, heat rolling off him in waves and clashing against my back. Against my best judgment, I twirl and stare at him.

"Dark desire smolders in his tormented gaze, more frightening in its intensity than violence itself. His jaw clenches as he works faster, harder. Then his gaze, brazen, possessed, forged in hell, widens as it devours my body." I watch as he hungers over me. "His face says it all. He's never wanted anyone more than he wants me. It's taking him every ounce of restraint not to pounce and take me like the animal he is. But it's not our time. Not now. Maybe not ever."

"It makes me want you even more. It makes *you* want me even more," he says between his shaking breaths.

"He's right again. I crave him," I say, forsaking all shame, and hop to sit on top of the vanity counter. I hike up my skirt, in my head his hands are doing the job, and spread my legs.

"Holy hell," he rasps.

"His stare dips to the view I've allowed. He must have imagined spreading me wide countless times. Does it live up to his expectations?"

"What the… Your underwear. It's soaking, for God's sake." He runs a hand through his wet hair. "This is torture."

"Then let me put you out of your misery." I hook my fingers in the elastic of my panties and push them down to my ankles. Then I slide my feet out of them and let them drop on the floor.

"You!" He snarls at the sight of me naked underneath my skirt and lunges forward.

I gasp, fear and arousal roiling inside me. Is this where I burn?

He stops an inch away from me and bangs his palm against the bathroom wall. "How is this putting me out of my misery? I can feel the heat coming from your pussy, Reagan. My cock is only a couple of thrusts away from taking what it's always craved."

"And yet you can't touch me, not until I tell you to." I lean in and whisper, "Maybe not even then, my protector."

He shouts in pain and slams his palm again multiple times against the wall. His eyes squeeze shut as he sucks in a breath through his teeth. Then he picks up my underwear and narrows his gaze at it. When he peers back at me, he smirks. "These are mine."

A gasp escapes me when he sharply inhales my scent out of the fabric, and then his tongue darts out and, slowly, licks the wet spot staining it.

As if he's eating me, I squirm. But no. I've

started this game. I can't let him win. If there is no redemption, no absolution from the demons we embrace in the shadows, then I'll savor the chaos. If he's the devil, then I'm his queen.

Instead of pressing my thighs, I spread them wider. Then I slither two of my fingers between them. "You can't come until I do."

His face twists with rage. "You can't do this to me."

I rub my clit. "Watch me."

He does. He stays still, growling and cursing both of us to hell and beyond, until my fingers are covered in my orgasm.

"Your turn," I whisper.

Eyes pinned to my wetness, he balls my panties in his fist and raises them to his nose and tugs at his hardness.

One.

Two.

Three.

Four.

I approach his ear. "Good boy."

His rugged groans of pleasure rasp against my neck as his climax spurts hot and sticky on my inner thighs.

"As he marks my flesh with his release, I burn my name through the woven depths of his soul, a mark never to be erased." I hold his gaze. "Mine."

CHAPTER 40

Birdie

Marcus presses a finger to his ear, and a frown crosses his face. "It's that detective again asking to see you, Birdie."

I look up from the book I'm reading and adjust my glasses. I have a pretty good idea why Torrance is here. It's been five days since Butterfly Man's last note, six since I've seen Gia alive.

My eyes meet Tristan's. He's sitting on the couch polishing a military knife like a sociopath. Sometimes, I want to chuck a book at him. We've barely spoken after the *shower scene*, but now is not the time for radio silence.

"I'll see if I can dismiss him," Marcus says.

"No." Tristan coaxes the blade to a mirror-like sheen. "Let him in."

Marcus glances at me for confirmation, and I nod once.

Tristan stands, knife swishing against the cloth in hand, as Torrance's hulking frame fills the living room entrance. The two men regard each other warily before Tristan puts his weapon back in his ankle sheathe.

The detective greets me and then stretches a hand toward Tristan. "Detective Jacob Torrance, Oak Bluffs PD. And you are?"

Tristan's eyes shoot daggers at the detective. "Tristan Morra," he says tightly, ignoring Torrance's outstretched hand. "Mrs. Abel's head of security."

A charged beat passes as they stare at each other before Torrance drops his hand and inclines his head at me. "How many bodyguards do you have? I counted four so far. Two at the gate, the guy from the last time I was here and your *head of security*. Are there more?"

Yes, Tristan first came with four bodyguards. Marcus, Brandon, Dixon and Riley, and then he added a new member after we received Butterfly Man's last note, Maddison or Morrison or whatever.

I steel myself, fingers gripping the spine of the book. I've been preparing myself for this conversation for days, but there's something about being in the same room with this man that makes me nervous. "Is that why you're here, Detective? To count my bodyguards?"

"I'm just curious how many you need when the psycho stalking you and threatening to kill people to earn your love turned out to be a myth."

"Certainly, it is something more pressing than curiosity that brings you here, twice in one week."

Torrance chooses the seat closest to mine and makes himself comfortable. "Can I talk to you?" He glances sideways at Tristan. "Alone?"

"Is my client under arrest?" Tristan asks, his face made of stone.

The detective snorts. "We'd be having a very different conversation if she was."

"Then no. Absolutely not."

A grin stretches Torrance's mouth. He keeps it on as he peers at Tristan, weighing him in, a second too long. Then he switches his gaze toward me. "Does he speak for you?"

"When it comes to her security, yes, I do," Tristan answers.

Torrance doesn't take his eyes off me when he repeats, "Does he speak for you?"

A muscle pulses in Tristan's jaw. His lips part, but I raise a hand to stop him before he says anything we might both regret. "Why don't you say what you're here to say, Detective? There are cameras everywhere. He'll hear it anyway."

He regards me carefully, studying me like he's just done with Tristan. Can he hear my frantic heartbeat? Can he see through the mask about to smash into pieces if he keeps looking at me with those steely eyes? Finally, he gives a small nod, and I allow myself to breathe. "Very well. I'm here to—"

Tell me Gia is dead. Butterfly Man killed her.

"—tell you Saldana's case is closed. It's no longer a homicide investigation."

I blink, and then I blink harder. "What?"

"We found CCTV footage of the man that was in the car with her. He left the vehicle when she was still alive. We found other footage that confirmed Saldana was driving by herself a few minutes before the crash. There is no evidence that someone else was in the car with her when it happened."

"Does that mean her death is officially a suicide?"

"Yes, ma'am."

That doesn't make any sense. Not with the details he's disclosed earlier, the breadcrumbs Butterfly Man left on purpose to lead back to me. Torrance painted a very palpable picture of how Butterfly Man took Saldana and killed her, as if he were there with them every step of the way. He was certain Saldana was killed, and my stalker was the main suspect in her murder. Now, he's found new evidence that proves she killed herself and my stalker is a myth?

I don't know if I should be pissed or glad. Who is running that shit show? Saldana was murdered, and Butterfly Man killed her as a favor to me. The police couldn't be more wrong. And what about Gia? She's never missed a day at work or ghosted me before. Her disappearance can't be just a disappearance, not after those photos. How have they not found her yet? Does Butterfly Man still have her? Why has he not killed her yet? What is he doing to her?

Infinite questions jam my brain, seeking answers that I can't find. This is his narrative. He's always in control. He won't let me or the police find Gia until he wants us to. "What about the man in the car?" Who the hell is Butterfly Man?

"Unidentifiable male. No clear photos of his face anywhere. He's been very cautious, most likely because of his profession."

"What profession?" That requires masterful stealth skills, access to drugs and the ability to control police evidence.

"It can't be confirmed, but my friends at the station couldn't find a better theory than the one you proposed. He's a drug dealer."

Butterfly Man is not a drug dealer. He's too smart to be one. Besides, he's stalked me for so long he must know how much I loathe drugs.

He must know, no matter how delusional he is, I'd never accept to be with someone who sells them for a living.

But he's smart enough to pose as one.

Was Saldana not lying about having a drug problem? Was it real and Butterfly Man used it to lure her into her death? Is that how he is going to get Blake, too? Tristan exchanges a glance with me, and I can feel the detective's eyes on us.

"Are you all right, Mrs. Abel?" Torrance asks.

I push my glasses up my nose and set the book aside. "Yeah. It's just a lot to digest, but thanks for stopping by to let me know."

"I thought it would be best if you heard it straight from me, and I'd like to apologize in person, for the other day."

My brows shoot up my forehead. "An in-person apology from the police. That's refreshing. Yet too hard to believe."

"I understand your experience with the force, on multiple occasions, has been less than satisfying, but I hope that by coming here today I can prove that not all of us are the same."

"Like I said, too hard to believe."

"Well, who knows, maybe one day I can change your mind." He flashes his teeth at me. It's not that menacing smile he's given Tristan. It's nice and genuine. Detective Torrance, when he's not trying to trap people into a confession or thinks everyone is a suspect until proven innocent, can be charming. "If you'll let me."

Excuse me? Is this what I think it is? Is Detective Torrance flirting with me?

I wouldn't know. In books, I can write men who flirt in every way imaginable. In reality, I wouldn't see the signs if they were glowing in neon. I've only been courted by two men—monsters—my whole life. My gaze, reflexively, travels to Tristan. A man like him can tell if another is flirting with me.

Tristan is standing closer to me now. His posture is so stiff, and murder is written all over his expression.

Jealousy. Possessiveness. Yes, these signs I can read like an open book. Torrance is definitely flirting. *What the hell?*

"Now that my official business here is over," the detective smiles at me again, "I'd—"

"Better go," Tristan grinds. "You must be busy, so is she."

"Oh, I don't mean to keep you from," Torrance stands and points at the book I was reading, *Ravishing Her*, "what must be a very important read. By the way, I finished your book the other day."

I arch a brow. "The one you were going to give your sister?"

"Guilty. I started it out of curiosity, and I

couldn't put it down. You're quite the storyteller, Mrs. Abel."

So he keeps telling me. It's never sounded like a compliment. It's always felt like an insult. *You're quite the liar, Mrs. Abel.* Except for this time. The first genuine praise he's given me, and it's tarnished by that stupid name. "Thank you, and please, since your official business here is over, call me Birdie."

Tristan throws his murderous gaze at me. I pretend I don't feel the danger radiating from him or see his knuckles turn white as he clenches his fist.

"I will do that." Torrance's face lights with excitement. "Would you like to grab a coffee sometime, you know, to discuss the book with your new fan, who is gonna be very dedicated to your novels from now on?"

My lashes flutter. Is this happening? Is he asking me out? Right in front of my menacing bodyguard who is seething with jealousy?

Smash!

I jump, my heart leaping into my throat. Shards of porcelain scatter across the floor, the remnants of an 1860 Sèvres vase now lying in ruins.

"Oops. How clumsy of me. I must have accidentally bumped it." Tristan says without the least bit of remorse. "Was that expensive? I'll pay for it." He stands between me and Torrance. "Now, I believe you were leaving."

The two men stare at each other, the tension so thick I could cut it with Tristan's knife. Finally, Torrance inclines his head back at me. "How about dinner instead? Take a caffeine break and try a real meal for once? Pick you up tomorrow at eight?"

CHAPTER 41
Tristan

oncha de la lora.

CHAPTER 42

Birdie

etective Torrance shows up for our book club for two at eight o'clock sharp, or so I've been informed. It's Marcus who takes me from my room, but Tristan is the one waiting down the stairs with his permanent scowl. Torrance is nowhere in sight. He must be standing outside still. Tristan's orders.

I come down, and my gaze meets Tristan's. The lines between his eyebrows ease when he gets the full view of my little black dress. His face is everything a woman would like to see at her graceful stair descent after she's spent hours perfecting her look. But it lasts for one fleeting moment before his jaw hardens, and his brows hook tighter.

The second I reach him, he says, "If you let him touch you, he's dead." Then he marches to the front door.

Wow. Okay. This evening is going to be interesting.

Marcus accompanies me to the door. Tristan, who, based on his expression, must be picturing a hundred different ways to kill Torrance, barely makes room for me, his eyes never leaving the detective. Torrance, on the other hand, is waiting calmly in a dashing black suit with a bouquet of flowers in hand.

His charming smile makes a reappearance when he spots me. "You look absolutely gorgeous." He hands me the flowers. "These are for you."

The arrangement surprises me. No tacky red roses. They're purple and golden—glitter sprayed on demand—tulips. Tulips are my favorite flowers, and gold is my favorite color, but I don't think anybody knows that. Coincidence to match the purple or chosen on purpose? Perhaps he just has impeccable taste. "They're…lovely. Thank you."

A low growl rumbles next to me as Tristan pushes his jacket aside just enough to show his gun. Torrance puts a hand in his pocket and makes the same move with his suit jacket to show his weapon. "Shall we, Birdie?"

"Not before my team sweeps your vehicle

for any threats," Tristan says. "Unless you'd like to follow us to the restaurant, all by yourself."

"Is that what you want?" Torrance asks me. "I'm good with whatever makes you feel safest."

"I'll ride with you as planned. Let me put these in water first." I frown when I turn and face Tristan. "Mr. Morra, please help me find a vase other than the one you broke yesterday."

Once we enter the kitchen, I hiss, "What's wrong with you? You can't play *whose gun is bigger* with Torrance."

He shrugs. "You're right. It doesn't matter. You saw my *gun* and will never see his."

"For God's sake, this is serious. Stop threatening him. Have you forgotten he's a cop?"

"I don't give a shit who he is. It's you who forgot your divorce isn't final yet. Or now you're not scared Abel will find out and use your date against you?"

"This is *not* a date."

He snorts. "Yeah, the dress, the flowers, the dinner, they're all for a business meeting. How stupid do you think I am?"

"Tristan, you promised. Whatever we feel toward each other, it can't develop past what it is now. You can't pull that jealousy crap anymore."

His glare intensifies to the point of pain. "Then tell me why the fuck you said yes when he asked you out."

Because I can't wrap my mind around the sudden interest Torrance has in me or the change in Saldana's case. I believe Torrance is hiding something. His intentions for this dinner aren't entirely pure. Cops will do anything to get what they want no matter the means or how deceitful they can be. Perhaps he's fishing for information, and asking me out is his way of getting me to talk. He must think I'm a battered wife, desperate for any kind of attention, who will do anything for a man who promises safety and care.

So I'll play that role, let him believe he's playing me and winning, until I discover what he really wants. Then I'll make my move. I'll use him to find Butterfly Man before all is lost.

However, if I'm being paranoid and all of this is only in my head, if he's as genuine and good as he claims to be, Jacob Torrance can be the breath of fresh air I need in this suffocating web of lies.

I retrieve a vase from the cabinet and fill it with water. Then I put the flowers in it.

"You're driving me crazy. Answer me, Birdie." Tristan searches my face. "Do you like him? Is that why?"

Do I like Jacob Torrance? That's not a question I'm prepared to answer now. "As my head of security, your job is to ensure my safety, not police my personal decisions, intentions or interactions," I say in an attempt to set boundaries.

Tristan opens his mouth to argue, but I cut him off. "Unless you have credible reasons to believe Detective Torrance poses a threat, you need to stand down."

"I can't know that for sure because you didn't give me enough time to do a proper background check."

I sashay back to the man I've kept waiting more than he should. "It's a good thing you're coming with me then."

CHAPTER 43

Birdie

Per protocol, yesterday, Torrance gave my bodyguards the address of the restaurant he was taking me to, but I preferred not to know beforehand. I may be on a mission, but I might as well enjoy the whole experience.

I can't believe my eyes when we reach our destination. The Alchemist Bistro & Bar. The place where I was supposed to dine with Tristan and Marcus the day at the lighthouse, my favorite restaurant in Edgartown.

The flowers and the restaurant can't be a coincidence. How did he know all this information about me?

"A little bird told me this place was one of your favorite restaurants on the island," the detective says as we—and Tristan—wait in the car for the 'all clear' to enter.

My gaze narrows at him behind my shades. "A little bird?"

"It's just an expression. Oh God, is that offensive? I've never met a Birdie before. I'm so sorry. I should be more careful with…words."

"I'm not offended by your choice of words, Detective. I'm curious how you found out about The Alchemist being one of my favorite restaurants."

"During the investigations, I've learned where you usually like to hang out. You're the only celebrity on the island, and everybody is generous with info when it comes to you." He smiles sheepishly. "If you don't like it, we can find somewhere else. I just thought maybe you'd like an inconspicuous place to be…you know… At the café, I remember you were very worried. I don't want you to feel uncomfortable in case…"

In case Blake is watching.

Sweat beads the detective's forehead. He reaches to his side, and Tristan goes on full alert, hand on gun and all. But Torrance only gets out a book. "See? I even brought a new book for you to sign."

Oh. *Oh.* "That's…thoughtful."

He runs a hand through his hair; he's so nervous it's adorable. "Really? I didn't ruin the night already?"

I notice he has a lot of hair on his head for a man in his forties. How does it feel to have my fingers digging in those dark, thick waves? Are they as soft as they look? Do they smell as nice as he does, a blend of spice, wood, and something powerfully wild? I smile. "No."

From the backseat, Tristan sticks his head between us. "Her *husband* is not anywhere near the perimeter. We checked." He glares at me. "And the restaurant is clear. We're good to go."

Suddenly, I'm the only one sitting in the car. Then Tristan opens the door for me. By the frown on Torrance's face, I realize why they were racing each other out. Torrance wanted to be the one doing it, but my bodyguard wouldn't let him. It's the first time tonight Tristan manages to get a visible rise out of Torrance.

"Get a grip," I whisper to Tristan as I leave the car.

He clenches his teeth. "Just following protocol, ma'am."

Marcus is waiting at the entrance. The hostess, Stephanie, greets us with a wide smile. "Welcome to The Alchemist. Birdie, how lovely to see you again!" Her eyes flit over all of us, taking in the three men's imposing forms. "Table for four?"

"Two tables. There's a reservation under Torrance," the detective says.

"Of course!" There's a tremor in her high-pitched voice and a flush to her cheeks. I can't tell if she's afraid or aroused or both. "Right this way please." She sways her hips more than usual as she leads us to our tables. I catch Marcus stealing a glance, but the other two are busy glaring.

I get my usual table. The lights are dim, so I take off my shades. The detective manages to pull the seat for me before Tristan does. One Tristan. One Torrance.

My head of security sits at the next table with a glower so dark I think they'll ask him to leave for scaring customers. Marcus doesn't join us. He's on floor duty.

My books—the one I signed to the detective's sister and the other one he brought—nestle at the table side and stare back at me with their colorful sticky notes peeking out of the pages. "You actually read the book?"

"No, I just put these annoying things between the pages to think that I did."

I arch a brow at him and snatch the book to see if he's joking.

"Okay. That was a lame joke to tell someone with serious trust issues. I take it back," he says.

When I flip through the pages, a shrivel of joy sneaks up on me. Besides the sticky notes, there are highlights, annotations and vivid NSFW drawings of a couple of spicy scenes. I bite my lip on a smile.

"Yes, I read it, and I loved it, like I told you yesterday. I wouldn't lie to you, Birdie. Not about your work, at least. I can imagine how much you must value it."

I put the book back. "Thank you, Detective."

"Jacob," he prompts. "Please."

As we go over our menus, *Jacob* catches my eye and smiles warmly. I smile back. "What?"

"I'm trying to be a gentleman, but I can't take my eyes off you."

"Wow. What happened to the nervous guy in the car?"

"Believe me, I am nervous. I haven't done this in a very long time."

"This? What exactly is *this*?"

"Discussing a book with its author, what else could it be?"

"So you've done that before?"

"Yeah. Haven't you?"

"I have actually."

"See, it's very common. Everybody does it."

I laugh wholeheartedly, and he stares. My gaze drops to the menu. "Now, you're making me nervous."

"I'm sorry. It's just nice to hear your real laugh."

Come to think of it, I can't remember when the last time I laughed from my heart was.

The waiter comes for our orders, and Jacob

asks what wine I'd like to have. Is he drinking? I doubt he'll touch any tonight. *Trying to get my inhibitions low to find out all my secrets, Detective?* I politely decline. I need to be at the top of my game.

"Do you mind if I have some?" he asks.

Surprise hits me two folds. He is drinking, and he's so well-mannered he asks for approval. Am I supposed to fall for this shit? "What's next? Are you going to fight for my honor, too?"

Taken aback, the detective stares back and forth between me and the waiter. Shit. I didn't mean to say that out loud or in front of an audience. So much for keeping up the act. I blew my cover before I even started. I glance at the waiter. "Give us a minute please."

"Sure." The waiter practically runs away from our tables.

Tristan rises from his seat and reaches my side in one stride, raw animosity rolling off him in potent waves. "Is everything all right?"

I dart a glare at him. "Yes. Please return to your seat."

A vein pops in his neck as he studies my face, and then he scowls at Jacob. "If anything bothers you, you know what to do."

The signals. He trained me for the signs I should give to signal danger when I first hired him, and he's gone over them with me a million times since yesterday. There are several. Blink or tap my heel three times. Say the word Tango, which we later changed to Gatsby—it's more natural and covert to use a bodyguard's last name I won't use in any other context and can also refer to a novel.

But the ones that pertain to this event are the SOS text ready on my phone, which means the detective is being an asshole. Please engage. Another with a poop emoji if I just need Tristan to fake a phone call to get me out of the boring meeting.

When Tristan finally returns to his table, I peer at the detective. "Look, I'm not trying to be rude. I just have no filters sometimes."

"I noticed." Jacob puts the menu aside. "Did I say something wrong? Is this about the wine? I just needed a glass to ease my nerves. I swear I'm not an alcoholic or anything."

I should lie and use his words against him to come back from my fiasco, but my emotions are getting the best of me. While I understood what I was getting myself into, deep down, I was hoping I was wrong about the detective. I should have learned my lesson. In the land of deceit, hope is your worst enemy.

"I know what alcoholics look like, and you're not one. So no, it's not about the wine. It's about how considerate you can be, picking this place, how nervous you're trying to act around me, how polite you are, trying to give me the princess treatment. I don't know what you're trying to pull off here, Detective."

"I'm not trying to pull anything off." He locks his gaze with mine, sincerity dripping from his voice. "I mean, look at you and look at me. You're Birdie Abel. Of course, I'm nervous. It's not an act. And what you call the princess treatment is just me trying to treat a woman like you as she should. Being polite and considerate is the least I can do for you because you're not just a princess, you're a queen. Sitting here with you is a dream, and I don't want to ruin it." He purses his lips. "But maybe I'm trying too hard and already messed up."

He doesn't blink or fidget. Everything about him exudes respect and honesty, but I don't believe a single word. "Why don't you cut to the chase and tell me why you brought me here? We both know it's not to fangirl over my work."

He nods pensively. "I was hoping to tell you after that glass of wine, but… Here goes nothing." His hands clasp in front of him as he leans forward. "There was this girl that I met so many years ago. She…stole my heart without so much of a word. Just like in your book. But I didn't let myself believe my feelings for her were true. This was real life, not some fantasy to escape. This kind of love couldn't be real.

"So I didn't tell her how one look into her

eyes could take away my breath or what her smile did to me. I didn't take her pain away or make her dreams come true. I let her go, just like that. Watched her fall for someone else, and I didn't lift a finger to earn her love."

His eyes glisten, and his pained expression tears at me. Listening to a man like him, so masculine and powerful, talk about a lost love with such vulnerability demolishes my barriers and doubts until only compassion remains. Unexpectedly, I find myself blinking away my own tears.

"Problem is, that kind of love *was* real, but I only realized it too late," he continues, and I lower my head from his gaze so that my composure doesn't shatter completely. I know better than to let anyone see my real tears.

"Is that why you've never gotten married?"

"There is a story in everything. This is mine."

"But why are you telling it to me?"

"Because, after years of pain, despair and loneliness, I learned my lesson and decided that if I ever came across something remotely close to how I felt about that girl," he pauses until I lift my eyes to him, "I wouldn't let her go, no matter what it takes."

"Jacob…" His name tumbles unbidden from my lips.

"From the moment I saw you, there was something that pulled me to you. An urge to be in your world, to get to know you and be around you. However, my manners that you think are an act wouldn't let me approach a woman who wasn't single. Then the case happened. I was a cop, and you were a suspect. But now the case is closed, and you're getting a divorce. There's no more reason for me to wait. I've wasted so much time already."

"Does that mean this is a date? A real date?"

"For me, it is. Was I too subtle? Don't let my being polite and considerate fool you into thinking my intentions are entirely pure. While I read your book to get to know you, and with every page I fell in love with the story, I used it as an excuse to ask you out."

"Why would you do that?"

"I didn't think you'd agree to go out with me otherwise." He swallows. "If I'm not showing it right, let me say it straight. I like you, Birdie. And if you'll forgive my bluntness, I want you more than I've ever wanted a woman before."

My breath catches in my throat as his meaning sinks in. Does that mean all my suspicions are wrong? There's no ploy to get information, to catch me off guard? He wasn't trying to play me at all—he genuinely wanted to pursue...me?

A shaky sigh leaves his chest. "Please say something."

"I don't know what to say. But if what

you're saying is the truth, if your interest in me is genuine, you must understand that even after the divorce is final, I will need a very long time to consider being in a relationship again."

"I'm well aware, and I'm prepared to be as patient as you need me to be. I have a long way to go to show you I'm worthy of your trust, too." He leans in and inclines his head so that he can whisper in my ear. "And when the time is right, if you'll let me, I'll fuck your brains out like Domenico did with Nicky from page two-hundred and eighteen onward and show you nights more depraved than what Jocasta Larvin had with the Lazzarini duo combined."

I cough wildly, my skin licked by flames.

He rests his back against the chair and pours water in my glass, a playful smirk on his lips. I take a sip, my stare clashing with Tristan's. He's on edge, eyes flickering between me and Jacob, anticipating, so I wave a hand and mouth, "I'm fine."

I chance a glance at Jacob. "You sir are naughty." The characters he's mentioned are from the most erotic romances I've ever written. I don't know which is sexier, the scenes that portray my darkest sexual fantasies or the fact that he's thoroughly read them that he remembers their page numbers.

His shoulder lifts nonchalantly as he studies the menu again.

"Suffice to say, you've read more of my

books than the one I gave your sister."

"I'm burning through your backlist at this point. You hooked me with that first introduction to your universe. You are very creative with your…words."

I clear my throat, pressing my thighs together. "If you ever decide to leave the force, I'll hire you to illustrate my NSFW artwork. They sell like crazy, and your drawings are spot on. I'll make you famous."

A touch of color rises to his face. "You saw that, huh? I was saving them for our third date."

"Ambitious much? What makes you think there will be a second date let alone a third?"

He grins as he sets the menu aside. "A little bird."

"The same bird that told you about the restaurant and the flowers?"

"What about the flowers?"

"Tulips, purple and golden tulips."

His shoulders slump. "You hate them. I should have gone with red roses. I knew it."

"No, Jacob. That's not what I'm saying. I loved them."

Dumbfounded, he purses his lips. "Full disclosure, I'm not a flower man. I Googled the best kind to bring on a first date and most advice said no roses, especially red, so I remembered, in your book, the main character loved tulips and thought you might like them, too."

"And the colors? Those were not in the book."

"The lady at the flower shop chose them. Personally, I felt the glitter was too much, but she said it was a fancy touch, so…"

Jacob knew nothing about my favorite colors. It was only luck.

With a chuckle, I revel in the spark that ignites in his gaze, giving myself a break from the weight of reality. As the last of my doubts has dissipated, I can finally enjoy the night and the possibilities that come with this man who sees and wants me—just me. Whatever complications may arise, whatever risks I might face, they will have to take a backseat until I go home.

He points a thumb behind his shoulder. "Can I tell the waiter to come back for our order? I'm starving."

"Yes, please. And on second thought, I'd like to have a glass of red wine."

"You got it, baby girl."

Wow.

When the waiter leaves with our order, Jacob asks, "If you didn't think this was a date or a *fangirl* dinner, what did you think it was? Why did you think I asked to meet you?"

I shrug. "Something stupid that doesn't matter anymore."

CHAPTER 44

Tristan

At five in the morning, the house is silent except for the faint wind and waves sneaking in from the beach, but sleep continues to elude me. Images keep flashing through my mind—Birdie laughing at something Torrance says, his lips lingering too long next to her ear as he whispers his bullshit, the unmistakable spark in her eyes that screams she's into his crap.

I toss aside the covers. There's no point in trying to get some shuteye. Might as well make myself useful and let Marcus sleep. I get dressed and make my way out.

"Sir," Brandon says. He's outside Birdie's bedroom, not Marcus. "Is everything all right?"

"Where's Marcus?"

"He asked me to take over until morning. He wasn't feeling well. Probably something he ate."

"Okay. I'll make some coffee and take your place. You can go back to sleep when I come back up."

"Thank you, sir. I was worried she'd wake up and see me. She doesn't like me very much."

I stare at him in question.

"She said I looked like someone she hated. Maybe a replacement will be best."

"Don't be silly. You're one of the best details in the firm. You're needed here."

His brows hitch, but he nods like the obedient soldier he is. "Yes, sir. Thank you for your trust."

Downstairs, I enter the kitchen. As soon as I turn on the lights, I freeze. There, taunting me on the countertop, is a crystal vase filled with a dozen purple and golden tulips—Torrance's last-ditch effort at winning Birdie's approval. My jaw tightens as I approach them, each lush petal smug at my inability to reciprocate such a romantic gesture.

It'd be so easy to sweep the vase to the floor. Despite the churning urge to obliterate the evidence of another man's attempt to steal her for himself, I settle for glaring at the flowers as if looks alone could shrivel the cocky blooms.

Why did she agree to go on that date? When we went home, she said she suspected Torrance was lying about the case. Pretending to like her and asking her out were tricks to get information from her. She went along with it to find out his intentions, but it turned out she was wrong.

Her motives are legitimate—I've suspected the same. That's not the whole truth, though, if there is any honesty in her words to begin with. There's something else only she knows that drove her to accept the detective's invitation.

Is it just an attempt to reclaim some sense of normalcy amidst the madness? It doesn't make watching her drift further from me any easier.

Is she trying to move on from what we have with someone she can be with when Abel and Butterfly Man are gone? Does she like Torrance? Her soft smiles and blushing cheeks say she does. My fingers curl inward until blunt nails bite into my palms.

"No, this can't be it," I say to the fancy ass coffee machine as I press its buttons. I know her well enough to realize she's neither reckless with her emotions nor trusts easily. Even if she likes him, she's too smart to put her secrets at risk for a juvenile crush. She's too mature to have a juvenile crush in the first place.

God, she's driving me crazy. I should have never made her that promise. What was I thinking?

That Birdie does not belong to you, no matter how your traitorous heart might wish it so? That if you can't excise this jealousy entirely, you can at least force it to silence until you've ensured her freedom to pursue happiness—whatever that might cost you?

"Well, I didn't think I'd have to watch her date someone else. I didn't think I'd be tormented by visions of another man taking what's mine."

She's not yours.

"Shut up." On my phone, I check the security feed of her bedroom. She's sound asleep. How could she be after what she did to me? I want to tie her to her bed and punish her until she learns never to make that mistake again. "Your wholehearted laughs and sweet whispers don't belong to him. They're mine. All mine."

She's not yours!

"Shut up!" I smash the cup. The glass shatters against the tile floor with a piercing crash, shards scattering in every direction. Searing pain lances through my hand as the scalding liquid splashes over my reddening skin. I groan a curse, cradling my throbbing palm.

Reports of the noise I've made and requirements for immediate situation check come in over the radio. I wash my hand and lift my sleeve to my mouth. "Morra here. I broke a cup in the kitchen. Damages are minor. No need to engage. I'll handle the situation myself. Back to your positions."

Three chuckling 'copy' and one 'yes, sir" come through as I clean myself up.

What the hell was that? Lashing out like some unhinged maniac? I squeeze my eyes shut, drawing in a shuddering breath as I wrestle for control. I'm better than this, stronger than whatever this pathetic jealousy is trying to reduce me to. If I let these volatile emotions consume me, I'll be of no use to anyone, least of all Birdie. She deserves far better than some unraveling hothead watching over her, than to be trapped in the crosshairs of his possessive darkness.

A long, resigned sigh flees my chest as I peel off my stained shirt and make my way over to the supply closet to grab cleaning supplies. I must get rid of the mocking evidence before Birdie sees it in the morning light.

I kneel amid the shards, the stinging in my palm dulling to a throbbing ache. A fitting punishment for allowing my weaknesses to make me unworthy of Birdie's trust.

A muffled thump from my phone grabs my attention. I glance over at the live feed from Birdie's bedroom. One second, her sleeping form is bundled under the comforter, the next, she suddenly bolts upright, her body rigid.

I snatch up my phone, snag my gun and sprint towards the stairs. My feet pounds over the hardwood. Adrenaline spikes through me as I reach the hallway. I ignore Brandon and burst through Birdie's bedroom door. The click of his gun follows mine as I sweep the muzzle right to left.

"Tristan!" A sheen of sweat glistens on her brow in the dim light filtering through the windows.

"What's wrong? Are you hurt?" I demand, searching the room for any signs of danger.

"No." Her eyes, wide and wary, dart between me and Brandon. "But you scared the hell out of me. What's going on?"

Just a nightmare then. No external threats. I nod for Brandon to leave and holster my gun. "You were sleeping, and then you bolted upright terrified. I thought there was a breach."

As Brandon exits, she turns on the light on her nightstand. "You were watching me sleep?"

"Don't make it creepy. It's my job."

Her gaze sweeps me from head to toe and lingers on my torso. "And you like to do that part shirtless?"

"Jesus Christ. I poured coffee on my shirt. I was cleaning the mess when you woke up in the middle of your sleep looking like you were about to be murdered. Next time, I'll get fully dressed before addressing a situation where you could end up dead."

She doesn't take her eyes off my half-naked body and licks her lips.

"Stop," I hiss. "You can't look at me like that."

"Like what?"

"Like you want me, after you made me watch you date someone else. I'm sick of your games." Is that the purpose of going out with the detective? A cruel game she's forcing me to play to watch me burn? For vengeance? For punishment? Or is it a competition, may the best man worthy of her attention win?

"Now who's making this creepy?" She frowns at my hand. "I was looking at that. Did you burn yourself?"

"It's nothing. Go back to sleep."

"It's not nothing. It's flaming red. I have ointment in the bathroom." She pushes out of the bed, the spaghetti straps of her lavender nightgown falling down her shoulders, her pebbling nipples almost popping out of the satin.

My blood pounds in my temples at the idea of anyone seeing her dressed like that. I move and block her from the camera range. "Could you put a robe on or something?"

She arches a brow at me.

"Please."

Laughing under her breath, she rounds the

bed and grabs the robe lying on one of the armchairs in the corner. She disappears inside the bathroom for a minute and comes back, covered up, with an ointment tube and bandages in her hands. "There."

"Thank you."

"Do you want me to take care of it?"

I grit my teeth. "I can handle it. You get some rest."

"I can't."

"I'll make you some anise tea. It'll help."

"No. I need to go get the mail. Now."

My face scrunches in confusion as I check the time. "Excuse me? It's five forty-seven a.m."

She swallows, her eyes haunted. "Have you noticed I don't have a mailbox here? I only use a P.O. box, and it's Gia's job to pick up my mail and bring it to me. With Gia being *detained*, it's been a week since I received any correspondence. I could be missing very important messages here."

Butterfly Man's notes. It's been a week since he sent the last one, and she's been anxiously waiting for a move he hasn't made yet. Or has he?

I've turned this house into a fortress he can't infiltrate. He can't come anywhere near it, her car or her. The only viable solution to send her more notes is the mail. "Shit."

"Yeah, shit. I don't know how I could forget something like that." She stalks to the dressing room. "Fix your hand and put on a new shirt while I get dressed. We have no more time to waste."

"I'll sit this one out. I'll get a team ready to take you there, though."

"What? Tristan, I don't know what I'm going to find in the mail. You have to be there with me. You're the only one I can trust with this."

"Then don't open anything until you return."

She crosses her arms over her chest. "Is this some sort of payback?"

"Payback? For what?"

"You know what."

In two strides, I close the distance between us until the warmth of her exhales ghosts over my skin. "You mean for going out with another man, laughing at his silly jokes and blushing at his dirty whispers?" I shrug, enjoying the sight of her flustered. "That's your thing, Birdie, not mine." But maybe I should start punishing her for her mistakes from now on. I glance at her throat, picturing my hand around it. How red will her face turn when I choke her? What sounds are she going to make? How long will it take her to beg? What will she beg for?

Gulping, she squirms. "Then why would

you not come with me?"

I let her sweat a little more, my mind swimming in images of what else I can do to her in punishment. That pretty head is full of potential.

"Tristan?"

I blow out a breath and retreat from her proximity before I lose my mind. "Marcus has food poisoning from eating at your favorite restaurant, and my hand is burnt. If there's a chance of facing any kind of danger on your trip to get the mail, it's best if the details protecting you aren't compromised."

Because even when she infuriates me the most, I'll still do what's best for her. Even when she provokes my demons out to play, I'll always put her safety first.

<h1 style="text-align:center">CHAPTER 45</h1>

<h2 style="text-align:center">Tristan</h2>

In the control room, Marcus appears on the monitors, entering the kitchen. Then the aroma of cumin and herbs fills my nostrils. I leave one of the men on surveillance and go to Marcus. "You should be in bed. Food poisoning isn't a joke."

"It's not food poisoning. It's my lactose intolerance biting me in the ass after that bowl of ice cream. Literally." Marcus heats water. "I'll be fine, though. My grandma used to make this herbal remedy for me whenever I ate dairy. It worked like magic. I'll drink it and make myself useful again."

I chuckle, leaning against the counter. "Why would you eat ice cream?"

"Detective asshole said it was vegan.

Newsflash, it wasn't." He grabs a teaspoon of honey and adds it to his cup. "Where's Birdie and Gatsby? And what happened to your hand?"

I fill him in, leaving out the details he shouldn't know. "Come again about Torrance and the ice cream."

"I was circulating the floor when he was going to the bathroom. He told me I should eat something and recommended ice cream for dessert. He said it was the best vegan ice cream on the island." The kettle wheezes, and he pours the water on the herbs. "I should sue that place."

My gaze narrows. "Or the detective."

Marcus stares at me. "Do you think it was intentional? He lied on purpose to get me sick?"

"Anything is possible. We can't rule anything out. I never liked that asshole. There's something off about him that I can't place, especially after his background check returned nothing. He's a ghost. I can't even find where he served before he transferred to Oak Bluffs."

"How would he know I was lactose intolerant? He ran background checks on Birdie's details, too?"

"Two days ago, he was asking how many she had." He lied to Marcus, the only detail with lactose intolerance on the team, about the ice cream. He'd watched me break a vase when he asked her out; he must have deduced I was jealous. He left those fucking flowers to mock me, counting on my temper to induce another reaction that might incapacitate me, too. A gnawing suspicion tugs at my gut. Marcus's conveniently timed illness is just a little too coincidental. "What if he's singling us out?"

"Why?"

My whole body snaps into high alert as I fish my phone out of my pocket. "To get her alone without either of us. An easy target to take." Swearing, I call Brandon. "Pick the fuck up."

"Wait, you think Torrance is the stalker?"

"And I've just sent her out there into his fucking trap all alone."

CHAPTER 46

Birdie

re you safe?
My head leaning against the car window, I ask each of the Victorian houses lining up across the shoreline, as if I could see the people that lived in them.

I step into their worlds, into their heads, with no boundaries, and I see them in ways others do not. My mind races with mini stories about each house, where I make their residents all happy and safe at home. There's something inspirational about the idea of loving, functional families. I even let myself envy them for having what I've never had.

Talk about an overactive imagination. My parents always told me I had one of those. He did, too. They didn't mean it as a compliment. They didn't mean it. Period. My imagination was their excuse to make me the villain of their story, to justify what they chose to do. To me, it was a weapon. The only weapon I could have.

I jump back into the mini stories, where nothing is unacceptable or too far-fetched, like families that protect their children and husbands that take care of their wives, instead of scaring them for life.

My weapon deters the memories but doesn't take away the anxiety of the present. What's more frightening? Finding a note from Butterfly Man in the mail or the lack of thereof?

Tristan said the targeting of Gia and Blake would make catching Butterfly Man easier. He has a team watching Blake like a hawk and sends one of the men to Gia's house every other day, waiting for Butterfly Man to make a mistake. But nothing ever happens.

Blake has been living like a hermit in his office. No one visits him but the food delivery people and his dealer, who looks nothing like the man in Saldana's car photos and doesn't wear face masks with or without butterflies either. As for Gia, every time it's the same report. Neither she nor her car is there.

Watching Gia and Blake has been a dead end. Just like the background checks on the list of people I interact with daily; none of them has any ties to Florida.

I've never thought I'd say that, but I'm praying to find a message from my stalker in the mail. Ever since he sent those photos, I've been waiting for the next step. Different photos of Gia and Blake, covered in blood this time, miraculously making their way into my house. News about their bodies rotting in a ditch, hopefully not after they pumped their blood with lethal drugs and drove themselves into a tree—a pattern will draw more attention from the police and circle back to me—but, at this point, I'd take anything. Anything is better than the silence, the ignorance, the nothingness, the waiting that squeezes the life out of me ever so slowly.

Does that make me evil? My eagerness to see Gia and Blake dead? If I am, what does that make them?

I'm not delusional. In the stories of the people who hurt me, I'll always be the villain. In mine, I'm just tired of being a victim. For once, I want to have a happy ending, and if that makes me evil, so be it.

Why don't you kill them already? Gia has been missing for a week. I don't know how many texts Tristan can send me from the burner, pretending to be her, before the lie crumbles into a plot hole. *Make your move, so I can make mine.*

My phone rings. Jacob's name on the screen stares me in the face. Why is he calling so early in the morning? Oh my God, did the police finally find Gia's body?

I hesitate between the red and green icons, my heartbeat thumping in my ear. Should I take this call? At this hour? Without Tristan by my side?

Anything is better than the waiting. Don't be a coward and take control. Holding my breath, I answer. "Hello?"

"Shit…uh…didn't think you'd pick up. This call was intended for your voicemail." He chuckles nervously. "Good morning."

"What's wrong, Jacob?"

"Nothing! Nothing at all. I was called at the station a couple of hours after our date, and I'm just about to hit home. I thought I'd leave you a good morning message so you could hear it when you woke up." He swears under his breath. "It was a bad idea. I'm so sorry. I didn't mean to wake you. In my defense, I've always thought you're one of those people who turns off the sound of their phones when they go to sleep."

I am. Is he really that intuitive? The early morning sun casts long shadows on the road ahead, mirroring the doubt creeping into my mind. "*That's* why you're calling before it's even seven a.m.?"

"Can you go back to bed and pretend it was all a dream, and maybe not hate me a little?"

Finally, I exhale a sigh, in disappointment rather than in relief—they haven't found Gia yet—that turns into a chortle at the end.

"You're such a dork. A romantic dork."

"Does that mean I'm off the hook?"

"I wasn't even sleeping, so yes, you're off the hook."

"Phew. Wait, what are these sounds? Are you outside…*before it's even seven a.m.?*" His tone changes from humorous to wary in a split-second. "Is something wrong? Are you okay?"

"Yes, I'm fine. I…just couldn't sleep so I went for a drive."

"Alone?"

"You know better, Detective." I throw the same thing I told him when he offered to give me a ride at the café, where we first met in Oak Bluffs.

He grunts. "Little bird is a castle, always watched or watched over."

"Have you just quoted from my book…and changed the protagonist's pet name for his love interest to fit mine?"

"Are we impressed yet?"

"I'll give you a point for memorizing that line, but, Jacob, for the sake of any possible future together, don't ever call me little bird. That's Blake's pet name for me."

"Copy that. Jesus, I'm royally fucking up today. Is there any preference for other pet names I could use?"

Oddly, I'd love to hear him call me by my real name. Reagan, just Reagan. But I can't tell him that, just like I can't tell him the real reason I'm out or where I'm going. "For now, Birdie will suffice."

"Okay. Birdie, would you like to grab some coffee and tell me what's keeping you up at night? I can bring it over wherever you are to make it easier for your bodyguards. Just send me your location, and I'll be there in no time."

Although the genuine concern in his voice makes me want to share my worries about Butterfly Man, to trust Jacob will be on my side and help protect me, I can't shake off the suspicion that this call might be more than just a romantic gesture.

Is Jacob really worried about me, or is this a clever ploy to pinpoint my location? He sounds too eager to know where I am.

The weight of my secrets and trust issues presses down on me all at once. Even after my doubts about Jacob cleared up on our date last night, I can't stop thinking what if he isn't who he claims to be.

When I don't answer right away, he asks, "Am I asking you out again too soon?"

"No. That's not it. I just have a lot on my mind today. Rain check?"

"Sure. I'll call you tomorrow."

Am I being paranoid, or am I right to be cautious? The line between trust and self-preservation has never felt so thin.

CHAPTER 47

Tristan

Marcus sets his cup on the counter and quickly works his phone. "She's not alone. She has details you've trained yourself, Tristan."

I pace the kitchen, my mind racing with the worst possible scenarios. "Then why the fuck aren't they picking up?"

"I'm tracking their route on the GPS. No unusual traffic. The two cars are intact."

The ringing clips in my ear. "Sir?"

A thread of relief courses through me when I hear Brandon's steady voice. "Report."

"Our principal is in her car with Riley. I'm following them in mine. I've just checked with Dixon. He's securing the destination. It's clear."

"Any sign of Torrance or suspicious vehicles?"

"Negative. Route is secure."

Thank God. She's safe, at least for now. "Brandon, what's your ETA to the P.O. box location?"

"Nine minutes, sir."

"Maintain present overwatch protocols but keep a sharp eye out for any anomalies. Comms checks every three minutes, updating locations at each new turn. Call in immediately if Torrance is spotted in the perimeter. Once you reach the destination, maintain tight perimeter control, but no need for heavy presence up front. Only you can accompany her for the mail retrieval, with the rest of the team providing mobile cover watch and securing intersecting routes."

"Me, sir?"

"Yes, Brandon. I trust you. This is your operation now."

"Copy. I won't let you down."

Marcus eyes me warily as I hang up. "Why him? She hates Gatsby."

"Every second she's out there is a risk. I want her to get that mail and head back in no time. When you do a job with someone you don't like, you do it as fast as possible, and you don't get new ideas about running other tasks either."

"Did she want to do something else other

than getting the mail?"

"Not that I know of, but better safe than sorry." If she doesn't find a note from the stalker, my gut tells me she'll try to do something to provoke him. That's why she went out on that date. I get it now. It wasn't a break from stress, a stupid crush, a punishment or a competition. She did it for Butterfly Man. He didn't make a move, so she made hers. What is more provocative than watching her going out with another man?

"And Torrance? You really think he's working an angle here? Setting up an ambush because he's Butterfly Man?"

"I don't know what to think, but he's up to something. I can feel it." I rest my hands on the counter and exhale a long breath. "Whatever it is, it puts Birdie at risk. Until we know the full scope, we're playing this by the book."

The radio crackles. "Sir, you're needed in the control room. There's something you need to see."

"What now?" Marcus huffs, taking his cup with him, and comes with me to the control room.

On the monitors, two vans are parked a few feet away from the house. One has MVTV printed on the doors, and the other has a huge red 5 with the word LIVE above it.

"Are these news channel cars?" Marcus

asks. "Did Birdie book an interview or something?"

"She doesn't do interviews," I say distantly, searching the websites of these channels. I freeze at the first search result.

Fatal Karma For Copycat Scribe After Author's Maniac Fan Vowed Payback!

"What the hell?" I scroll down the headlines. There's more than one.

Literary Feud Explodes In Fatal Crash After Psycho Fan's Death Threats!

Plagiarism Scandal Turns Tragic: Copycat Writer Dies in Suspicious Crash

Deadly Crash Fuels Speculation Over Author's Deranged Stalker

Question Marks Surround Death of Plagiarist After Author's Fan Threats

Marcus peeks his head and glances at my phone screen. "Guess the cat is out of the bag. Our low-key celebrity has turned into a real one overnight." He shakes his head, watching the monitors. "What's next, paparazzi or another homicide investigation?"

More cars approach the premises, and people with cameras and microphones spill out of them. "Fuck. Marcus, you and Morrison secure the front gate. Form a barricade and don't let anyone of these vultures come close. I'll handle the backside."

My phone chimes with a text message from

Brandon. *Mail retrieved safely. No sign of Torrance. On our way back.*

I call him as I sprint to the backyard. "Switch cars with Birdie."

"Is something the matter?" Brandon asks.

"Don't tell her that, but there's press outside the house. You'll drive her car to the front gate, linger in the driveway and let the press hover around you while I sneak her in through the back. Do not let the reporters take her photo. I repeat, no photos under any circumstances. Your jobs depend on it."

"Yes, sir. Will switch cars right away and keep you updated."

This is a nightmare. The case was closed. Who leaked this shit?

CHAPTER 48

Tristan

"Seven years. Even with my little share of fame, even when I knew that day was going to come eventually, I've managed to avoid them for seven years. Now, I'm one photo away from having the life I've built tumbling down over my head." Birdie's fingers stroke her lips absently as she stands by her office windows, watching the reporters from behind the curtains. "Any idea who is responsible for this circus?"

I have a theory. "Not yet, but we're on it. I won't let them come near you I promise."

She gives me back my suit jacket; I've used it to cover her as I snuck her inside the house, just in case someone was hiding with a camera. "Don't make promises you can't keep."

"I know what I'm saying, and I'll always keep my promises to you."

"Tristan, they have a photo of the stalker's note. The one he left on my pillow. How the fuck did they get their filthy hands on it when there's only a handful of people who have seen it?"

"Someone leaked it. On purpose."

"Who? Me, Gia, Blake, one of your men? You?"

"With all due respect, I don't appreciate the accusation in your tone. Every man in the team, including me, has signed an NDA. You could sue the hell out of us and the firm. We'll all be out of business. If you don't trust me and my men, trust that none of us is that stupid."

"Well, it can't be me, Gia is *indisposed*, and Blake hasn't left his office in days, having crack for breakfast."

I fold my arms over my chest, fuming. "There are cameras covering every inch of this house. You're more than welcome to review the footage to check if any of the men who are supposed to protect you have broken into your office and taken a photo of that note."

Her arched brow speaks volumes. "There's one blind spot, where you and I stayed for hours analyzing the notes. I was too distraught to notice if you took a picture of them. If you did, I couldn't prove it."

Fuck you. "Are you for real? Why would I do that to you?"

"Because of Jacob. He's a cop and a decent man that's earning my trust, fully capable of protecting me from an abusive husband and a stalker, and you're afraid he'd replace you. So you stab me in the back and tip the press because he has no jurisdiction over them. That kind of danger only *you* can handle."

There is no way in hell I'd betray her like that. Where the fuck is this coming from? One night with that bastard and he manages to brainwash into distrusting me? This doesn't make any sense. Birdie can't be that stupid or naïve. "Do you actually believe that bullshit?"

"Every crime has a motive. No one else on the list of people who know about the note can benefit from this circus but you."

I glare at her, fighting the urge to shake her to snap her out of the trance he put her in. "Your list of suspects is missing one, Mrs. Abel."

Her eyes twitch at the name; she deserves to feel a fraction of my anger. Then her hands fall on her hips, and she lifts her chin, challenging me. "Who?"

"The police. Didn't you report that note? They have a copy. I wonder if you know someone there who was particularly interested in pursuing the dismissed stalker case, who tried to solve Saldana's case with a theory about your alleged stalker killing her and failed.

"That can't look good for a guy who has just transferred to a new precinct and needs to prove himself among his peers. We don't even know why he transferred. He's forty something with no wife or kids. Why start somewhere new, in a small town on a remote island of all places? Did he ask for it or was he forced to do it because he fucked up? I'm guessing the latter, and he's doing everything in his might not to fuck up again, even if it means throwing you under the bus."

"I can't believe you right now. You're going to say anything to throw *him* under the bus."

"You can't believe that a cop would screw you over, but you can believe I betrayed you like that after everything we've shared, after everything I've done to protect you?"

"You're giving me no choice, Tristan. I don't trust you anymore, and I can't let you protect me if I can't trust you."

I've thought watching her on a date with another man was the most difficult thing I had to go through on this job, but I'm wrong. Her questioning my loyalty hurts more than anything. To hear those words from her, to see that look in her eyes, to know that I've lost her like that, is excruciating.

"You're making a mistake. Can't you see? That's exactly what he wants. Think for one goddamn minute before you ruin everything."

"Oh for God's sake, Look at me." She blinks three times.

My body goes fully alert. That's her danger signal. My hand flies to my gun out of instinct. What's going on? How could she be in danger here?

She glances at my gun and shakes her head. Then she flashes her phone at me and puts her index finger on her lips. "I don't want to hear you say another word about Jacob. Do you hear me?"

I silently read the text on the screen.

Know it's not u. Don't trust Jacob. He called when I was getting the mail. Sounded so adamant on knowing where I was. What if he's tracking me somehow & trying to make meeting me look casual so I won't suspect he's watching me? Could be wrong about this but my gut tells me I'm not wrong about the press. He did it for the case like u said. What if he bugged my phone yesterday when I wasn't looking to listen to our conversations to get evidence?

My eyes widen at her and gesture for her to give me the phone. "I hear you, Mrs. Abel. Loud and clear."

With a nod, she hands me the phone. I run to the control room and check her device for

any threats. Her fists clenching and unclench-
ing, she joins me and stares at the computer.
"How long does it take?" she mouths.

"A few minutes," I mouth back, more anxious than her to know the truth. If that asshole
has bugged her phone, so help me God…

She takes a pen and a notepad from the
desk and scribbles something. I lean forward
and read it. *I feel like my heart is going to explode. I
can't watch. I'll wait for you outside at our spot.*

Her footsteps echo out of the room, and
I use the time to review the situation I haven't
had time to process. For a scary minute there, I
thought she meant what she said about believing I betrayed her. It was all a part of her plan
to nail Detective asshole. That woman never
ceases to surprise me.

My heart beats faster with every percentage
the scan progress line reaches. *C'mon. Let's get
the son of a bitch.*

A box pops on the screen. The scan is complete, and the results are there.

Fuck.

CHAPTER 49

Tristan

"It's clean." Birdie's face lightens up. "Really?"

She's so happy her detective hasn't bugged her phone, and it hurts my heart. That bastard is winning her over, earning her giggles, her trust and soon her love. Call me selfish, toxic or plain fucked up, but I don't want her to be happy with someone else.

"I'm sorry about the things I've said in the office. You know I trust you with my life, Tristan," she says.

"A little heads-up next time. You scared the hell out of me, you know. To think for one moment that I won't be here to protect you…"

She smiles at me. "I should have, but I wanted you to react genuinely in case he was listening."

"What if he was? The things you said about the stalker and his notes, Torrance would have known everything and used it against you."

Smirking, she saunters toward one of the benches and makes herself comfortable on it. "He couldn't. He'd have obtained that information illegally, which makes it inadmissible in court. Without solid evidence to back his theory, which he can't get because we'll never let him have it, it'd have been my word against his."

Despite my pain and frustration, I can't help smiling back at her in admiration. She had it all planned. Calculated every step and considered every possibility. She's so smart and beautiful and sexy and—

"Can you stop looking at me like that?"

"Like what?"

She tilts her head to the side, her hair cascading smoothly over her shoulder, and I picture her exactly like that, but her mouth is forming an O while she's sitting naked on my lap. "Like you're falling in love with me."

That ship has sailed. I'm not falling. I've already drowned deeply and can't be saved.

My throat bobs with a swallow as I drag my gaze away. "Here's your phone back. I'll…go."

"Go where? Sit. Now that Jacob isn't another person I should be wary of, thank God because I have my share of those, we still need to figure out who tipped the press."

"Your phone being clean doesn't prove anything about Torrance's honesty. He's not stupid to bug your phone when you have me. He knows I'll check." I fill her in about the ice cream lie and my doubts. "Listen, it can't be a coincidence you and I have the same suspicions about him at the same time. He's up to something."

Her face darkens in a heartbeat, all the happiness and relief forgotten. "What are you trying to tell me?"

"That he gave that photo to the press, tightening the circle around you while pretending to be trustworthy so you'd seek his help and open up to him, telling him everything…or worse."

"Worse?" Blood drains from her face. "Do you think Jacob can be Butterfly Man?"

"Lying to Marcus to incapacitate him, calling that time of the day, those flowers…"

"The flowers?"

I won't tell her what happened in the kitchen because of them, but I'll tell her this. "Gold and lavender are your favorite colors. He got the purple two shades too dark, but it still counts. He can't be that lucky."

"He said the lady at the flower shop picked them." She muses. "You know my favorite colors?"

I have an eye for details, especially when it comes to the people I care about. "I've been living with you for some time. It's my job to notice things. But don't change the subject. Something is off about Torrance. I mean, you said it yourself when he came questioning you about Saldana. It felt as if he was there."

"But he wouldn't be telling me these things if he was the stalker. He'd close the case as suicide from the start like he'd planned."

"Or he did it so you could come up with this conclusion."

She glowers at the ground, and then she shakes her head. "No. it's too easy. Like you said, he's not stupid. If he were Butterfly Man, he wouldn't choose my favorite restaurant, flower and colors on our first date. Besides, Jacob doesn't fit the description of a stalker. Have you seen the size of him? He's huge, hard to miss, can't hide in plain sight or lurk in the shadows. And he's a cop. If he wants to have me, there are other power moves he can use to get me." She lifts her gaze to me. "But you make a legitimate argument about the press and the ice cream lie. Also…"

"Also what?"

"He said something today, a quote about me being a castle, always watched or watched over. Watched over by the bodyguards, and I thought he meant watched by Blake because the first time we met I shared my concerns about my husband always watching."

"But he could mean the stalker or the press he knew would be here because he tipped them."

Her fingers fumble with her phone. When I glance at the screen, she's calling Torrance.

"What are you doing?"

"There's only one way to find out why he lied or if he's the one responsible for the media chaos." She puts the call on speaker.

Ring.

Ring.

Ring.

Ri—"Birdie?"

"Yes, Detective. Who else? Do you not have my number saved?" She chortles.

"I do. I just didn't think I'd hear your voice again after my last call. I'm so glad you called."

I roll my eyes. *Burn in hell.*

She puts on a flirtatious face even when he can't see her. "What can I say? I have a big heart, and I believe in second chances, so how about that coffee? Bring it over to my place?"

"You got it. I'll be there in forty minutes give or take."

"Great. I'll be waiting." She hangs up and stands. "When he arrives, don't let him in right away. Let's see his reaction when he finds the reporters."

I nod once.

Her lips purse as she casts a distant look at the beach. "By the way, my trip today was futile. There were no notes from Butterfly Man."

CHAPTER 50

Tristan

I stand beside Birdie in the control room, my eyes fixed on the monitors. Every car that approaches slows down, then speeds away at the sight of the media circus. Until a familiar SUV approaches.

"There." I point at one of the screens. "He's here."

Birdie leans in. "It's showtime."

We watch as Torrance's vehicle comes to a stop just short of the reporter line. His face visible on the high-resolution camera, he grimaces in concern. It's not the reaction I expected.

He doesn't get out immediately. Instead, he pulls out his phone and makes a call. His brow is furrowed, his free hand gesturing animatedly as he speaks.

"What's he doing?" I mumble.

"I don't know, but he looks worried. Genuinely worried."

"He knows we can see him. Of course, he's acting worried."

After a few minutes, Torrance ends the call and sits there, staring at the reporters. He makes no move to engage with them or to approach the gate. Instead, he reverses his SUV and parks it down the road, out of sight of the cameras.

"Is he leaving?" Birdie asks incredulously.

Her phone rings, grabbing our attention. "It's him," she says. She puts the call on speaker when she answers. "Hey."

"Hey, um, I'm outside, but… Are you aware there are reporters outside your house?"

"Hyperaware."

"Okaaay. Are you all right?"

She exchanges a glance with me. "Yes. Why would I not be?"

"Because you're a private person, and I've never seen the press camping outside your house before. Besides, you couldn't sleep last night and had to go out so early in the morning. Something must have happened."

"You mean you don't know?"

Torrance pauses. "Shit. Please don't tell me I caused this with our date. They took photos and spun lies, didn't they? How? I took every precaution... Ugh, I'm so sorry, Birdie. I didn't mean to get you in trouble. Did your husband contact you? Did he hurt you in any way?" Agitation pulses in his voice at the end.

Her lips pursed, she lifts a shoulder at me, as if asking, "You think this is still an act?"

If I'm being honest, the guy sounds genuinely concerned, but I'm not going to be vocal about it.

A satisfied smile appears on her face at my scowl. "No, Jacob. Why don't you come inside, and I'll explain?"

"Sure. But do you think it's a good idea with their cameras there? I don't wanna cause any more damage."

"You won't. I'm waiting for you."

When she hangs up, my eyes revert to the screen. The detective appears on another camera, walking towards the gate with a coffee tray in his hand. He's keeping his head down, clearly trying to avoid drawing attention to himself. As he reaches the crowd of reporters, he pauses, visibly taking a deep breath, before he pushes through them without engaging.

When he reaches the intercom, he presses the button. The buzz echoes through the house, and I look at Birdie, waiting for her signal. She nods, her face a mixture of guilt and anticipation.

"Let him in," I radio.

On the monitors, the gate opens, and the guards make sure only Torrance is in. Marcus's gaze shoots daggers at the detective, and he takes his time searching Torrance thoroughly. Before Marcus lets him in, he opens the six coffees on the tray one by one and smells them. "Why six?"

Torrance shrugs. "For all of us. Birdie, me and her security. If there are more of you inside, please send my apologies. You can share, though."

"Is there dairy in all of them?"

Confusion crosses Torrance's face. "Except for mine, I think so, yes."

"And why is that? Are you lactose intolerant?"

"No," Torrance says warily, "I'm vegan. What is this all about?"

"Please take your cup from the tray."

Torrance sighs impatiently and does as he's told.

Marcus puts the lids back on the cups and throws another glare at Torrance. "The rest will be inspected before being served. Let's hope it's just milk in them. Enjoy your coffee, Detective." Then Marcus ushers Torrance inside the house and tosses the coffee tray in the garbage.

I snort a laugh.

"He didn't need to do that." Birdie gestures

at the monitor. "I know Marcus must hate Jacob for giving him diarrhea, but it's obviously a mistake. Jacob being vegan explains everything. He must have thought the ice cream *was* diary-free even if he was misinformed. That's why he ate it, loved it because, let's face it, vegan ice cream must taste like crap, and recommended it to Marcus."

If he didn't lie to Marcus on purpose, got lucky with the flowers, didn't tip the press and his morning call was purely coincidental, it means he's squeaky clean and we're back to square one. It means he's a good guy, and she's going to fall for him because that's what she deserves. A good guy.

"Let's not jump to conclusions before I check his story." My fists clench as I head out. "Stay here until I'm done with him."

Torrance puts his detective face on when he sees me in the hallway. "Where's Birdie?"

"She'll join us shortly." I guide him to a seat in the living room. "Did you enjoy your ice cream last night? My friend here tried it based on your recommendation, and he said it was amazing."

Torrance unbuttons his suit jacket and sits, setting his coffee on the table in front of him. "That's good to hear. It was so delicious."

"I don't remember seeing vegan options on the menu, though. Why did you say it was?"

"Many restaurants will have the option to switch ingredients to accommodate dietary restrictions even if they're not on the menu. You just need to ask, and that's what I did. I asked the waiter if they could serve vegan ice cream, and he said yes." His eyes dart between me and Marcus, who still has a murderous glare on his face. "Will either of you tell me why the hell are you interested in my diet, and why it's more important than filling me in on the press situation out there? And where is Birdie?"

"I told you she'd be here shortly." I pointed at the taunting vase in the kitchen. "What's the name of the flower shop where you got those?"

"Why?"

"Security reasons. Name and location please."

"Give me your number. I'll share it with you."

"Just show me on your phone."

He scoffs and fumbles with his phone. Then he shows it to me. "There."

I take a screenshot. "Where were you before you transferred to Oak Bluffs?"

"SON OF A—" Birdie yells, and a loud thud follows.

Marcus, Torrance and I rush to the control room. I barge in first, guns out. There's a chair broken on the floor. I jump over it and securely press Birdie against the wall, covering her with my body. My eyes roam the room, assessing for intrusions or breaches, but there's no one in the room except Dixon on surveillance. "What happened?"

Dixon throws his hands in front of him. "Mrs. Abel smashed the chair."

I spin and get out of her personal space. Her face is crimson, and her knuckles are white. "Birdie, what's wrong?"

"Blake," she seethes, shoving her phone between us.

There's a text from him on the screen. *I got your divorce papers, little bird.*

"It's him. Blake gave the press the note."

CHAPTER 51

Tristan

What's one word for a man who beats his wife, controls her, lives off her, cheats on her, and now that she's trying to break out of his prison, now that he can't get any more pieces of the cake, he reveals her secrets to ruin her life in revenge?

Dead.

If Butterfly man doesn't kill that piece of shit, I'll do it myself.

Against my advice, Birdie has tried to call him. She shouldn't have any contact with him. We don't know what else the sneaky bastard is up to; he can twist her words and use them against her. He never picked up, though.

She's been on the phone for the last

eighteen minutes in her office, figuring out if it's just Abel who is in on the press conspiracy or her agent and publisher are backing up the scandal for more sales of her books.

"My agent has no clue what's going on, and she'll see what she can do to contain the situation. My publisher, on the other hand, doesn't answer my calls. What does that tell me?" She tosses her phone on the desk and places her hands on her hips. "How could they do this to me? Why? I've made my publisher multiple seven figures, and Blake would have lived as a king for the rest of his life with the money he's made working with me if he hadn't spent it all on drugs and whores."

When I see her like that, I wish I could zip open my chest and let her crawl inside where I could shelter her from the cruelty of the world. "I'm so sorry, Birdie. When money is involved, people do nasty things."

"But why do I have to be the one that pays for their greed and vice?" She rubs her mouth like a warrior ready for blood. "None of that. Not anymore." Then she makes another call.

"Who are you calling again?"

"My agent."

"You said she didn't know anything."

Birdie turns her back at me, as if she didn't hear me. "Martha, I've just got off the phone with Blake. He told me everything."

My eyes narrow at the back of her head. Why would she lie?

"I told him if he came clean, I'd consider reassigning him as my manager, and he sang like a canary. He confessed that he did it. You know who helped him?" Birdie twists and smirks at me. "My publisher. Blake recorded their conversation together, and I listened to every word. You know what that means." She opens the speaker.

"A lawsuit is in order," Martha says.

"Exactly. But I have a good heart. If the house will settle, I won't go to court or destroy their reputation on social."

"I'll make sure your message is delivered. How much are we talking about?"

"Half of what I've made them."

Martha clears her throat. "Half?"

"Not a dime less, and my rights reverted back to me." She ends the call, pride and victory dancing in her eyes.

"Do you think they'll fall for it? What if Abel tells them the truth?" I ask.

"They won't believe him, and they'll settle because they're guilty. But if they don't, I'll go to Blake and offer him exactly what I said I offered him. He'll run to catch that bone like the dog he is and sell them out," she stretches on her toes to reach my ear, "but we both know he'll run out of breath before he gets one bite."

She walks to the sofa bed nonchalantly, unaware of the havoc she's wreaked in her wake. I watch her in awe, as if I'm seeing her for the first time, and fall in love with her dark side as much as I have with her light. She's the verse I can't write but I'll spend a lifetime trying. A story I dare not tell without crossing the line between sanity and madness, inspiring quests I never knew I longed for.

"You're a masterpiece." One, for now, I can only admire from afar.

Her lips stretch with a sated smile as she sits. "Well, thank you, Tristan. Can you bring Jacob in, please? I need to apologize for doubting him."

Just like that, I go from picturing myself worshiping at her feet to spanking her while my hand is squeezing her throat.

When I let the detective in, he's talking to someone on the phone. He wraps it up as he takes a seat right next to her. How dare he invade her space like that? I should be the only one allowed to sit there. I can't stand the way his eyes roam over her face, drinking in her beauty that should be mine alone to appreciate. Every cell in my body screams to rip him apart, to make him suffer for daring to breathe the same air as her. What happens if I tear him away from her side and throw him against the wall?

I imagine the satisfying crunch of his bones breaking under my fists, the way his blood would paint the floor, the things he'd say to beg for his—

"Tristan?" Birdie brings me back to reality.

I clear my throat. "Sorry, did you say something?"

"Yes. Could you please give us a minute?"

My *what the fuck* stare tightens at her, but she doesn't budge. From the corner of my eye, I see Torrance smirking.

Bending more than necessary to whisper to her, I smirk back at Torrance, and then I whisper, my lips less than an inch apart from her ear, "If he doesn't wipe that smirk off, I won't just do it for him. I'll rearrange his face in a way he can never smile again."

She inclines her head and whispers back. "You're out of line, again, breaking your promise when you literally just said you'd always keep your promises to me."

One day, I'll punish that mouth that challenges me, those lips that mock me, so close to mine, so primed for the taking, and yet off-limits. "It's funny how you seem to remember only one of them and forget the rest. Remember what I said would happen if you let him touch you. Don't test me, Birdie. My patience has its limits."

As I wait outside her office, I watch them

on my phone. I could listen to their conversation, too, but I choose not to. Maybe she's testing my trust. Maybe I don't trust myself if I hear something intimate between them. I can't let him provoke me into doing something stupid that could ruin everything between me and her. I can't let him win. I can, however, think of how many ways to kill Jacob Torrance that can pass for an accident. Twenty-three.

I catalogue each interaction between them, filing it away to replay later in agonizing detail. Every smile she gives him, every word, inspires another way to end his life.

Earlier, I said she deserved a good guy, but he doesn't deserve her. No one does. I've memorized her every habit, her likes and dislikes, breathed in her art, learned her darkest fantasies without her having to verbalize them for me, and she shared sacred moments and secrets with me she'll never have with him. What does he know about her, really? He can't possibly understand her the way I do, can't worship her the way she should be worshipped.

If only she could see how perfect we'd be together. If only I could make her understand that no one would ever love her as deeply, as completely as I do. No one has what it takes to give her what she needs from a man like I do.

One day she'll realize it. She has to. And if she doesn't see it on her own, I'll make her.

Torrance comes out, somehow looking even taller than he already is, and strides down the hall without a word. Then Birdie leans against the doorframe next to me, playing casually with her necklace.

"Why did you tell me to leave? And where is he going?" I ask.

She rests her back against the frame, her eyes daring, piercing, peeling me layer by layer. "You mean you didn't listen?"

"No. I only do when you authorize it or a threat is detected. It's protocol, Mrs. Abel."

Her lips curve up at the corners. "Fair enough, Mr. Morra."

"Are you gonna tell me what's going on?"

She nods for me to come inside and walks toward the windows. "Tell the guards to let Jacob talk to the reporters. He said he could deal with them. Let's see if he comes through."

"If he's flashing a badge to shoo them away, it can backfire. Normal people can get away with calling the cops on the press, but celebrities get slayed on social media for it."

"That's not what he's about to do. Just tell the men to let him through and watch."

"You're the boss." I turn on my mic. "Let him through."

The previously hushed murmurs of the reporters camped outside the gate swell into a roar of questions and demands as Torrance steps down the porch. Microphones thrust forward like accusing fingers, and camera lenses glint in the morning light, each eager to capture every expression he makes.

He puts his shades at the barrage of flashing bulbs. Clearing his throat, he raises a hand to quiet the clamoring crowd and marches to the gate. "Good morning. I'm Detective Jacob Torrance of the Oak Bluffs Police Department. Thank you all for coming. I'm here to make a statement on behalf of my department to provide an update on the investigation into the death of Katie Saldana, age 26, whose body was found in a vehicle that crashed into Ocean Park on March 5th, 2025."

The reporters fall into an anticipatory hush. Only the rustle of wind through the oak trees lining the driveway and the distant call of a seagull break the sudden silence.

"Can he do that?" I ask.

Birdie's gaze drifts outside the windows. "He's been on the phone with his boss asking for permission, and he's cleared to give a statement."

"After a thorough investigation," Torrance begins, "including comprehensive forensic analysis, toxicology reports, and accident reconstruction, we have concluded that Mrs. Saldana's death was not the result of foul play as initially suspected.

"The evidence we've gathered indicates that Mrs. Saldana suffered a fatal drug overdose while driving, which led to the subsequent car crash. Toxicology reports show lethal levels of psychedelic amphetamines in her system at the time of death. The medical examiner has officially ruled the cause of death as drug overdose.

"While this case did not involve murder, it highlights the ongoing drug crisis affecting our community. We urge anyone struggling with substance abuse to seek help from local support services. We extend our deepest condolences to Mrs. Saldana's husband, family and friends during this difficult time. This case is now closed. We appreciate the public's assistance and understanding throughout our investigation. I'll now take a few questions."

A commotion erupts, but the detective points at one of the reporters in the middle to speak.

"What about Mrs. Abel's stalker and their threats? Have you investigated them?"

Torrance glances toward the office, and Birdie nods once behind the curtain, as if he could see her. She must have known that question would pop up. What did she tell him to say? Is she revealing the big bad Butterfly Man secret to the public? Is that why she told me to leave the room, knowing I'd never approve of that plan security wise? Is she provoking Butterfly Man to come out and play with an even bigger move? "What did you do, Birdie?"

"I'm controlling the narrative."

Torrance's expression remains neutral. "We've followed up on the report Mrs. Abel filed on February 15th, 2024, concerning receiving a rather disturbing note from an anonymous person. The note, while concerning, appears to be an isolated, one-time incident, and we've found no evidence linking it to Mrs. Saldana's death. That case was closed weeks before the unfortunate event."

Another reporter shouts out, "Is Mrs. Abel in any danger? Why are you here at her residence?"

"We take all threats seriously, but there's no evidence of any danger to Mrs. Abel. As I said, the incident was never repeated, and no stalking claims could be proved. As a courtesy, Mrs. Abel has agreed to let me share with you some private details about the report.

"Mrs. Abel's safety is not currently at risk because we've identified the person who sent the note, who thought at the time it was a harmless joke. Since it was a one-time incident, and due to the nature of their relationship, Mrs. Abel decided not to press charges. But rest assured we've taken every legal precaution to ensure it won't happen again."

"Who is the person who sent that note?!"

"What is the nature of their relationship?!"

The shouts and screams demanding to know who Butterfly Man is and how Birdie knows him ricochet against the walls.

"What the hell?" I stand in front of Birdie. "That's what you told him to say? Are you crazy?"

"Watch your tone," she says ever so calmly.

"You told Torrance, the fucking police, about Butterfly Man!"

"No, I only told him my assistant tried to prank me, and my greedy husband played along, thinking it was a good publicity stunt just like the police called it. Then I asked him to feed the press that story without disclosing any details, and he generously agreed."

"Lying to your agent about your junkie husband to get back at your publisher is one thing, but this? This is beyond dangerous, Birdie. We don't know how your stalker will respond to this."

"That's exactly the point." She meets my gaze, her eyes determined. "We need to flush out Butterfly Man, make him react. This controlled release of information might just do that and, simultaneously, drive away the prying eyes of the reporters." Her eyes return to Torrance as he handles the press. "I played it your way, Tristan, but it didn't work. We need Butterfly Man to make a move, to slip up. It's the only way we'll catch him."

I watch her profile, illuminated by the morning light filtering through the curtains. Her determination is palpable, and despite my reservations, I can't help marveling at her courage. That woman has some ovaries on her, and she's not afraid of playing with fire.

Outside, Torrance wraps up the circus. "Due to privacy concerns, we won't be disclosing further details about Mrs. Abel's personal circumstances. Please know that this is the only statement Mrs. Abel will give. Thank you all for coming. No further questions at this time."

As the reporters begin to disperse, Birdie turns to me. "See? They're leaving. Step one done."

"Now what?"

"Now we wait. And we watch very, very carefully."

The game has changed, and Butterfly Man's next move could be the one that finally brings him into the light or burns us all in flames.

Torrance returns to her office, so full of himself, and she welcomes him as if he were a triumphant soldier after a vicious war. But what does he know about wars?

She grins at him. "You saved the day, Detective. I can't thank you enough. How can I repay you?"

"That smile on your face is the best reimbursement ever," he replies, and bile rises to my throat.

"At least, let me make you some coffee. The one you bought must be cold."

"If that buys me some more time with you, then I'd love that very much."

Seriously, my stomach has just flipped. "Shouldn't you get some sleep, Mrs. Abel? It's been a stressful day, and you didn't sleep well last night."

She throws a dismissive wave at me. "I'll be fine after getting that coffee."

"Actually, your bodyguard is right," Torrance says. What is he doing? Trying to win me over too? *That will never happen, forro.* "You should rest. And…I was thinking, maybe this weekend, we can go somewhere…you know, to rejuvenate after all that stress."

Her face lights up with interest. "What do you have in mind?"

"How about Cape Cod? Or Vermont?"

"That sounds—"

Like something that will never happen in your lifetime, motherfucker. He's trying to get her to fuck him after one date and one favor? Guess *that smile on your face* isn't the best reimbursement ever after all.

"—lovely."

No. No. No.

"Great. I'll send you options, and you can choose the one you like the most," he says and then looks at me, "then I'll send you the itinerary and all trip information for the security check."

Smashing his bones and painting the floor with his blood won't be enough. I'll make him watch me fuck her like he never can before I tear him limb to limb, and then fuck her again on each part of his corpse.

The images in my head are so soothing I grin from ear to ear. "Who's gonna be paying for this trip?"

"Tristan," Birdie scolds.

"I am," Torrance answers before I have to explain to her that another cop could be taking advantage of her fortune because, shockingly, it doesn't seem to have crossed her mind. "It's my idea. Of course, I'll cover all expenses."

Because you expect to get your dick wet in return. "We'll need at least four rooms, one for you, one for her, and two for us, maybe more if I decide to bring additional details. You sure you can afford it on your detective salary?"

"Yes, Morra, I'm sure. Being my age with no family to provide for has a few perks when it comes to money." He gazes at her. "Lunch tomorrow?"

She nods with a smile. "It's a date."

"Have a good day, Morra." He smirks at me

on his way out.

I shoot her a death glare. "How many times have I told you not to test me, Birdie, and you haven't listened?"

She saunters toward her desk. "I stopped counting."

"Then I hope you're prepared for the consequences." I march out of the house and follow Torrance as he walks out of the gate.

He stops midway to his car. "Looking for something, Morra?"

"Just ensuring your safety exit, Detective. You don't know what might be lurking in the shadows or who."

He chuckles. "I can handle myself."

"Better safe than sorry. Just like I won't let *anyone* come near Birdie, I can't let anything happen to her guests."

He approaches me and nods, smiling like a goddamn creep. Then he bends his head down to my side. "At some point, you're gonna see I'm a better man for her than you'll ever be. Deep down you know I can protect her more than you can."

"Why? Because of your training and guns?" I scoff. "Look around you, Detective. The youngest one in my team has received more training and has access to more guns than you. Your badge doesn't amount to much here. If anything, it's a disadvantage."

He glances at the mostly vacant area outside the gate. "Didn't look that way to me today."

I scoff again, keeping the blazing war inside me buried. "Enjoy the little time she allows you with her while I live in her house all day and all night, where I sleep in the room right next to hers or stand outside her bedroom at night, one step away from answering her if she needs *anything*."

A cold fire ignites in his metallic gaze. "She's not yours to have."

"Or yours. Consider this your one and only warning, Detective."

He doesn't deserve her, and neither do I, but I'll take her anyway. She doesn't belong to Abel, Torrance or Butterfly Man. She belongs to me.

Reagan will be mine.

CHAPTER 52

Birdie

omething isn't quite right.

My eyes snap open, and my heart is about to explode. Two nights in a row, I'm yanked out of my sleep with a terrible feeling shooting my anxiety rate through the roof. Yesterday, it was because I thought I missed Butterfly Man's note. Tonight…I don't know.

Although I should feel safer I have Jacob in my corner along with Tristan and his team, and more in control after the moves I've made this morning, I can't shake the feeling something bad is going to happen, like the sudden death of your favorite character in a book.

What are you up to, Butterfly Man?

Without getting up—I don't want Tristan to barge in again—I reach for my phone on the nightstand to check the time. 1:36 a.m. Great. I only got two hours of sleep. I guess stress and fear do that to you.

Emotions are little tricky things. As a woman who, at a very young age, has been taught not to show her emotions—or there will be heavy consequences—for self-preservation purposes, I've learned to keep them locked. With time, however, there was no closet big enough to contain them, no lock strong enough to hold them back. That's why I write. I let my feelings out in my stories, a safe haven where they roam free without the fear of being caught.

Opening the nightstand top drawer, I glance at the many journals and notepads hogging most of the space. I need an outlet for the emotions that are tearing me apart. Tempted, I brush my fingers over the engraved leather cover of the journal on top.

Swiftly, I draw my hand back and shut the drawer. If I start writing, I won't stop, and I need to get some sleep. So I open the second drawer and settle for the next best thing to blow off some steam. The rose.

Unpopular opinion, but wands, dildos and even bullets aren't my best friends. The idea of inserting anything that runs on batteries inside my vagina is terrifying, and if I'm being honest, nothing works better than my own fingers while my all-time favorite written smut scenes play all together in my head. The rose, though, has changed my perspective about sex toys. Whoever invented it must be a woman as she clearly understands the female body anatomy and the annoyance a cock-shaped toy—anything man related in general—could bring.

Glancing up at the security camera, I hesitate to start. What's Monarca's protocol on intimate privacy? I don't think it's detailed in the contract, and I've never bothered to ask. Sexual pleasure in any form has been at the bottom of my priority list since my performance for Butterfly Man. The last thing I want is another self-pleasure scene caught on camera.

Should I put a towel on the camera and text that I need a moment? *Could you be more obvious, Birdie?* I blow out a frustrated breath. "I just need to get some sleep."

My eyes dart between the camera and the drawer. "Fuck it." I slip the rose under the covers. It's a covert toy—hopefully the men don't know what it's for—and the room is dark. If I stay very very quiet, no one will even notice.

The team in the control room, maybe, but you know Tristan is also watching, and he will notice.

I don't care. It won't be the first time he sees me come. My need for some shut eye is bigger than my shame.

And if he comes in? Right in the middle of it? Or

just when you're at the edge and desperate for release? Will you have the clarity to tell him to leave? Will he have the decency to listen?

Images of shirtless Tristan barging in while I'm spread open, a sex toy between my thighs, play in my head. My whole body throbs with forbidden desires. I close my eyes, and I see it. The hunger that will spurt in his intense gaze, the swelling in his pants that will grow with every undulation of my body as I chase my pleasure. Every contort of my face, every gasp, an invitation, a call to everything primal in him to take over. To punish. To claim.

I bolt out of the bed and lock the door.

"Okay. He can't come in. Let's do this. Nice and quick." I slide under the covers, pulling them over my head, and give my back to the camera. Setting the rose on my favorite mode, I pull down my panties.

As soon as the vibration hits my wetness, my dirty imagination does its thing. Vivid visuals of my antiheroes come alive, in my room, in my bed, touching and tasting every inch of me, doing, together, naughty wicked things to my body, each in their way.

Then it sneaks up on me. A face I haven't written, fully masked with a neon butterfly for a mouth, peeking in from the dark like a flash of lightning that disrupts the night.

My heart skips a beat as my eyes snap open.

The rose humming its vibrations along with my accelerated breathing are the only sounds in the room, but for a second there, in sync, another breath joins mine.

I pause the toy and sit upright. In the darkness, my gaze bounces from one wall to the next. "Are you there?" I whisper.

When silence answers, I swallow and switch on the light on the nightstand. Bracing for the worst, I hold my breath and look around like a maniac. Except no one is there. It's just me, alone, with made-up monsters to fuck me to sleep.

"It's all in my head. You're not here. You can't be." *But I can feel you getting closer, watching me, as if you were here, in the same room with me.*

I switch off the light and bury myself under the covers. With the rose back in position, behind my eyelids, I banish my familiar dirty friends and stare at the neon butterfly. A beautiful, terrible trap I'm falling into.

My fingers tremble as I restart the toy, the vibrations seem to intensify at the perverse fantasy. The terrifying glow pulses, a symbol of my madness, a hypnotic reminder of the danger that both frightens and entices me.

I imagine his breath on my neck, phantom fingers trailing across my skin. My own touch becomes his, and I shake at the thrill it gives me. The line between fantasy and reality blurs.

Butterfly Man isn't a fictional villain written to entice. He's a stalker obsessed with me to the point of murder, and I'm soaking the sheets with my arousal picturing him in a scary mask claiming me.

"This is wrong," I whisper to myself between gasps, even as my nipples harden painfully against the satin of my gown, and my legs spread wider in desperate need. The thought of him watching my fingers between my thighs, drinking in my vulnerability and darkness, comes into play, and it sends a shiver down my spine. Is it revulsion at the violation or the desire for more?

How many times has he replayed that scene? How many times has he touched himself to it? What sounds did he make when he came? Did he groan or growl? Did he break with my name on his lips? If he did, which one?

The neon butterfly smirks at me, mocking me with its silent glow. Then the mask vanishes, but the smirk stays, one I'm so irritably familiar with. Tristan's.

No. My eyes twitch as I shake the intrusive flickers of his face off my head. *I won't go there.* I reprimand myself as if masturbating to a killer is acceptable but to my bodyguard is an unforgivable sin.

Frustration huffs out of my lips. If I crave

a villain, why do I not stick to the harmless ink-on-paper kind? If I desire a hero, why do I not rely on fiction to deliver one who isn't morally gray?

But it's not about the choice between villains and heroes. The truth is, I'm tired of fantasies. What I crave is something real. Butterfly Man is real. Tristan is real.

Jacob is real, too. Why is he not an option? He's good, handsome, sexy, gentleman on the street, freak in the sheets and has proved he'd do anything—

"Don't stop." A strained whisper rips the silence as shadows congeal and take form beside me.

A gasp rips out of my throat as my heartbeat bursts my chest. Eyes wide, I jolt to open the lights, but forceful weight pins me to the mattress. Arms flailing, I open my mouth to scream.

My voice clashes against a firm grip unheard. The scent of leather fills my nostrils, and my wrists are squeezed together above my head. I kick as hard as I can, but my strength is nothing against the weight rendering me immobile.

My eyes squint to adjust in the dark in hopes of making out any details about him. A shadow around his head. A hoodie perhaps. His face and figure are a silhouette of black. I can't see the glint of his eyes or the outline of his features. There's only a flicker of a color where his breaths come out. He must be wearing a mask. Butterfly Man's mask. Exactly how I've pictured him, except the butterfly isn't glowing.

"No, darling. No kicking, no screaming, none of that," the voice rasps, low and gruff and menacing, but, a part of me notices, it doesn't threaten me, not outright anyway. "You'll be a good girl for me and stay quiet. No need to tell anyone our little secret. I'm not here to hurt you. I never will. You know that. But I won't hesitate to hurt anyone who stands in the way between us, like those bodyguards…"

Panic floods my system as the reality of the situation crashes over me. He's here. Butterfly man has found a way to break into my house again. That breath I've heard… He's been here in my bedroom all this time, watching me, and now, he's pinning me down to my bed in the middle of the night, threatening to kill anyone I ask for help.

To be continued…

Thanks for reading book 1 of
The Storyteller's Bodyguard series

Please **leave a review** of the
book and **Preorder** book 2,
XOXO, Little Butterfly and
book 3, **Z for Butterfly Man**

Special Edition Hardback of
this book is available on https://
njadelbooks.com

Also by N.J. Adel

Dark Mafia Romance
Forbidden Cruel Italians

The Italian Marriage
The Italian Obsession
The Italian Dom
The Italian Son

Steamy Forbidden Contemporary Romance
Off-Limits Italians

The Italian Heartthrob
The Italian Happy Ever After

The Night Skulls MC series

Furore
Tirone
Dusty
Cameron
Night Skulls Mayhem

Standalone MC Romance

Savage Crown

Romantasy

Veils of Desire and Darkness

About the Author

N. J. Adel, the author of Forbidden Cruel Italians, Night Skulls MC and Veils of Desire and Darkness series is a cross genre romance author. From chocolate to books and book boyfriends, she likes it DARK and SPICY. Mafia bosses, psycho anti-heroes, bikers, rock stars, dirty Hollywood heartthrobs, supes, smexy guards and men who serve. She loves it all.

She is a loather of cats and thinks they are Satan's pets. She used to teach English by day and write fun smut by night with her German Shepherd, Leo. After Leo passed away, she only writes dark and twisted books.

9 798990 293540